WITH RED HANDS

Also by Stephen Woodworth

THROUGH VIOLET EYES

With Red Hands

Stephen Woodworth

A DELL BOOK

WITH RED HANDS
A Dell Book

Published by
Bantam Dell
A Division of Random House, Inc.
New York, New York

Book design by Lynn Newmark

Dell is a registered trademark of Random House, Inc., and the colophon
is a trademark of Random House, Inc.

ISBN 0-7394-4991-5

Printed in the United States of America

I feel doubly blessed that
my first reader also happens to be
my favorite writer:
my darling wife and dearest colleague,
KELLY DUNN.
The magic touch she brought to
this novel is but a twinkle
of the miraculous joy with
which she has transformed my life.
For that and so much more,
I dedicate this book to you,
beloved Partner in All Things.

WITH RED HANDS

1

The Consultation

PRESCOTT "SCOTT" HYLAND JR. FIDGETED IN HIS CHAIR, discomfited by the oxford shirt and Dockers he wore. Left to choose his own wardrobe, he'd be in a wife-beater T-shirt and board shorts, but Lathrop insisted he go for the preppie look.

"And lose the rings," the attorney had commanded, referring to the silver bands that pierced Scott's ears and eyebrows. "The press will be on your tail twenty-four/seven until this thing is over."

Scott smoothed his left eyebrow. The holes were already starting to close. Lathrop had accomplished in five minutes what his parents had failed to do in three years.

If only Dad could see me now . . .

The thought unnerved Scott, and he pushed himself straight up in the chair, focusing on what the lawyer was saying as if his life depended on it, which it did. Although Scott was still technically a minor at seventeen, the D.A.'s office had pushed to try him as an adult in order to seek the death penalty.

"I don't need to tell you, we've got a lot of points against us." Malcolm Lathrop leaned forward in his leather-upholstered throne and consulted some papers on his desk as if reviewing a grocery list. "Although your parents' bedroom appeared to have been ransacked, almost nothing of value

2 ∘ **Stephen Woodworth**

was taken, and every other room in the house was left untouched—including yours."

Scott shifted in his chair and said nothing.

Not a single ruffled hair disturbed the perfect rayon wave of Lathrop's pompadour. "Then there's the broken window, where the 'burglar' supposedly entered the house. Unfortunately, the police found glass fragments *outside* the window, not inside. And as for those little accounting 'mistakes' you made at your father's business—well, the less said, the better."

Scott picked at a hangnail but still said nothing. Lathrop had forbidden him to say anything more about the case, even in private.

The attorney rose and strolled around the enormous walnut altar of the desk. "The good news is, we now have your parents on our side."

"My parents?" Scott's scalp prickled. In his mind, he saw his dad slumped back against the headboard of the bed, a crimson impact crater in his chest, while his mother sprawled on the floor nearby, the left half of her face blown off, her skull bleeding brains . . .

Lathrop regarded the boy as if he'd just slouched out of a cave. "You *are* familiar with the North American Afterlife Communications Corps, aren't you?"

"Yeah." Last year his dad had dropped a bundle on a brand-new painting by Picasso or some other dead guy. It looked like something you'd stick on your refrigerator with Snoopy magnets.

He'd seen NAACC dead-talkers in cop shows and movies, too, of course. Purple-eyed freaks known as Violets, they'd allow murder victims to take over their bodies and speak with their voices. But if the killer wore a mask, the victims' testimony wouldn't matter . . . would it?

"The Corps' conduit for the L.A. Crime Division recently contacted me," Lathrop informed him. "He's kindly offered to summon Elizabeth Hyland and Prescott Hyland Sr. to testify at the trial."

Scott's face went numb as the blood drained from it. "But . . ."

Lathrop held up his hand. "Not to worry. They'll tell us the *truth* about what happened that night." He propped himself on the edge of the desk and folded his arms, putting on a more sympathetic face. His eyes remained keen and cold, however. "We know you were framed, Scott. Can you think of anyone who'd want to kill your parents and set you up to take the blame?"

Scott suddenly felt like an actor who'd forgotten his lines. "Sir?"

"How about your dad's business partner?" Lathrop glanced at a sheet of paper on the desk. "Avery Park. Our private investigators found that he has no credible alibi for the night of the killings. And he does stand to gain by your father's death, doesn't he?"

"Yeah. I guess." The lawyer's insinuations gave Scott the queasy sensation of being hypnotized: Lathrop was telling him what to believe.

"Never fear, Scott. We won't let him get away with it." Lathrop tapped a button on the intercom beside him. "Jan, would you show in Mr. Pearsall?"

A moment later the office door opened. With the poise of a game-show model, Lathrop's receptionist ushered a pudgy, troll-like man resembling an alcoholic undertaker into the room and shut the door behind him. Scott stood to greet him, but the man crossed the ocean of carpet with an unhurried air, hands in his pockets. His pear-shaped body made the jacket of his cheap suit limp on the chest and tight at the waist, and his toupee looked like a dead poodle, its permed hair three shades lighter than the coarse brown brush of his mustache. A pair of Oakley sunglasses sunk his eyes in shadow.

"Scott, I'd like you to meet Lyman Pearsall, the conduit I told you about."

At Lathrop's prompt, Scott shook the newcomer's hand. He noticed how Pearsall grimaced at the touch, the man's lips moving as if he were silently repeating a phrase he didn't want to forget. Scott shivered, remembering how the Violets in the movies would always mumble some sort of mystical gobbledygook whenever dead people were around.

"Mr. Pearsall has requested a two-million-dollar retainer for his services," Lathrop said. "But I can handle him for now, and you can deal with it when you inherit your parents' trust later this year."

"Sure." Scott stared at Pearsall's flabby face, the submerged menace of his unseen eyes. "Thanks."

Lathrop indicated the twin chairs in front of him. "Let's all sit down and get to know each other, shall we?"

He moved back around behind the desk while the other two seated themselves, still staring at one another. Pearsall casually removed his sunglasses.

His violet irises burned Scott's face with invisible fire.

"Now then, Mr. Hyland," he said, his voice a cobra's rasp, "tell me everything you remember about your mom and dad."

2

Two in the Sandbox

NATALIE KNEW THE SESSION WAS GOING TO BE BAD, even before Corinne Harris opened the black leather-bound case containing her dead father's pipe. She could tell from the moment she set foot in Corinne's immaculate living room, each object placed with fanatical precision, the white carpet brushed so that every shag bristle bent north, like compass needles. She could see it in her host's eyes as they avoided looking into Natalie's own violet irises, could sense it in the way Corinne stalled for time with small talk and excessive offers of hospitality.

"I've made some lemonade." She set a tray of finger sandwiches on the glass-topped coffee table. "Or I could brew some coffee? Or tea?"

"No thanks. Water'll be fine." Natalie smiled at the tumbler sweating on the coaster in front of her.

"Oh . . . fine." Like a parakeet alighting on its perch, the woman settled herself at the far end of the sofa, knees together, and interlaced her thin fingers. "So . . . you said you have a daughter?"

"Yes. Callie. She'll be six next June."

"That's such a sweet age!" Corinne gushed.

"And your kids?" Natalie inquired, more from politeness than curiosity.

"Both teenage boys, I'm afraid. Tom's seventeen, Josh fifteen. They were adorable before the skateboards and rap music. Now they give Darryl fits." She smiled as if apologizing for her own sense of humor. "You and your husband must be thrilled to have a little girl."

Natalie's smile flattened. "Callie's father passed away before she was born."

Corinne put her hands to her mouth in horror. "I'm sorry! I had no idea."

The faux pas stung like a stiletto between Natalie's ribs. "It's all right," she said, although it was really all wrong. Dan should not have died barely a week after they fell in love. It wasn't fair.

"Mmm. It must be hard for you." Corinne's lips quivered with an unasked question. No doubt it was the same question everyone wanted to ask when Natalie told people about Dan: *Do you still talk to him?* A better question would have been *Does it matter?* She might as well have tried maintaining a marriage with no more connection to her lover than a long-distance phone card.

The hemorrhage of sorrow threatened to bleed onto her face. Eager to drop the subject, Natalie took a sip of water and swirled the ice cubes in the glass like tea leaves in a cup. "When did your dad die?"

Corinne's mouth crinkled. She'd managed to avoid any mention of Conrad Eagleton since Natalie had arrived, but now she could no longer pretend that she was simply enjoying afternoon tea with a friend.

"Sixteen years ago."

A knot tightened in Natalie's stomach. When Corinne had phoned to schedule the appointment, she'd sobbed into the receiver as if prostrate before her father's corpse. "How old was he?"

"Fifty-six." Corinne smoothed her skirt. "He had a bad heart."

"And why have you waited so long to contact him?" Natalie asked, although she could guess the answer.

Corinne shrugged and gave an airy giggle. "I don't know. There was Darryl and the kids to think about. Darryl . . . he'd think this's all a big waste of money."

"Your husband doesn't know?"

"He doesn't need to." She crossed her arms in adolescent defiance. "It's my money. I saved it up from my allowance."

Allowance? Natalie thought. *Hubby Darryl sounds like a real peach.* "You sure you're ready for this? Reconciliation with a dead loved one is never easy."

"I just want to show him that I've changed. That everything turned out okay."

Natalie nodded. "Did you find a touchstone?"

"I think so." With the care of a museum curator, Corinne lifted the small oblong black case from the coffee table and pried open the lid. "Will this work?"

The pipe lay cushioned in dingy green velvet, its darkly grained wooden bowl pointed downward like the butt of a dueling pistol. Deep bite marks scarred the tip of its black plastic stem, and Natalie could smell the sweet yet stale cherry scent of tobacco that seeped from the case. Despite the countless times she'd summoned souls, she still felt the familiar twinge of dread.

"Yeah. That'll do."

Actually, she could have used Corinne herself as the touchstone, for every individual or object a dead person touched during his or her lifetime retained a quantum connection with the electromagnetic energy of that person's soul. Natalie, however, preferred to use a personal item from the deceased because physical contact with a Violet made most clients uncomfortable.

With a deep breath, Natalie twisted her long sandy-blond hair into a bun, which she fastened in place with a plastic hairclip. Having real hair was one of the perks of working in the private sector. When she was a member of the NAACC's Crime Division, she'd been required to keep her head shaved so the electrodes of a SoulScan electroencephalograph could be attached to the twenty node points on her scalp. The device would then confirm when a dead person's soul inhabited her brain. Fortunately, she didn't have to bother with that now; seeing Natalie with a bunch of wires sticking out of her head would probably make a client like Corinne Harris run screaming from the room.

Natalie took the pipe from its case, silently mouthing the words of her spectator mantra. The repeated verse would hold her consciousness in a state of suspension, yet allow her to eavesdrop on the thoughts of the inhabiting soul while it occupied her mind:

> *Row, row, row your boat,*
> *Gently down the stream.*
> *Merrily! Merrily! Merrily! Merrily!*
> *Life is but a dream . . .*

An encroaching numbness prickled in her extremities, as if her fingers and toes had gone to sleep. Memories that weren't hers sifted into her skull. Natalie pressed the pipe between her palms and shuddered.

Conrad Eagleton was knocking.

An old Cadillac Fleetwood Brougham sat before her with its hood up, billowing steam from its blown water hose. The summer sun baked her balding crown, and the armpits of her dress shirt sagged with sweat.

She was late. She'd miss the meeting, and Clarkson would get the contract. Twenty years with the same company, and this is what I end up with! Crappy car, lousy job, miserable life! She kicked the Caddy with her patent-leather dress shoe, kicked it until her toes crumpled with pain and her heart spluttered like the burst water hose. . . .

Natalie's pulse stammered in sympathy. Conrad Eagleton's bitterness throbbed in her temples as he relived his fatal heart attack, and she hastened to calm her autonomic functions before her own heart gave out.

Row, row, row your boat . . .

With long, yogic breaths, Natalie slowed her rabbit-quick heartbeat back to its normal rhythm. Through fluttering eyelids, she saw Corinne wave her hands excitedly and leap to her feet.

"Wait! Wait! I forgot something."

She fluttered out of the living room, leaving Natalie to squirm on the sofa in semiconsciousness. Corinne returned with a framed family photo of her, Darryl, and their two sons.

She brandished the portrait as if it were a report card lined with A's. "He'll want to see this."

Natalie didn't answer. Her tongue felt like a dead slug in her mouth, and her hands tightened on the pipe until its stem snapped. She dropped the pieces in her lap.

Life is but a dream . . .

With the clinical detachment of a psychiatrist analyzing someone else's nightmare, Natalie watched as Conrad Eagleton opened her eyes and gaped at the spotless white interior of the living room and the aging woman he didn't recognize as his daughter. "What the hell . . . *where am I?*"

The martinet bark quavered with fear. *Easy, Conrad,* Natalie cooed to him in the mind they now shared. *There's nothing to be afraid of.*

Eagleton clapped Natalie's hands over her ears, trying to shut out the internal voice. In doing so, he touched the soft skin of her cheeks, noticed the fine-boned grace of her smooth ivory arms. Her delicate hands trembled as he looked down at them. "What's happened to me?"

Corinne leaned forward, her eyes and mouth round O's of awe. "Daddy?"

Conrad shrank from her. "Who are you?"

Her lips curled into the crescent of an uncertain smile. "It's *me*, Daddy. Cory!"

He squinted at her puffy, pleading face. Dye kept her hair brown and Botox erased her crow's feet, but she couldn't hide the subtle drooping of her cheeks and chin and the perpetually tired look in her eyes.

"Cory? You were only twenty-four when . . ." His words fell to a whisper. "Has it been that long?"

Fidgeting in the ensuing silence, Corinne snatched up her family portrait as if grabbing a fire extinguisher. "Tommy's almost grown up now," she said, pointing to the older boy. "Darryl's been a wonderful father to him. And this's Josh. I think he looks like you."

Conrad snorted. "You found some schmuck to take care of you, eh?"

Corinne's smile guttered like a wind-struck taper. "But you'd like Darryl, Daddy. He's a city councilman, and . . . well . . ." She spread her hands, inviting him to admire the impeccable décor of their handsome town house.

Conrad stood, hands on hips, and gave the room a cursory inspection. "I'm surprised he was willing to take you. Especially when you already had a kid with that loser . . . what was his name?"

"Ronnie." Corinne hugged the framed photo to her chest. "That was a long time ago."

"Some things never change. How long you think it'll take you to drive this one away?"

"Daddy!"

Cut her some slack, Conrad, Natalie chided him.

"Shut up!" He pounded Natalie's fists against the sides of her head. "You have no idea what she did to me!"

Right then, Natalie considered faking the rest of the session. She could push Conrad out of her head with her protective mantra, then play his role for Corinne, giving her the reconciliation she longed for. *Tell them what they want to hear,* Arthur McCord, her cynical Violet mentor, once said. *They like it better than the truth anyway.* But long ago Natalie had vowed never to lie to her clients the way Arthur had to his, so she let Conrad Eagleton's wrath erupt from her mouth.

Corinne seemed to shrink into her corner of the couch. "Daddy, what's wrong? What're you talking about?"

"You know damn well what I'm talking about!" Natalie's wiry frame vibrated with his anger. "You're a worthless leech, Cory, and you always have been."

"That's not true!"

"The hell it isn't! Why d'you think your mother stuck me with you? She knew. Probably why Ronnie dumped you, too. And this idiot"—he flailed a hand toward the photo she held—"what's-his-name, Darren? I *pity* him."

"But I've *changed.*"

"Yeah, just like you'd 'changed' when you came crawling home from Seattle with Tommy in your tummy."

"I know I made a mistake, but I've settled down now . . ."

"Settled down, or found someone else to sponge off?" He pointed to the hard gray world outside the living room window. "You think I would've been out on the I-5 in hundred-degree heat if I hadn't had to support you and your stupid kid? I worked myself to *death* for you."

"I'm sorry! I'm sorry!" Corinne blubbered. "I never meant to hurt you."

His laugh was the inextinguishable crackle of a fire in a coal mine. " 'Hurt' me? Cory, you *killed* me." He loomed toward her. "You hear me? You killed me, and if you think you can make it all better with your pathetic apology, you're even more hopeless than I thought!"

You're not being fair, Natalie interjected.

"*Fair?* What do you know about *fair?*" Conrad shouted at the ceiling—a rebuttal to God. "Is it fair that I had to come home after working thirteen-hour days to cook and clean up after her? Is it fair that women wouldn't give me the time of day because I had a brat hung around my neck?"

Corinne wheezed sobs like a leaky accordion.

That's enough, Natalie warned Eagleton. *If you don't apologize right now, I'll send you back.*

For a moment, fear short-circuited his anger. Like most souls, he dreaded the black void of the afterlife.

Then he surveyed the sterile whiteness of the living

room, the gray day outside the window. The rosebushes that lined the front flower bed had been pruned to a skeleton of thorns, the lawn mowed to crew-cut shortness. His gaze returned to his daughter, and he ground Natalie's teeth.

"Send me back if you want. There's nothing here for me anyway."

Corinne flinched as if slapped, bawling like a colicky infant.

The Lord is my shepherd, Natalie recited, *I shall not want . . .*

With the words of the Twenty-third Psalm, her protective mantra, circling in her head, she mopped Conrad Eagleton's consciousness from her mind. He didn't fight her, but his hatred left the acid sting of bile in her brain. As sensation returned to her limbs, Natalie dropped heavily onto the couch, still shaking with feverish rage.

Corinne didn't even lift her head from her hands. Dampness seeped between her fingers. "I didn't even tell him I love him."

Natalie massaged her temples. "He didn't give you the opportunity."

"No wonder he hates me." The daughter tightened herself into an armadillo ball.

Whining little brat, Natalie thought, then shook the words out of her head. Conrad's contempt still hissed through her neurons like quicklime, but she ignored it and moved to put an arm around Corinne's shoulders. "It's not your fault."

"It *is!*" Corinne's fingers knotted around clumps of her hair. "I never listened to him, never appreciated him." She spoke with such venom that she, too, seemed possessed by her father.

"You may have made some mistakes," Natalie said quietly,

"but that doesn't mean you didn't love him. And it doesn't mean he shouldn't love you."

Corinne blotted her eyes with her wrists. "I thought if I could talk to him again, tell him I was sorry, we could make it all right."

"Sometimes you can never make it all right." In her mind, Natalie saw her own father smile and wave over his shoulder to her as he left her crying on the front steps of the School, condemning her to a quarter century of NAACC servitude. Her tone hardened to a diamond's edge. "You just have to go on and make your own life right."

The words didn't console Corinne Harris, née Eagleton. Perhaps nothing could. She wept herself dry, muttering self-recriminations.

"It's okay," Natalie murmured over and over as she cradled the woman in her arms. "It's not your fault."

Eventually Corinne lapsed into silence, her open eyes as blank as a desert sky. When several minutes passed without a word, Natalie gingerly pried herself from her client's embrace and rose from the couch.

"I'd better go now. You know where to reach me if you need to."

Corinne didn't respond. Natalie let herself out of the house.

The session had lasted so long that she was late to pick up Callie at day care. Hunched forward with her perpetual death grip on the steering wheel, Natalie ran a yellow light for the first time in her life. The tan Chrysler LeBaron that had been tailing her all day accelerated through the red light to keep within a car length of her. In her rearview mirror, Natalie saw the driver, a black man with wraparound eyeshades, shake his head.

"Sorry," she apologized, as if George could actually hear her from inside the LeBaron.

She slowed her Volvo to a few miles an hour below the speed limit and crawled through the surface streets from Tustin up to Fullerton. Taking the 55 north might have been quicker, but freeway traffic still made her skittish. Natalie had been too afraid of auto accidents even to get behind the wheel of a car until she turned twenty-seven, but the duties of parenthood had ultimately forced her to learn to drive. Flexing one cramped hand, then the other, she wondered if she'd ever get used to piloting one of these death machines.

She glared at the traffic ahead, but it couldn't take all the blame for her anxiety. The session with Corinne had been a disaster, and for the thousandth time Natalie questioned whether she did any good as a family counselor. Especially when she was barely on speaking terms with her own dad. Even now, she burned with the memory of the day he abandoned her. . . .

To her five-year-old imagination, the granite-walled grounds and glowering Victorian façade of the School looked like a fairytale castle—but not the happily-ever-after kind. It looked like the sort of castle where an evil witch would imprison you until a prince came to your rescue.

"I don't like it here, Daddy." The soles of her tennis shoes skidded on the flagstones as he pulled her toward the semicircular stone steps that led to the entrance. "I want to go home."

"Don't be silly, Natalie. We only just got here." Rather than yanking her arm to keep her moving, Wade Lindstrom picked her up and carried her to the oaken double doors. "You'll see. You'll like it once you start making friends."

He gave her his salesman's smile and pushed the button of

the intercom on the wall next to them. A buzzer sounded, followed by a voice that sounded equally impatient. "Yes?"

"Natalie Lindstrom, here for enrollment," her father said into the speaker.

"Ah, yes. We've been expecting you. One moment, please."

Disbelief alone kept Natalie from crying. Daddy couldn't leave her in this scary place.

"Will you come visit me?" she asked softly.

He laughed and chucked her under the chin. "Of course, sweetheart."

"Soon?"

His smile wavered. "As soon as I can. They like to keep you to themselves for a while. Until you adjust."

"What about Mommy?"

The cheer ran from Wade's face like melting greasepaint, and he set her down. "I told you, honey. Your mother is . . . sick. She's going to be in the hospital a long time."

"Did the Thresher get her?"

He glowered at her. "Where did you hear that name?"

"You were talking to Grandpa on the phone about it. You said Mommy wouldn't be in the hospital now if she hadn't messed with the Thresher case. Who's the Thresher?"

"Never mind. Forget you ever heard that name. It's nothing for you to worry about."

One of the massive doors groaned open. Wade turned toward it, relief cleansing his expression when he no longer had to stare into her questioning eyes.

The man who emerged from the door was about her father's age, with a bald scalp and funny-looking ears that stood almost straight out from the sides of his head, like an elephant's. Dressed in a white robe, he spared barely a glance at Wade before casting his violet gaze at Natalie.

"Ms. Lindstrom! It's a pleasure to welcome you to the Academy." He bent at the waist to extend a hand to her. "I'm Simon McCord, one of the primary instructors here."

Natalie took her fingers from her mouth long enough to shake the professor's hand.

He frowned slightly at her spit-slicked touch and dabbed his hand dry on his robe. "I know we'll get to be good friends."

She said nothing, struck dumb with fear, awe, and a growing curiosity. Simon was the first Violet she'd seen outside her family.

Wade put out his own hand, trying to catch the professor's attention. "Good to see you again, Simon—"

"Professor McCord."

"Yes, of course. We're delighted that you'll be teaching Natalie." Wade gave up on the handshake. "Nora always spoke very highly of you."

"Dear woman—I hope she's not suffering." Professor McCord folded his hands with pious detachment. "You've submitted the necessary enrollment paperwork, I trust?"

"Sure."

"Then I think we can get little Ms. Lindstrom settled in." He took hold of Natalie's hand.

Wade looked like someone had just knocked the wind out of him, but he gave Natalie his closing smile—the one that sealed a deal—as he squatted to kiss her on the cheek. "It's going to be great, kiddo. You'll see."

She rubbed her nose, which was starting to run. "Come back soon, okay?"

He exchanged a glance with Professor McCord, his lips white. "We'll see. Love you, sweetheart."

"Love you, Daddy."

He hugged her once more and descended the steps. She

didn't cry, however, until he paused about halfway down the
front walk to wink and wave at her.

"Now, now—no tears," Simon chastised Natalie, drawing her
into the open maw of the School. "You should rejoice. You're
among Family now."

Brakelights the color of anger flashed in front of Natalie,
jolting her back to the present. She panic-stopped, and rubber squealed behind her as the LeBaron screeched to a halt
inches from her rear bumper.

Natalie glanced again in the rearview mirror at George's
frowning reflection and exhaled her bottled tension. *God, I'm*
starting to act like a real L.A. driver. I better relax before I get both
of us killed.

Not for the first time, she toyed with the idea of giving up
Violet work entirely. Everyone else had ordinary jobs. Why
not her?

But what else could she do? Being a conduit was the only
profession she'd trained for. As a freelancer, she could earn
thousands of dollars for a single session and still spend most
of her time at home with Callie. If she chose not to capitalize
on her unique skills, she'd probably have to take on full-time
office or retail work.

There was always her art, of course . . . but not many
artists made enough to support a family.

Maybe she should go back to work for the Corps, she
thought. No doubt they'd welcome her with open arms and a
steady paycheck. But they'd also want Callie, and Natalie
wouldn't allow that. Not yet, at least.

It was nearly four thirty when she pulled into the parking
lot of the Tiny Tykes TLC Center, a former preschool that had
been converted to a private day-care facility. George, she saw,
parked the LeBaron on the street outside.

Out of habit, Natalie switched off the engine and dug her contact lenses out of her purse. Once she put in the first one, though, she paused and cast an ashamed glance at her eyes in the rearview mirror—one blue, one violet.

What a wonderful role model you are, she silently sneered at her reflection. *Bet Callie can hardly wait to get her first pair of lenses.* Nevertheless, she went ahead and put in the second lens before getting out of the car.

A fresco of three gigantic alphabet blocks with the letters "TLC" masked the entire front wall of the day-care center, the dark windows camouflaged in the design of bright primary colors. By this time, the indoor activities would be done for the day, so Natalie headed straight for the small playground to the right of the school building. The overcast sky and waning daylight dyed the grass gray, and the few toddlers who remained rode the merry-go-round and teeter-totter with winter lethargy.

Seated on an orange plastic chair far too small for her, a plump woman rested her folded arms on her belly and darted her eyes from the children to her wristwatch and back again. Catching sight of Natalie, she heaved herself forward to get to her feet and hurried to meet her. "Ms. Lindstrom! Ms. Lindstrom!"

"Hi, Ms. Bushnell. Sorry I'm late."

"No, no problem-o." Panting between words, Ms. Bushnell pulled a folded glossy brochure out of the back pocket of her plus-size jeans and thrust it into Natalie's hands. "I got some info on that school I told you about."

"Oh. Thanks." Natalie grimaced at the photo of the forbidding Victorian mansion on the front cover. Cursive script below it read: "The Iris Semple Conduit Academy: An Introduction." She, of course, knew it better as "the School."

"They've got good people there." Ms. Bushnell tapped the picture. "Experts. I'm sure they could help Callie. You know . . . with her education."

"Uh-huh."

"And it's all free! They'd pay for everything."

"I'm sure they would."

"I really think it'd be the best thing for her." Ms. Bushnell's genial face adopted a look of matronly concern. "The fits, the way she talks to herself or zones out completely—ordinary schools simply aren't equipped to deal with those things. And it can be upsetting for the other children."

Natalie nodded, her jaw tightening.

"At the Academy, she'll have a chance to meet kids . . . like her. I'm sure she'll find it easier to make friends there."

"Mmm. You're probably right." Natalie folded the brochure in quarters and crammed it into her purse. "I'll give it some thought."

Ms. Bushnell beamed. "Want to help however I can. She's a darling little girl."

"Thanks." Natalie gave her a plastic smile and moved off toward the square wooden cell of a sandbox in the far corner of the playground.

A small girl with her brown hair tied up in pigtails crouched there on the miniature dunes. Her denim overalls powdered with white dust, she pushed a blue plastic bucket with both hands to bulldoze sand onto a growing mound in front of her. After patting the sand into an igloo-shaped hill, she used a stick to stir shallow holes in the dome, her singsongy voice drifting on the air like the notes of a distant calliope.

". . . .make a room for you, and one for Mommy, and one for me . . ."

Natalie frowned as she drew close enough to catch the words. Callie apparently sensed her displeasure, for she stopped talking and scrunched up her face as if making a birthday wish. Her violet eyes wide, she looked up at her mother with the exaggerated innocence of a child who's been caught playing with matches.

"Hey, baby girl." Natalie squatted beside the sandbox. "Whatcha making?"

Callie prodded the mound of sand with her stick. "A house."

"Uh-huh. And are we going to live there?"

"Yeah."

"Just you and me?"

Her daughter's lips puckered. "Yeah."

Natalie drew a deep breath. "Who were you talking to?"

Callie continued to jab the stick in the sand. "Nobody."

"Was it Daddy?"

Her daughter's eyes remained downcast.

Natalie sighed. She'd asked Dan to leave their daughter alone. *She has to live her own life,* she told him, and he agreed . . . or so he'd said.

"Honey, I told you not to talk to Daddy at school. If he knocks, just tell him to go away."

"He doesn't knock. I call him."

Natalie stared at her, amazement mingling with apprehension. She knew that Dan had occasionally inhabited Callie ever since she was a baby. In fact, Callie's first word had been "Da-Da." But now she'd evidently figured out how to use herself as a touchstone to summon Dan whenever she wanted.

She needs to be trained, Natalie thought. Summoning the dead without knowing how to get rid of them was dangerous. Callie could lose control of her body for hours or even days if the inhabiting soul refused to leave on its own. In the mean-time, it could make her do whatever it wanted. Natalie had found that out the hard way.

She clawed at the School nurses with six-year-old fingers as they dragged her into the infirmary and onto a padded table. "No! I won't go back!" the soul inside her shrieked, the scream grating the back of Natalie's throat. "You can't make me go back!"

A-B-C-D-E-F-G . . . A-B-C-D-E-F-G, Natalie repeated desperately, but the alphabet mantra didn't help. Imprisoned inside her own head, she couldn't even speak the letters aloud. The invading soul's will was stronger than hers.

Helpless to stop herself, she watched her feet rabbit-kick one of the nurses in the stomach. He snarled and slammed one of her legs down on the table, lashing it in place with a leather belt. Working together, the two nurses managed to bind her other limbs as well, after which they forced the electrode-lined loop over the crown of her head. Insulated wires ran from the headband to a console on a cart beside the table, and a large red button lit up on the unit's control panel.

"NO!" Natalie heard herself scream again. Her body twisted in its restraints like a mouse mired in a glue trap.

The first nurse slapped the red button as if starting a Laundromat dryer, and Natalie's thoughts dissolved in lightning . . .

"We'll talk about this later," she told her daughter. With a grunt, Natalie hefted Callie out of the sandbox and carried her toward the parking lot. "Right now I'm starving. How about a pizza?"

The cloud of guilt lifted from the girl's face. "With olives and pepperoni?"

"You bet."

"Yay!" Callie raised her little fists in a touchdown Y.

Natalie chuckled. *She has his smile.*

Her face fell at the thought, for the resemblance was bittersweet. In one sense, Dan could be closer to his child than any parent on earth; in another way, he was worse than dead to her, his presence merely a reminder of his absence.

Natalie hugged Callie to her chest. *We're haunted, baby girl, but we love the ghost. What are we going to do?*

An older woman in a business suit stepped into their path. "I was hoping I might catch you here," she said. "Motherhood agrees with you."

Natalie squinted at the woman's stern, bronze-colored face, at the graying hair tied back in a French braid. "Inez? Why on earth . . ."

"I need your help." Inez took a thick padded envelope from under her arm and held it aloft. "Scott Hyland's trying to get away with murder."

3

To Hear a Who

NATALIE SET CALLIE DOWN. "I'M RETIRED, INEZ."

Her old friend, now a deputy district attorney for Los Angeles, nodded. "I know. That's why I need you. I don't want the Corps to know about this."

Callie gripped her mother's leg, peeking shyly at the stranger, and Natalie stroked her hair. "If it's not the Corps' business, why should it be mine?"

Inez Mendoza waved the envelope. "Are you familiar with the Hyland case?"

"Only what I've read in the papers. Sounds pretty open-and-shut to me."

"To me, too. The evidence we've got against Scott Hyland's so massive, we weren't even going to bother putting ourselves on the three-month waiting list to get a Violet. Then Hyland hooked up with Malcolm Lathrop."

Natalie snorted. "Figures."

"Last week Lathrop quietly submitted the defense's witness list for the trial. Lyman Pearsall's name was at the top of the list."

"Lyman?" She knitted her brows in distaste. Natalie had met Pearsall only on a couple of occasions and had found him an unctuous little man prone to petty complaints. "How did he end up on the case?"

"Apparently Lathrop demanded conduit testimony. Specifically, *Lyman's* conduit testimony."

"But what does he hope to gain by summoning the victims in court? You'd think that's the last thing he'd want."

"You'd think. Maybe Lathrop wants to confuse the victims in front of the jury, to surprise them with questions that make them contradict their own testimony, thereby introducing reasonable doubt. That's why I want find out what Scott Hyland's parents have to say before we go to trial—without letting our man Malcolm know about it." She looked at Natalie expectantly.

"I'm *retired.*"

"I know. That's why you're the only one who can help me. The Corp has refused to give me access to anyone but Pearsall."

Natalie shook her head. "I have enough problems with the N-double-A-C-C. It sounds to me like you have nothing to worry about anyway. If you're convinced Hyland did it, cross-examining his parents will only help your case."

"I know, but . . . there's something else." Mendoza reached into the padded envelope and withdrew a folded newspaper article. "I've worked with Lyman Pearsall on several cases; since you left, he's been the primary Violet for the L.A. Crime Division. We never liked each other much, but he did the job. Then, last year, this happened." She shook the clipping open and handed it to Natalie.

RIES GOES FREE, the headline read. KILLER WAS HISPANIC, VICTIM SAYS. Below it, a photo of Avram Ries showed the handsome blond defendant hugging his attorney as the jury delivered its not guilty verdict.

"Honey, why don't you go play for a few minutes?" Natalie gave Callie a distracted nudge, and the girl wandered off with wary reluctance.

"We had a mountain of evidence against Ries," Mendoza said as Natalie skimmed the article. "Even a DNA match with sperm samples taken from Samantha Winslow's corpse. Then suddenly Lyman Pearsall appeared as a conduit for the defense. He summoned Winslow in court, and she told the jury she was actually strangled by a Mexican man. Ries' lawyer admitted that his client had had sex with Winslow, who was a prostitute, but convinced the jury that the sperm match alone did not prove that Ries had anything to do with her death.

"Three months after he was released, some cops on patrol in Griffith Park pulled up behind what they thought was a couple of teens making out in a car. They found Ries in the backseat on top of a naked body. He'd wrapped the dead woman's bra around her neck. Even used the same kind of knot we found in the bra around Samantha Winslow's throat."

Natalie returned the newspaper clipping, trying not to let Inez see her wince. "SoulScan confirmed Lyman's inhabitation, didn't it?"

Inez conceded the fact with a nod.

"Then maybe the first victim told the truth. Maybe Ries only killed the second woman."

"Do *you* believe that?"

Natalie could only shrug. The coincidence sounded pretty far-fetched to her, too. "You got a better explanation?"

"Not yet. But I'm as sure that Avram Ries committed both those murders as I am that Scott Hyland shot his parents. And I'll be damned if I'm going to let Pearsall get Scottie-Boy off."

With her square jaw set in ferocious determination, Inez resembled Patton on the front lines. Natalie suppressed a smile. The passing years obviously hadn't mellowed the prosecutor. "If you think Lyman is behind this, why not ask the Corps to check him out?"

"I did. They told me he has a perfect track record and left it at that. They evidently don't appreciate anyone who questions the credibility of Corps Violets.

"That's why I came here, rather than going to your house." Inez glanced over her shoulder, no doubt certain that Corps Security agents were spying on them. Employing a non-Corps Violet in a criminal investigation was a felony, and both Inez and Natalie could go to jail if caught.

Good thing she didn't see George, Natalie thought wryly.

"I trust you," Inez said. "If *you* could summon the Hylands . . ." She let her eyes finish the proposition.

Natalie looked at her old friend, then at Callie, who now sulked on the rim of the merry-go-round, watching them with anxious boredom. "I'm sorry."

"I thought you might feel that way." Inez dipped her hand in the envelope again and withdrew a small clear plastic bag. "That's why I brought this."

Natalie took hold of the bag by one corner, as if accepting a dead rat. Inside it a chintzy charm bracelet had knotted itself into a ball of bangles.

"It belonged to Marcy Owen, Ries' second victim. She wouldn't have died if we'd managed to convict him. Maybe she can convince you." The prosecutor indicated the label on the bag, which bore a phone number. "If you change your mind, call and say you'd like to take advantage of our special offer. I'll know what you mean."

She walked away before Natalie could object. Growling, Natalie shoved the plastic bag into her purse, where it lodged in the folds of the School brochure. "Inez!"

The prosecutor glanced back.

"Good luck."

Inez cupped a hand to her mouth to amplify her reply. "No such thing!"

She proceeded to her blue Subaru Legacy—no doubt the same one she owned six years ago—and drove off.

Callie crept back to her mother's side. "Who was that, Mommy?"

Natalie stooped to pick her up. "Just a friend. Someone I used to work with."

"Does she have a job for you?"

"No." She carried her daughter toward the Volvo. "It was nothing."

When they got home with their pizza, Natalie took Callie inside, then put a couple of pepperoni and black-olive slices on a paper plate, grabbed a can of Coke from the fridge, and went out to where the ever-present LeBaron rested by the curb in front of the condo. George swiveled his head toward her, eyebrows arched over his wraparound shades, and rolled down the driver's-side window.

"Hey, Nat. What's this?"

"A little snack, since they've got you working through dinner again." She handed him the pizza and soda.

"Thanks. Think I would've starved without you by now." His Easter Island face split with a smile. Four years ago Natalie had used just such a snack to break the ice with the man the Corps had assigned to intimidate her, and they'd been fast friends ever since.

She leaned on the windowsill and peered inside. "What book you listening to? Another Clive Cussler?"

"Nah. Taking a break from him." He picked up one of the

white cassettes from the seat beside him. "Now I'm learning 'Fluent French in Forty Days.'" He cleared his throat. *"Bonjour, madame! Je suis heureux de faire votre connaissance. Où est la salle de bains?"* He enunciated each syllable, grinning proudly.

"Wouldn't Spanish be more practical in L.A.?" Natalie asked dryly.

"Yeah, but that wouldn't give me an excuse to take Monica to Paris, would it?"

They both laughed. Natalie jerked her chin in the direction of the rumpled spiral notebook beside him. "How's the novel coming?"

"Pah! I'll finish it when I retire." He peered down at the plate of pizza that now sat on his lap, the tiki-like solemnity returning to his face. "Nat, I don't wanna seem ungrateful for the hospitality, but I can't talk to you any more."

Natalie's smile faded. "What do you mean?"

"They're turning up the heat on you. I could lose my job." He scanned the street, looked over his shoulder—the watcher afraid of being watched. "Thought I should give you a heads-up."

Natalie frowned. "Is it because of Inez?"

"Who? Nah, it's your little girl. They want her."

"I know." Her hands tightened on the car's door frame. "They wouldn't just . . . take her, would they?"

George didn't answer right away. "Not without some sort of justification," he said at last. "You know the Corps; they like to maintain the appearance of acting within the law. But they'll jump at any chance to take her into 'protective custody.' Won't happen on my watch, but I can't say the same for Madison and Rendell."

Natalie nodded, already starting to quiver. Arabella

Madison and Horace Rendell were the other two Corps Security agents assigned to shadow her around the clock.

George leaned forward until she could almost see the weary eyes behind the shades. "*Garde-toi*, Nat. *Et attends ta fille*. Watch your daughter."

Natalie backed off from the LeBaron and ran into the condo without bothering to say good-bye. George would understand.

She was relieved to find that Callie still sat at the kitchen table. She'd pulled all the olives off the piece of pizza in front of her and scraped them into a big pile to eat one at a time.

"Is it good, baby girl?" Natalie asked, sliding a slice for herself onto a paper plate.

"Mmm-hmm!" Callie dropped another olive into her open mouth. "Can we go to McDonald's tomorrow?"

"No. And make sure you eat some of the cheese and bread, too."

Natalie looked down at the grease pooled in the pepperoni on her own slice and could almost feel the cholesterol collecting in her aorta. In her mind, she saw Dan thrusting a similar dripping mozzarella mess at her during one of their hurried lunches together. *C'mon . . . you know you want it!*

The ghost of a grin rose on her face. Given how many times she'd lectured Dan about his junk-food habit in their brief time together, he'd find her present diet incredibly funny. There was a time when she wouldn't have even considered such garbage food. Callie, however, had no such culinary inhibitions, for TV commercials and the other kids at day care had introduced her to all kinds of empty calories: pizza, tacos, peanut butter and jelly sandwiches, and even, God save us, McDonald's. To keep her happy, Natalie learned to eat the stuff and sometimes even enjoyed it.

Tonight her old revulsion returned. She left the pizza untouched on her plate and got a cup of yogurt out of the fridge. Her appetite didn't improve, however. She ate a few spoonfuls, but mostly just stared at her daughter.

After dinner, they went upstairs, and Callie demanded that her mother read her Dr. Seuss' *Horton Hears a Who* for the thousandth time.

"Is Daddy a Who?" she asked when Natalie closed the book and tucked her in bed, surrounded by Mr. Teddy and her other stuffed bears.

"Yeah," Natalie said with a sad half smile. "Sort of."

"And we're like Horton?"

Her mother considered the elephant that conversed with tiny creatures no one could see. "You could say that."

Callie nodded, as if this explained a lot. "Sometimes I hear other Whos," she confided.

Natalie eased herself back onto the bed. "Besides Daddy?"

"Uh-huh."

"How many?"

"Lots." She curled her hands around her mouth and whispered into Natalie's ear. *"Some of them aren't very nice."*

Natalie sighed. *You knew this was coming,* she reminded herself, but the thought didn't help. She'd done her best to shelter Callie up to that point. In fact, she bought this ugly, cookie-cutter condo simply because it was brand-spanking-new and therefore less likely to be a touchstone for deceased former residents. Even then, however, she realized her daughter wouldn't be safe for long, for the dead resided everywhere.

"I know you said not to talk to Daddy," Callie went on, "but he makes the bad ones go away. He comes in and pushes them out of my head."

"You don't need Daddy to get rid of them." Natalie gently

lifted her daughter's chin until their eyes met. "The next time the bad ones come, I want you to say your ABCs. Say 'em over and over without stopping until the bad ones go away. If that doesn't work, *then* call Daddy. Okay?"

Mouth twisting with doubt, Callie bobbed her head.

"You'll see. You can keep 'em out all by yourself." She ruffled Callie's hair, which now hung in loose curls, and kissed her forehead. "Good night, sweetheart."

"Night." Callie gave her a peck on the cheek.

Before she left the room, Natalie decided to make sure the windows were securely latched. Madison would be on duty now.

"Mommy, why do you change your eyes?"

Natalie paused with the curtains half drawn, cursing herself for forgetting to take out her contacts when they got home.

"Because people who can't hear Whos don't understand us," she told Callie without turning around. "So sometimes I have to pretend that I can't hear them, either."

"Oh."

"But we don't have to pretend with each other." She took one of the contacts out and winked at Callie with the violet eye. "I promise."

"Uh-huh." Callie lay like an overturned turtle under a shell of teddy-bear comforter. The dejection on her small face squeezed Natalie's heart.

"Love you, Mommy."

"Love you, too." Balancing the blue lens on her fingertip, she bent and kissed Callie's forehead again. "Sweet dreams, honey."

She shut the curtains and retreated from the bedroom, leaving the bedside lamp on in case Callie had . . . *problems* during the night. Easing the door shut behind her, she replaced the contact in her eye before descending the stairs.

The answering machine by the kitchen phone told her she had four messages, and Natalie didn't want to hear any of them. Nevertheless, she pressed PLAY but kept her finger poised on the SKIP button.

"Hi, there! This is Errol Wingard from Iris Semple Conduit Academy," a canned voice chirped. "We were wondering if you'd given any more thought to your child's enrollment in our school. As you know, she'll receive a full scholarship plus benefits—"

Natalie hit SKIP. The same recorded spiel every day! As bad as the Corps was, Natalie never thought they'd stoop to telemarketing.

Now the answering machine seethed with Corinne Harris' anguish. "You *fraud.* How *dare* you say such awful things in my father's name! I want my money back, you thieving bitch, or I swear I'll have Darryl—"

SKIP.

Natalie sighed. Corinne evidently found it easier to believe she'd been duped than to admit her father hated her.

"Hey, kiddo . . . it's me," the third message began, the man's tone embarrassed and . . . penitent? Natalie tapped on the SKIP button, but didn't press it.

"Sunny and I are in L.A. on a business trip and were wondering if we could treat you to dinner." He cleared his throat. "Don't know if you've still got my cell phone number, but you can reach me at—"

SKIP.

Her jaw clenched, Natalie was about to erase the fourth message unheard, particularly when it began like another School sales pitch.

"Good evening, Ms. Lindstrom. I was calling to ask whether you'd had a chance to consider our special offer."

Special offer. The words jarred Natalie's memory. The woman speaking was Inez.

"Feel free to contact me if you have any questions. My number is . . ."

Natalie snatched her purse off the table and dug out the plastic bag containing the charm bracelet. The recorded voice repeated the phone number on the bag's sticker.

"Remember, this is a limited-time offer, so please call today." A sinister emphasis edged the commercial blandness of Inez's tone. No doubt she feared that the Corps had tapped Natalie's phone. No doubt she was right.

Natalie shook the bag, and the bracelet ran in rivulets of silver chain beneath the plastic. Tiny plastic blocks, like miniature dice, alternated with the charms, black letters painted on each of them, spelling out a name: MARCY.

Maybe she can convince you.

I can't deal with this right now, Natalie told herself. *I've got enough problems of my own.* She toyed with the idea of tossing it in the kitchen trash along with Callie's half-eaten pizza and that infernal School brochure.

He'd wrapped her bra around her neck.

"Curse you, Inez." Natalie ripped open the bag and poured the bracelet into her palm.

She'd barely recited two words of her spectator mantra when her legs went numb. Dizzy and nauseated, she dropped onto a kitchen chair as Marcy Owen's memories bled into her brain. A runaway teenager fleeing an abusive father shacks up with an abusive boyfriend, only to have him pimp her for rent and drug money. One night she turns the wrong trick, and a blond, blue-eyed john twines her bra around her neck and pulls. A common-enough story for a murdered prostitute, and all the more tragic for being so familiar. But Marcy had one thing most murdered prostitutes didn't.

A son.

In her mind, a baby in grimy footie pajamas appeared, his tiny hands stretching upward to touch the matted fur of a thrift-store teddy bear, his blue eyes wide with awe. "Bobby," Natalie heard herself say.

Like an internal home movie, the memory's point of view swung from the baby's crib to the sofa, where a thick-limbed man in a bowling shirt and boxer shorts calmly lit a crack pipe. A bittersweet chemical smell like shorted circuitry filled the room, and the man coughed, his bloodshot eyes blinking with exhaustion. Gary, the boy's father—and now his sole parent and guardian.

Equally helpless to save the child, Marcy and Natalie sobbed as one. When Marcy leapt from the chair, looking for a way out of the house, Natalie shifted to her protective mantra. The charm bracelet slipped from her fingers.

The dead woman's soul dissipated back into blackness, leaving Natalie limp and alone. One murder, two victims.

She couldn't let another murderer go free.

Tear trails drying on her cheeks, she picked up the kitchen phone, dialed, waited.

"Libra Enterprises," Inez answered. "How may I help you?"

"You called earlier about a special offer." Natalie glanced at Marcy's bracelet, which lay on the floor like a silver worm. "I'd like to accept."

4

A Crooked House

LYMAN PEARSALL WAITED IN A BURGER KING IN LAKE-port, drinking coffee and eyeing the ebb and flow of diners around him for more than three hours, until well after sunset. Satisfied that none of the restaurant's patrons lingered as long as he did, he exited out the rear door to where his battered '89 Bronco crouched alone in the far corner of the parking lot.

Although none of the other cars from the Burger King followed him out onto the street, Pearsall drove in aimless detours along the roads that slithered through the hills surrounding Clear Lake. As he had during the entire nine-hour drive from L.A. up to northern California, he watched the rearview mirror to make sure no one tailed him. He had to be careful, now more than ever. The Corps had backed him up in the Ries case, but that didn't mean they trusted him.

When no headlights trailed in his wake, he turned onto a rural lane flanked by groves of craggy walnut trees. The road's potholes brimmed with water from recent rains, and the Bronco rocked and bounced each time its tires bottomed out in one of the miniature craters. Before long, Pearsall found himself rolling through two inches of standing water.

On the right, the orchard gave way to a row of houses, each one surrounded by its own moat, an archipelago of drowning islands. Their porch lights and windows were dark, their driveways empty. Here and there, a real estate agent's FOR SALE sign rose from the swamp of a front yard like a white flag. The channel that ran behind the homes had flooded with the winter's El Niño deluge, and the few residents who still lived on the street had all sought shelter elsewhere. That was fine with Lyman. Perfect, in fact.

The road ended in a crude cul-de-sac, where the silhouette of a two-story house hunkered among a stand of willow trees that swayed in the breeze like sea anemones in a rising tide. The binocular blots of the Bronco's headlight beams swelled in size on the house's façade as he drove up to it. Metal glinted in one of the upstairs windows. Wrinkled aluminum foil lined the inside of the glass, as if the room's occupant wanted to block out all external light.

Pearsall parked the Bronco in the detached garage and jumped down from the cab. Stagnant floodwater soaked his work boots and the cuffs of his jeans as he slogged around to open the rear door and tailgate. Looping the plastic handles of several Kmart bags over his left wrist, Lyman shoved a few rolls of chicken wire under his arm and grabbed one of the fluorescent lanterns with his right hand. He left the tailgate down and waded out of the garage and up to the front porch with his first load.

The air in the front hall was damp and stale with the scent of mold, and the dust that hung suspended in the lantern's grayish light made the entire room seem submerged in seawater. Stepping inside, Pearsall felt the familiar queasiness return as his internal organs all slid to the left inside of him. A previous flood had eroded the soil under the building's foundation, and the bare hardwood floor canted to one side like the deck of a sinking ship. "A fixer-upper," the real estate agent had called the house when she sold it to him two years ago. She could barely disguise her delight at being rid of the place. Lyman didn't care about the mold or the home's permanent list, however. The house was cheap and isolated, and that was all that mattered.

Pearsall grunted up the central stairway, lurching against the banister whenever the building's lean threw him off balance. He reached the second-floor landing, steadied himself, and shuffled around the corner to the left, where doors led into each of the three upstairs bedrooms. The one in the far right corner bore a large *X* of red duct tape that marked the bedroom whose windows were frosted with foil. The red *X* served as a reminder not to enter the room, but the tape was unnecessary; Lyman remembered only too well what resided in that room and why he should never go in there.

He proceeded through the door nearest to him into a bedroom which, like the rest of the house, had no furniture, no light fixtures, and not even a bare curtain rod for decoration. Lyman dropped his supplies inside and took the lantern back down to the Bronco for the next load.

It took several such trips up and down the crooked staircase before he was ready to begin work. Puffing with exertion, he plopped down on the lid of his metal tool chest and wolfed a king-size Snickers bar, washing it down with tepid Coke from a two-liter bottle.

This is the last one, he told himself again. *After this, I'm out of it for good.*

Despite the chill of the unheated house, Pearsall was sweating. He pulled the curly toupee off his head and wiped the perspiration off his bald scalp with his shirtsleeve.

The job took several hours, made more difficult by the

fact that he only had the light of his two fluorescent lanterns to work by. First came the initial layer of aluminum foil, which he tore off the rolls in long sheets and fastened to plaster or wood with a staple gun. These he used to cover every bare surface in the room: walls, windows, floor, ceiling. The cocked angle of the house made his ladder unstable, and he nearly fell off it twice.

Over the foil lining he unfurled the metal web of the chicken wire, nailing it in place so it would lay flat. Next, a layer of rubber matting to act as an insulator, then another layer of chicken wire and an inner lining of foil for good measure.

Exhaustion weighing on him, Lyman plopped down on the tool chest and surveyed his handiwork, looking for chinks in the room's metallic seal. It was already past midnight, and Pearsall considered quitting for the day. But, no, he needed to test the cage and make the final preparations at once.

Nevertheless, he dawdled, sipping listlessly from his Coke bottle until he'd emptied it. Dread increased his fatigue, and the longer he waited, the more weary and reluctant he became.

"Get on with it."

In the dripping emptiness of the house, the sound of his own voice startled him. He hadn't intended to speak aloud. Now alert and agitated, Pearsall pushed himself to his feet, mumbling his protective mantra.

> *"One penny, two penny, three penny, four,*
> *Five penny, six penny, seven penny, more . . ."*

He reopened the tool chest, removed the metal tray on top, and shone one of his lanterns into the compartment below. Three Ziploc plastic bags lay inside atop a pile of assorted screwdrivers, hammers, and wrenches. The first bag contained a man's black silk dress sock, the second a woman's hairbrush. He took these out, but left the third bag inside.

Pearsall had carefully measured and cut the metal and matting on the back of the bedroom door so that they would make a nice tight seal when he shut the door, which he did now. Entombed in the foil-gilded bedroom, Lyman unzipped the first bag and took out the dress sock while whispering his spectator mantra.

Several minutes passed, but no one knocked. The electromagnetic soul of the sock's former wearer couldn't pass through the metal and rubber barriers of the room's sealed lining. The cage was secure.

Satisfied, Pearsall put the sock back in its bag and set it on the floor along with the hairbrush. He pushed the bedroom door open again and cleared the chamber of everything but the two plastic bags and one of the fluorescent lanterns. Out in the hallway sat a plywood construction a bit larger than a telephone booth, open on one side, that was also covered in layers of foil, rubber matting, and chicken wire. Pearsall shoved the flimsy booth until its open side fit snugly against the frame of the bedroom's doorway and duct-taped foil over the crack where the booth's plywood met the wall's plaster. The enclosed entrance to the bedroom now resembled the safety airlock one passed through to enter a biohazard chamber.

The front of the booth featured a screen door, also covered in insulation and foil, that would slap shut automatically if released. As he stepped inside the booth, Lyman propped the door open with a plastic ruler tied to the end of a roll of twine. With the original bedroom door open as well, he backed into the bedchamber, unspooling string. When he reached the spot where he'd left the Ziploc bags, he cut the string and tied the frayed end around his right wrist.

Careful not to pull on the string, Lyman picked up the plastic-wrapped sock and hairbrush. He was taking a big risk. Violets who summoned more than one soul at the same time sometimes suffered seizures, their brains trying to serve too many masters at once. Even his protective mantra might not wrest control of his flesh from the invading entities in time.

This is your ticket out, he told himself, ripping open both bags. *After this you're free.*

Reciting his spectator mantra, he clutched the sock in one hand and the hairbrush in the other like the positive and negative poles of some gigantic battery.

The souls responded to his call. He barely had time to yank the string before his body collapsed into a quivering heap.

The plastic ruler popped out, and the foil-covered screen door slapped shut, sealing the cage. It couldn't contain Pearsall's screams, however, which resounded through every room of the crooked house.

Some time later, Lyman clambered out of the bedroom and into the narrow confines of the plywood booth as if pursued by wolves. He slammed the door and leaned against it, panting his protective mantra. Although his instincts told him to run from the house and never return, he waited in the booth until his heart stilled its jackhammer arrhythmia.

He had to be sure.

Patting his pants pockets, he withdrew the sock from one of them, pressed it between quivering hands. Nothing. Then the hairbrush. Nothing.

With the relief of a demolitions expert who has defused a bomb, Lyman stepped out into the hall and ripped the booth free of the wall, dragging it to one side for possible future use. He then slapped an *X* of red duct tape across the closed bedroom door.

Lowering himself with a groan, he sagged to the floor for several minutes, unmoving, his head aching from lack of sleep. The damp chill of the house leeched the remaining strength from his limbs, and the constant reek of mold made his throat and nose feel raw and coated with scum.

"Hope I don't catch anything," Lyman muttered, snorting mucous. The thought struck him as so funny that he giggled hysterically.

Wanting nothing more than to flop into a nice warm bed at a local motel, he got to his feet and bent over the open tool chest, which now rested in the hallway beside the second fluorescent lantern. One Ziploc bag still lay in the chest, a dark *V* enveloped in its plastic. As Pearsall lifted it from the box, the open jackknife grinned at him in the lantern's sickly light.

Again Lyman considered waiting until morning, when sleep and sunlight had cleared his mind. But he knew that if he put it off, he might change his mind, and he'd come too far for that.

He slid his hand into the bag and pinched the ebony handle of the knife between his fingers. Not that he needed a touchstone to summon this particular soul. He *was* the touchstone now.

Howdy, Lyman, a voice in his head purred.

Pearsall dropped the knife. The speed of the inhabitation unnerved him, as if a person he'd called on the phone turned out to be standing right behind him. He tried to say his protective mantra, but his lips and tongue had already gone numb.

"Need my help again, eh?" he heard his own voice say. "Well, you know how to purchase my services."

A bystander in his own body, Lyman Pearsall saw himself stoop to pick the jackknife off the floor. He watched himself kiss its blade, then fold it shut and tuck it into the back pocket of his jeans.

5

Fielding Offers

THE DAY AFTER CALLING INEZ, NATALIE ARRANGED FOR a babysitter to watch Callie for the afternoon and scheduled an appointment with Liv, her hairdresser. She could've done the job herself at home with a pair of scissors and her electric razor, but figured she might as well donate her two-foot blond tresses to the local "Hair Care" program that made wigs for kids undergoing cancer treatment.

Someone ought to get some use out of it, she thought morosely as she regarded her reflection in the salon's mirror. Liv had already tucked the nylon sheet around Natalie's neck and now braided her hair into two heavy ropes.

"Last chance to change your mind." Arching her pierced eyebrows, Liv snipped the air with her shears.

"Go on. Get it over with."

Liv sawed at the first braid with the crux of her scissors, and Natalie shut her eyes. She didn't open them again until her cranium ceased humming from the whine of the electric clippers.

She'd been through this before, of course. At the School, they'd shaved her head at age twelve so Dr. Krell could locate her node points. Hidden by hair for five years, the twenty tattooed spots still dotted her scalp, showing where to attach the SoulScan electrodes. As Liv brushed away the last of the clippings, Natalie stared at her own bald reflection, alarmed at how the years had hardened her features and hollowed her eyes. Would Callie look the same way when she passed thirty—a skull-faced mutant who only served as a mouth-piece for the deceased?

If only Dad could see me now. . . .

"Hey, honey," he said, as if in answer.

In the mirror, Natalie saw Liv turn toward the voice, and there beside her stood Wade Lindstrom, as timid as a rookie vacuum-cleaner salesman on his first doorstep. He'd lost weight since she last saw him, and folds of loose skin drooped from his face. Filaments of silver infiltrated the amber hair on his crown, while his temples had gone completely white.

Natalie suppressed a groan. "Dad, how did you—"

"I stopped by your house. Callie's sitter told me where to find you." His hands seemed rooted in the pockets of his sports coat. "Hope you don't mind."

"Why should I mind? This way you can admire my new 'do." She stroked her bare scalp.

"You going back to work for the Corps?" He failed to conceal the note of hope in his voice.

"You wish." No doubt Dad would be delighted if she patched things up with the N-double-A-C-C: because she walked out on them, he'd been blacklisted from all those juicy government contracts he used to enjoy.

Diplomatically silent, Liv whisked away the nylon sheet, and Natalie dug through her macramé handbag for money to pay her. "What can I do you for, Dad?"

"My dinner invitation still holds, if you're interested. I fig-ured you'd . . . be too busy to call, so that's why I stopped by."

"Uh-huh." She handed Liv two twenties and waved away the offer of change. "How long you in town for?"

"Just till Tuesday. But if I get this contract, I might be making regular trips to L.A."

"Mmm." Natalie opened the wig box she'd left on the counter and took out a roll of double-sided wig tape. She tore strips off the roll and pasted them onto her brow and temples. "Visited Mom yet?"

Wade cleared his throat. "Haven't had a chance. Meetings all week."

"Uh-huh. Well, we couldn't miss those, could we?" She lifted the old blond wig from the box, shook it out, and set it on her head as if donning a tiara. A few shades lighter than her natural color, it was the closest approximation of her real hair among the wigs she owned. She didn't want to startle Callie with a radical change in her appearance. "I'm pretty busy myself," she said, preening before the mirror.

"I realize it's short notice. But it's been a long time, and since it's a Saturday night, I thought maybe . . ." Wade shrugged.

Natalie's upper lip curled. "I suppose Sheila's going to be there."

"Yeah, Sunny and I are still married. Sorry to disappoint you."

She faced him for the first time. "You hardly saw me for more than twenty-five years and now you're buying me dinner. Why bother?"

"I have a granddaughter now. I'd like to get to know her."

"You have a daughter, too. You should get to know *her* sometime."

His milky-blue eyes never left her face. For once Natalie wished she'd left her contacts out. Dad always had trouble looking at her violet irises—they reminded him too much of Mom. No doubt that was one of the things he liked about

Sheila: nice, dull eyes as brown as her bottle-brunette hair. Darling "Sunny" would never end up in a loony bin, not with a vacuous psyche as spotless as her kitchen floor.

Natalie grabbed her purse and wig box and waved to Liv. "See ya in a couple years, girlfriend."

Wade's voice followed her to the salon's front door. "I could help keep her out of the School."

She paused, her hand on the door handle, and gave him a hard look. His cloudy eyes seemed sincere yet shrewd. A master negotiator, Wade Lindstrom always got the better end of a business deal.

"If you want to discuss Callie, we should meet without her there," she said. "And I only have the sitter for this afternoon."

Wade took a hundred-dollar bill from his wallet and held it out to her. "Contribute that to her college fund. I'm sure she'll stay a few extra hours."

Natalie made no move to take his money. If she was going to do this, it would be on her terms.

"The Spicy Thai. Corner of Lemon and Orangethorpe." She chose the restaurant because she knew it would give him heartburn. "Be there at six."

She left the salon without waiting for a reply.

Natalie seriously considered not showing up. Maybe that would teach Dad what it was like to wait for the attention that never came—payback for all those weekends he was too busy with "business" to visit her at the School. She only wished she could be there to see the forlorn look on his face as he and Sheila sat alone in the empty restaurant while the waiters put the chairs on the tables. God knows Natalie had worn that look enough in her life.

But she had to think about Callie. Maybe Dad could provide for her. He'd certainly made enough money in his life.

Natalie wanted to make some kind of statement, though, so she went home and switched her blond wig for one with a glossy, unnatural obsidian sheen. "Rebel black," they called it back in the eighties. She exchanged her white blouse and blue jeans for a black minidress and fishnet tights, her sneakers for Doc Marten boots. For the finishing touches, she took out her contacts, applied heavy mascara, eyeliner, purple iridescent eye shadow, and black lipstick. There wasn't time enough to paint her nails, but she compensated by wearing all the cheap and jangly silver chains and plastic bracelets she could find in her jewelry drawer.

By design, she arrived at the restaurant half an hour late. Wade and Sheila Lindstrom awaited her inside, seated on red vinyl-upholstered benches by the cash register. The way they blanched when Natalie smirked at them made the whole trip worthwhile.

"Hope I haven't kept you waiting," Natalie said casually.

It took them a moment to get to their feet.

"No problem, honey." Wade forced a chuckle. "We just got here ourselves."

"Hey, Sheila." Natalie put out her hand, bracelets clattering. "Glad you could make it."

"Natalie." Her stepmother gave her fingers a light squeeze, her mouth stretched as if exposing her teeth to a dentist. "You look . . . well."

"Nice of you to say so." She evaluated Sheila's knee-length skirt, square-shouldered jacket, eternally brunette bob. "And you're as stylish as ever."

"Let's get a table." Wade pushed them toward the host, who waited, menus in hand, to seat them.

For the first fifteen minutes, they talked only about what food to order. Natalie made several recommendations—panang, moo phad prik-pao, drunken noodles. All the spiciest dishes.

"Go with it." Wade slapped his menu shut. "I'm doomed whatever we get."

Their server, a teenage Thai girl whose black hair was streaked with auburn highlights, jotted Natalie's suggestions on her pad, tore the sheet off, and passed it through a long rectangular window into the kitchen.

Drumming on the table as if playing the bongos, Wade surveyed the restaurant walls, which featured framed posters of Tiger Woods on the fairway. "Not your typical Oriental décor."

Natalie leaned back and crossed her legs. "You were expecting paper lanterns and pagodas?"

"Callie's such a lovely girl," Sheila interjected with helium happiness. "So much bigger since we last saw her. And so bright!"

"Thanks." Natalie aimed her reply at Wade. "Home schooling, you know."

He bit his lip and nodded.

"Wade's always saying how he'd like to spend more time with her." Sheila patted his shoulder in spousal camaraderie. "That's why he's working so hard to get this West Coast contract."

"I heard. How *is* business, Dad?"

"Slow. Things are tough in the private sector, but we've got some long-term servicing revenue from climate-control systems we've already installed, and if it's a hot summer this year, our sales may go up." He squeezed juice from a lemon wedge into his ice water. "No government deals, of course."

Natalie's mouth twitched. "That's the Corps for you. Quick to forget a favor, slow to give up a grudge." Despite the fact that she'd helped catch the Violet Killer and dozens of other murderers, the NAACC had chosen to punish her and her entire family for her decision to leave the service. They wanted to make an example of her—a warning to any other Violets who might want to defect.

The server arrived with their meal, leaning between them to set heavy oblong platters of food on the table. "Anything else I can get you?"

Wade laughed. "A fire extinguisher."

His nose wrinkled as the scents of curry, ginger, and chili steamed up into his face. Natalie noted with sly satisfaction that he popped a Rolaids tablet in his mouth before they'd finished half the meal, while Sheila attempted to guzzle ice water with dozens of tiny ladylike sips.

Natalie displayed a bit of curry-drenched beef with her fork. "Like the food?"

"Oh, yes." Sheila picked at some of the pork. "The sauce is so . . . rich. I really can't do it justice." She took another nibble of rice and nudged her plate away.

Wade levered a hank of noodles to his mouth. "How're you doing?"

This was the moment Natalie always dreaded. When Wade Lindstrom asked *How're you doing?* he wanted to know how much money you were making. In her father's arithmetic, financial security equaled contentment equaled happiness. Every problem could be solved with a sufficient amount of money. Every problem, that is, except for his first wife's insanity and his only daughter's bitterness.

"Things are great." Natalie acted surprised that he'd even thought otherwise. "It's strictly freelance work, but I've been able to make my payments on the condo. Plus I get to stay home and take care of Callie most of the time."

"Good thing. Wish I could've done the same."

"You could have."

Wade coughed a piece of beef gristle into his napkin. "I saw you as often as I could. As often as the School would let me."

"You could have seen me every night if you hadn't sent me there in the first place."

Sheila's smile lines slanted downward. "Your father's always done his best for you. You've never wanted for anything."

"Only a family."

"That's not fair! We were *always* there for you. If you hadn't been so stubborn—"

"Relax, honey. Natalie's right."

Sheila glowered at him but pinched her mouth shut.

"I know you feel like I abandoned you," Wade said, "but your mother and I discussed it when you were born and thought it'd be safer for you to have School training when you got old enough. Nora went through exactly what you did, and she thought it was the best thing. It was her decision as much as mine."

Natalie studied his expression like a cardplayer gauging an opponent's bluff. "You put me there, even after you saw what happened to her."

"I know. I was overwhelmed by Nora's breakdown. Told myself I didn't want you to see her like that, that I didn't have the energy to care for both a kid and a mental patient."

He tore another chalky antacid tablet from the roll and placed it on his tongue. "Truth is, I didn't know *how* to take care of you. I convinced myself the School could do it better."

"Maybe you were right."

"Maybe I was wrong." He leaned toward her. "I know it's too late for me to be a father, but I can still be a grandfather. Please give me a chance."

The clink of china from the kitchen swirled in to fill the lull in conversation. The server swept by to check on them, sensed the tension, and discreetly withdrew.

Natalie leveled her violet gaze, unblinking, at Wade. "Callie is one of us. If you couldn't handle Mom or me, what makes you think you can handle her?"

His eyes quivered, as if he were straining to win a staring contest, then flicked toward Sheila, seeking support.

"That's what I thought." Natalie got out of her chair, dug a couple of twenties out of her purse, and tossed them on the table. "Dinner's on me. Have a nice trip home."

Sheila sniped at her from behind, but Natalie sauntered out of the restaurant without bothering to listen.

She found driving at night nerve-racking at the best of times; tonight, the trip home was intolerable. The moment she left her father and stepmother, a perverse gloom of guilt descended upon her. Had she been too hard on them? What if Dad really did want to help Callie? Was she simply being stubborn, as dear Sheila claimed?

Why the hell should I feel sorry for them? Since when have they shown me any sympathy?

To justify her wrath, Natalie replayed the fiasco of the last birthday she'd celebrated with her family. Lucky number thirteen.

Her father stuck his head into her School dorm room and grinned. "Hey, kiddo!"

Natalie glanced up from her cot, where she'd been drawing on a sketch pad with a set of colored chalks. "Oh, it's you. What are you doing here?"

"Come on now! You don't think I forgot what day it is, do you?"

"Of course not. It's Tuesday." She went back to rubbing chalk on the page.

He sighed and stepped back from the door. "Give us a minute," he murmured to someone outside the room.

Wade returned with a department-store gift box topped by the rose of a red ribbon bow. "I'm sorry I haven't been able to visit, honey. The School says you're going through a very important transitional time right now—all the students' visits are restricted."

"Uh-huh." She scribbled out the figure she'd drawn, ripped out the page and balled it up, and started over on a blank sheet.

"I'm lucky they make exceptions for birthdays and holidays." Her father refreshed his smile and sat beside her on the bed, but his twitching eyes betrayed his discomfort. "How's it going?"

"Oh, swell." Natalie stroked the eggshell smoothness of her newly shaven scalp, tattooed node points dotting the skin like some new kind of measles. "Like it?"

He responded by handing her the package. "You said the School hadn't given you the wig they promised yet. I figured you might appreciate this."

Shoving aside her artwork, she unwrapped the present with the perfunctory quickness of an assembly-line worker. Inside the box sat a foam mannequin head that bore a flaxen blond wig on its snowball pate.

"Real human hair," her father pointed out. "The best money can buy."

"Gee. Thanks, Dad." Maybe now he won't be embarrassed to be seen in public with me, *she thought, stroking the carefully coiffed locks.*

"I thought you could slap that on and then we could take you to dinner."

She frowned. " 'We'?"

Wade's smile flickered. "There's someone I'd like you to meet."

He walked over to the door and leaned out into the hallway. "Sunny?"

A brunette woman of approximately her dad's age inched into the room. She wore the business attire of a corporate attorney and the makeup of a televangelist, her lipsticked mouth petrified into a smile.

"Natalie, this is Sheila Ferguson. She works in my office. Sheila . . . my daughter Natalie."

"Wade's told me so much about you, Natalie." Sheila delivered the words as if reading off cue cards. Like most non-Violets, however, she couldn't sustain eye contact with Natalie's purple stare, and her gaze darted back to Wade. "You're even prettier than the pictures he showed me."

"Thanks." Natalie knew very well she wasn't pretty. So far, puberty had stretched her height without plumping her figure, making her gawky and boyish. The School had started shaving her head less than a month ago, and whenever she looked in the mirror, she saw a cross between a chemotherapy patient and a concentration-camp inmate.

"Natalie wants to be in the Corps' Art Division," her father said when no one else spoke. "She'll be working with the likes of Rembrandt and Da Vinci someday."

Sheila still held her handbag over her chest like a breastplate. "My, how exciting! I'd love to see some of your pictures."

"Here." Natalie flipped back a slab of pages in her sketchbook and held it up. "What do you think?"

Sheila's mouth crimped in puzzlement. "The detail is . . . remarkable."

"How about you, Dad?" Natalie tilted the portrait toward him. "Does it look like her?"

Wade turned ashen. "Yeah. It does."

"I did the best I could from memory." She studied the sketch of her mother critically. "I haven't seen her since I was four, so I wasn't sure how close I came."

Wade looked away, but Sheila bent closer to the picture, anxiety furrowing her forehead. "What is that?"

She indicated the figure that towered behind Nora Lindstrom's frightened-rabbit visage. Its U-shaped head resembled the mask of Tragedy, but the black crescents of its eyes and mouth slanted with fury rather than sorrow. The sinuous vines of its arms curled around to embrace Natalie's mother, its hands composed of long lethal needles aimed at Nora's skull.

"That? That's the Thresher." Natalie stared at the drawing, short of breath, and nearly forgot about her dad and the usurper pretending to be her mother. "I dream about him a lot. But Dad can tell you more about him than I can."

He scowled. "Drop it, Natalie."

"Why? If Sheila's going to be a member of the family, she should know what she's getting into. And she's certainly sucking up like she wants the job."

Bristling, Sheila bobbed her mouth open, only to shut it when she glanced at Wade.

"Get dressed," he snapped at his daughter. "We're going to dinner."

"Fine. Have fun." Natalie picked up her tablet and resumed drawing.

*Her father seated himself next to her again, put his hand on
her shoulder. "Please, honey. I'll take you wherever you want
to go."*

She kept sketching. "Promise?"

"Yes."

"In that case, I want to see her."

*He defied her glare for a moment, but her violet gaze wore
him down. "Okay."*

Her dad actually kept that promise. They drove directly to
the private sanitarium in Manchester where Nora was hospi-
talized at the time. Sheila, of course, sulked in the car with
passive-aggressive politeness while Wade took Natalie inside
to see her mother. Afterward, she understood why he'd
wanted to shield her from Nora's illness for almost a decade.

The real Thresher turned out to be far worse than the
one Natalie's childish nightmares had conjured.

Rather than fueling Natalie's anger, the memories exhausted it. She pressed harder on the Volvo's accelerator, de-
siring nothing more than to soak in the shower before going
to bed.

The slender figure of Arabella Madison waited for her by
the condo's front door with the patience of an eviction notice.

"Not tonight," Natalie groaned as she pulled into the
driveway.

Since she had to drive the babysitter home, Natalie left
the car out of the garage. As she got out and stalked up to the
front step, Madison smiled and cast an amused glance at
Natalie's short skirt and fishnets. "Nice getup, Ms. Lindstrom.
Working nights now?"

"Very funny, Bella. Shouldn't you be off collecting newts'
eyes and frogs' toes somewhere?"

The Corps Security agent laughed. Dressed in black leggings and patent leather boots and jacket, she cocked her hip as if posing on a Parisian catwalk. "I'm sure Child Protective Services would be eager to learn of any new . . . *employment* you've obtained. Particularly if it sets a poor example for your daughter."

"If clothes were a crime, you wouldn't be walking the streets. Now, if you'll kindly get out of my way." She shoved the agent aside.

"Did you enjoy dinner with your father?" Madison asked while Natalie fished her keys out of her handbag.

Accustomed to being spied on, Natalie ignored her and unlocked the door.

"Must be hard for him without all those government accounts," the agent mused. "Of course, he has it easy compared to your mother, poor dear."

Don't look at her, Natalie thought. *Don't listen.*

"Too bad you couldn't afford to keep her in that private sanitarium. State hospitals can be so bleak."

"Good *night,* Bella." Natalie opened the door.

"We can amend the situation, you know. And you won't even have to come back to work."

Despite her better instincts, Natalie turned to glare at her. "Okay, I'll bite. What's the catch?"

"In appreciation of your years of loyal service to the Corps, we're prepared to recognize your early retirement." She sounded as if she were about to give Natalie a gold watch. "We'll restore your full benefits and reinstate your mother's long-term care insurance. No more harassment, no more surveillance. You'd never have to see me again."

"That's almost worth selling my soul right there. What do I have to do for it?"

The agent pouted her lips a moment, phrasing her response in proper legalese. "The agreement is contingent upon your daughter's enrollment at the Academy."

Natalie shook her head with a dry chuckle. "Why am I not surprised? See ya 'round, Bella." She stepped through the front door and moved to shut it behind her.

"We're going to get her anyway, you know," Madison called from outside. "Sooner or later. All we need is a reason."

Natalie paused, recalling what George had said about "protective custody."

"I'll keep that in mind," she replied, and slammed the door.

Natalie stormed through the living room and was halfway up to the condo's second floor before she heard Patti Murdoch, the babysitter, call to her.

"Uh ... I already put Callie to bed." The teen flashed a timid, brace-faced smile from the bottom of the stairs. "Were you going to take me home?"

"Oh ... sure." Her anger doused by embarrassment, Natalie shifted her weight between a higher and lower step, unsure whether to go up or down. "Look, could you stay another hour or so? I'll give you an extra ten bucks."

Patti peeked at her watch. "It's kind of late. If I could call my folks—"

"Sure. Thanks." Natalie hurried on up to her bedroom and shut the door.

Once alone, she tore off the rebel-black wig and paced the carpet, massaging her forehead as if kneading the thoughts beneath her cranium. The words of her spectator mantra bubbled into her mouth like a drowning breath.

"Come on, Dan," she muttered when her summons went unanswered for several minutes. "I *know* you're there."

But maybe he wasn't. Maybe he'd gone to that other place he'd talked about. . . .

She crammed that fear back into its appropriate box among the compartmentalized anxieties in her brain and kept calling for him, all the while cursing herself as a hypocrite. She always scolded Callie for being too dependent on Dan, and yet whom did Natalie herself run to every time she got depressed?

"Come to me, Dan. Don't cop out on me now."

At last, she felt the welcome prickling of her fingers and toes. Moaning with relief, she sank to the floor beside her bed and let his sense-memories wash over her as if sliding into a warm bath: tasting the wine he drank at their first dinner together, smelling the rose and salt of her own skin as he made love to her for the first time.

It's been a while, Natalie, he said. She was too keyed up to submit to full inhabitation, so he spoke to her in thoughts, like an echo in the caverns of her skull.

"I know." The voice in her head conjured the image of his face—ruffled brown hair and kind, tired eyes, a hard, haunted look but an easy grin. "You don't knock anymore."

I thought you wanted me to let you and Callie live your own lives. The wistful accusation in his tone made her wince.

"I do, but . . . I miss you."

I miss you, too. I spend all my time reliving our days together, but there were so few. . . .

"Please . . . don't."

I'm sorry. I wouldn't come to Callie, but she keeps calling me.

"She loves you." Natalie sniffed and giggled. "She's so much like you, I think I see you inside her every day." She curled her lips down around her teeth and bit on them until the welling sob subsided. "I'm glad she can know her father."

Me, too. Still, maybe it would be better if I went on—

"Do we have to talk about that tonight?"

But it's real, Natalie. The place beyond. I can feel it. It waits for all those who are ready for it.

She could sense the eagerness humming in Dan's soul, stronger than the last time he'd spoken of it. "Are *you* ready for it?"

It took him a long time to answer. *Maybe . . .*

A knot formed in Natalie's throat. "And this place . . . do you love it more than me?"

Dan became so still inside her that she wondered if he'd already abandoned her for Paradise.

No.

He didn't mention it again that night. Instead, he listened patiently as she wept about the problems massing around her—the Hyland case, the Corps, her father—and gave her the comfort she craved. But when he departed, he trickled out of her with the whispering finality of sand running through pinched glass, leaving Natalie as empty as if her own soul had followed his into the place beyond.

6

Visiting Hours

LIKE THE ILLEGITIMATE OFFSPRING OF A MUNITIONS factory and a penitentiary, the Los Angeles Mental Health Institute managed to retain an overcast grayness even in the glaring sunshine of a cloudless southern California morning. Natalie hunched over the Volvo's steering wheel and stared at the asylum, conjuring all kinds of reasons not to go inside. She'd be late for her meeting with Inez, the visit would only depress her, and Mom wouldn't remember it, anyway.

Now you're starting to think like Dad, Natalie chided herself. She grabbed the shopping bag from the seat beside her and got out of the car.

A feeling of moral superiority motivated her to make the trip to the sanitarium in the first place. She wouldn't abandon Mom the way Dad did, by God! Never mind the fact that she hadn't visited for almost three months; she'd simply lost track of time in the daily scramble to make a living. Now that she needed to go to L.A. anyway, she could easily swing by and drop in on Mom. She would *prove* she cared.

As she entered the institution's reception area, though, her sense of duty eroded under cresting waves of dread. Truth was, Natalie barely knew Nora Lindstrom.

Are you my best friend? a squeaky falsetto voice asked in her head. The sock puppet, whom her mother had named

Yo-Yo, cocked its white woolly head and peered at her with jiggly eyes. Both the puppet and the woman who wore it waited for an answer.

Yes, her four-year-old self had answered at the time. *Best friends forever.* She'd glanced down at the dregs of milk and sugar in her plastic teacup and asked, *Can we have some more?*

Not right now, the puppet had replied. *I have to go away for a while. But I'll be back soon.* And it sealed the promise with a terry-cloth kiss.

Natalie didn't see Nora again until the day Wade took her to the hospital almost nine years later.

The tea party was one of the only memories Natalie had of her mother—of the woman she had been before the Thresher destroyed her mind. It made a paltry counterweight to the reality of the mumbling wraith who now shambled through the Institute's corridors.

The foyer was white and bright, its floor tiled with beige linoleum. A young woman with brown eyes and a coffee complexion attended the reception desk, and she greeted Natalie with professional pleasantness. "Hi, there. May I help you?" She hesitated to acknowledge her by name as she usually did, reminding Natalie that the receptionist had never seen her wearing her blond wig.

"Hey, Marisa. I'm here to see my mom."

"Oh! Ms. Lindstrom—yes, we received your call this morning." She pushed a button on the switchboard in front of her, smiling at Natalie as she adjusted the headset in her right ear. "I thought it was you. You changed your hair."

"You could say that."

"Looks nice . . . hello? Natalie Lindstrom is here to see

Nora. Is she . . . ?" Marisa nodded at some inaudible reply. "Uh-huh. Okay. I'll let her know."

She punched another button and glanced up. "Your mother's still with her doctor. It'll be a few minutes, if you'd like to wait over there."

Natalie thanked her and went over to sit on one of the hard wooden benches Marisa indicated. The "few minutes" turned into more than half an hour, and Natalie cursed herself for not bringing a newspaper to read. Instead, she was forced to stare at the wide white door across from her, which had no knob or handle, only the flat plate of a dead bolt lock.

Too bad you couldn't afford to keep her in that private sanitarium, Arabella Madison sneered in her head. *State hospitals can be so bleak. . . .*

When Natalie first got assigned to the Corps' West Coast Crime Division in her early twenties, she had moved Nora to the rest home in Ventura, for she knew that if she couldn't visit her mother regularly then no one else would. For a mental health facility, it was a pleasant place, with lace curtains on the windows and prints of pastel Impressionist paintings on the walls. Nora especially enjoyed the private gardens, where Natalie would lead her on sunny afternoons to watch hummingbirds sip from the bells of the trumpet vines.

The minute Natalie quit the Corps, the NAACC, in retaliation, cut off her mother's health benefits as well as her own, and the Ventura facility informed her that they could no longer maintain Nora as a resident.

You shoulda seen this coming, kiddo, Wade chastised Natalie when she called for help. *No insurance carrier on earth will touch your mother with her preexisting condition, and Sunny and I can't afford to put up eighty grand a year to care for her. You're expecting a kid and you walk away from a good job with full benefits . . . what were you thinking?*

Natalie put her face in her hands. *I was thinking of Callie, Dad,* she told him again, as she had that day. *I had to do it, for her sake.*

A metallic clatter and the whine of spring hinges made her look up. Andy Sakei, a short but burly Japanese American orderly, leaned out from behind the door and smiled. "Natalie? Is that you?"

"None other." She crossed the lobby to join him.

"You changed—"

"—my hair. Yeah, I know. How're things with you?"

"Hectic, as usual." Once she'd stepped through into the locked ward, he shut the door and pulled his key from the dead bolt. The reel on his belt sucked in the key chain like a strand of spaghetti. "Cindy and I are expecting our second any day now."

"Congrats! Boy or girl?"

"We asked the doctor not to tell us. Ultrasound always seems like cheating." He gave a little-boy snicker, his high-pitched tenor a charming contrast to the camel-hump biceps that inflated the short sleeves of his white uniform.

He conducted her down a corridor lined with identical knobless beige doors to a room at the corner of the building. Somewhere in the ward, someone cried out; the acoustics hollowed out the howl, making it impossible to tell if the person was male or female, hysterical, angry, or anguished.

Andy ignored it. "Your mom's receiving her medication, but I can bring her down when she's done."

Natalie passed through the door he held open for her. "Is she . . . okay?"

He shrugged. "She gets a little anxious now and then. You know how it is."

"Yeah." Natalie pulled a bouquet of daisies out of the grocery bag. "Okay if I give her these?"

"Sure. You got something to put 'em in?"

She dipped her hand into the bag again and brought up a 44-ounce plastic Slurpee cup. Glass containers were forbidden in the hospital because the patients might break them and injure themselves.

Andy grinned. "That works. See you in a few."

He left, shutting the door behind him. Sighing, Natalie set her bag on the long table in the room's center and arranged her bouquet in the Slurpee cup, adding water from a bottle she'd brought with her. As she did so, her gaze drifted to the pads of drawing paper that lay in front of each plastic chair around the table.

The remains of an art-therapy session still splashed the top pages of each tablet, blunt crayons strewn across them like burnt matchsticks. The pictures ranged from realistic to abstract, some featuring delicate portraits, others stick figures and caricatures. Pacing around the table's perimeter, Natalie glanced at each drawing in turn and noted that despite their different styles, they all shared a common theme.

Families.

And none of them looked happy.

Here, a tiny white baby nearly vanished in the maw of an enormous black crib as a vast maternal shadow hovered above. There, an angry red grate of clenched teeth formed a father's mouth. In each case, the parents dwarfed the children, some of whom were missing eyes, mouths, entire faces.

The pictures reminded Natalie of the sketches she'd done

as a kid . . . and sometimes still did. Had her mother drawn any of these pictures? If so, was she depicting her own childhood or that of the Thresher, the man she imagined was inhabiting her?

Your mother may say some scary things, honey, her dad had warned her before that visit on her thirteenth birthday. *No matter what she says, remember: It's her illness talking. The Thresher is NOT REAL.*

The door opened, and Andy urged a frail wisp of a woman into the room. "This way, Nora."

Natalie's mother shuffled forward, her slippered feet barely visible beneath the hem of her shapeless flannel robe. Her violet eyes wandered over the objects around her without seeing them, yet would occasionally fix on emptiness as if seeing something beyond the walls. Allowed to grow out after her retirement from the Corps, her blond hair had gone gray and chaff-dry. Though the hospital attendants had done their best to make it cover her scalp, tattooed dots peeked through the thin patches where she'd torn the hair out in clumps.

Nora drifted to the left, and Natalie moved into her path, hoping to make eye contact. "Mom?"

Andy gently steered Nora to face her. "Look who's here! It's your little girl."

Nora gave a puzzled scowl, and her gaze zigzagged up to Natalie's face. "My little girl?"

"It's me, Mom. Natalie."

"Natalie . . ." Nora rolled the name on her tongue, like a wine taster attempting to identify an unfamiliar vintage.

The diaper scent of urine that emanated from her mother made Natalie's nose twitch, but she contrived a smile and proffered the bouquet in its Slurpee vase. "Look what I brought you."

The flowers held no interest for Nora. *"Natalie,"* she repeated with greater urgency.

Andy pulled one of the chairs out from the table. "Here, Nora. Sit here."

He gently pressed down on her left shoulder with one hand while pushing against the back of her knees with the other. Nora's body folded itself into the chair, and Natalie sat facing her. "How're you doing? I know it's been a while . . ."

Nora's eyes sought hers, locked in on them. "Natalie?"

She smiled. "Yes, Mom, it's me. I—"

Nora snapped her hand around Natalie's forearm like a manacle. *"Has he come to you?"*

For an instant, Natalie thought she meant Wade Lindstrom. "I saw Dad last night, actually. He said to give you his love," she added, wondering why she was lying on his behalf.

Nora's nails dug into her wrist. "He *will.* He *will* come." She levered herself forward until their noses nearly touched, and Natalie had the unsettling impression of looking at her future mirror image. *"Don't let him in."*

"Now, Nora, let's not get excited." Andy pried her hand loose and eased her back in the chair.

Natalie sighed and looked away. *It's always the Thresher,* she thought.

Nora rotated her eyes so far to one side that she seemed to be trying to peer into her own skull. "He's everywhere."

"Mom, please don't—"

"He's here *now.*"

"He's *not* here. You won't get better until you realize that."

"He's always here." Her mother curled forward, hands

spidering up to nest in her thinning hair. "He'll never leave. Oh, God, Natalie, I'm sorry . . ."

She shuddered as if sobbing and Natalie reached to comfort her, ashamed that she felt more embarrassment than empathy. "It's okay, Mom. Really."

Rearing back from her daughter's touch, Nora balled tufts of her remaining hair in her fists and shrieked.

Not today, Natalie silently prayed. But she knew it was already happening.

"Easy, girl." Andy squeezed Nora's wrists to loosen her hands. Natalie noticed that fingerprint bruises already spotted her mother's forearms.

Nora hissed, eyes shut, her face pinched into a spiteful sneer. "Eleven minutes, Nora. Eleven minutes I gasped and gagged and crapped my pants. And I'm gonna make you suffer *years* for every one of those minutes."

Although Natalie knew better, she covered her mouth, the Twenty-third Psalm circling in her mind.

"Hysterical inhabitation," the Corps called it. The strain of summoning the dead fractured the psyches of some Violets, who would feel souls knocking that weren't really there. Before the invention of the SoulScan in the mid-seventies, such psychosomatic inhabitations had sometimes convicted innocent people of murder.

Small wonder the jurors were fooled, Natalie thought. Nora Lindstrom had suffered her first hysterical inhabitation way back in '82, only moments after the Thresher ceased twitching in the gas chamber at San Quentin. Although SoulScan readings had since confirmed that her mother was delusional, even Natalie found it easy to believe that the Thresher was the puppeteer who made her mother list the atrocities he would commit as his revenge.

"You know better than anyone what I can do," Nora rasped, heaving her thin frame against the restraint of Andy's arms. "I'll work my art on everyone you love while you watch and cry."

Natalie had heard such threats ooze from her mother's mouth dozens of times, beginning with the visit on her thirteenth birthday. Back then, she'd run from the room sobbing when the Thresher vowed to fashion a crazy quilt from the skin of her torso. Natalie had since learned to hide her childhood revulsion behind a condescending adult pity.

But something different happened today, something for which she wasn't prepared. Evidently afraid he was about to lose control of his patient, Andy took a hypodermic from his shirt pocket, pulled the cap off with his teeth, and jabbed the needle in Nora's arm. The moment it pricked her skin, Nora opened her eyes and peered at Natalie from beneath lowered brows. An iceberg calmness settled upon her, and her mouth stretched into a grin.

"You're the daughter, aren't you? You've grown up since the last time I saw you." Nora reached for her with hungry fingers. "Let's get to know each other."

Recoiling from the hand as if it were leprous, Natalie flailed backward, barely managing to stay on her feet as she knocked over her chair.

He wants to get inside my head, the way he does with Mom, she thought, heartbeat stuttering. If his soul's energy came into contact with her body, she'd become a touchstone in the Thresher's quantum circuit, enabling his electromagnetic spirit to find her wherever she was, to knock whenever he wanted.

Nora's arm dropped to her side. "Another time, perhaps?" She cackled, a sleepy slur creeping into her words as the sedative kicked in. "I look forward to meeting every member of the Lindstrom family."

The cold clarity of her glare dimmed, and she sagged against Andy in boneless lassitude.

Natalie drew out the length of her breaths. *It wasn't really him,* she told herself. *It was just Mom, having one of her fits.*

But what did he mean when he said that she'd grown up since the last time he'd seen her? Natalie had visited her mom dozens of times as an adult, enduring Nora's hysterical inhabitations on almost every occasion. She should be like a sister to the delusional Thresher by now.

Unless that was the real *Thresher. Maybe the real one hasn't seen me since I was a kid. . . .*

Andy propped Nora's semiconscious form in the chair, resting her head against his belly, and unhooked the walkie-talkie from his belt. "Yo, Marisa. Can I get a gurney in thirteen A?"

"You got it," her crackly voice replied when he released the talk button.

"Thanks, girl." Hanging the device back on his belt, he glanced toward Natalie. "Sorry you came on one of her bad days." The orderly patted Nora's slack shoulders. "She usually isn't like this."

Natalie still stared at her mother. "God, I hope not."

A residual viciousness clung to Nora's face like a fungus, fading only when her expression slackened into a catatonic stupor.

7

No Answer

"SOMETHING ON YOUR MIND?" INEZ ASKED, UNCOIL-ing the wires of the SoulScan's electrodes.

Natalie settled into one of the motel room's chairs and removed the wig and tape from her head. "No. It's been a long time is all."

"Well, I hope it'll be an even longer time before you do it again."

The deputy D.A. tore strips of surgical tape from a roll and stuck them to her fingertips until her left hand curled with white tentacles. These she used to attach the first of the twenty quarter-size disks to the node points on Natalie's scalp.

Natalie shivered at the touch of steel, but not from the coolness of the metal. As much as she loathed the SoulScan, she didn't complain today, for she now wanted the extra security offered by the Panic Button.

You've grown up since the last time I saw you, Nora's voice rasped with husky lust in her head. *Let's get to know each other.*

Natalie hadn't told Inez about visiting her mom at the Institute; indeed, she arrived late for their meeting because she'd meditated in her car for half an hour, inhaling and exhaling yogic breaths to forget the homicidal gleam in her mother's eyes. She obviously hadn't breathed deeply enough, though, for Inez at once sensed the anxiety distracting her.

She hadn't told her friend about the visit from Arabella Madison, either, but Inez was well aware of the risks of defying Corps authority. Hence their decision to rendezvous in this shabby room at a Motel 6 near LAX, which smelled of long-dead cigarettes and pine-scented air freshener, rather than at the D.A.'s office.

When Inez had stuck the last of the electrodes in place, she rummaged through her open briefcase and scooped out a handful of ratcheted plastic bands.

Natalie shook her head, jiggling the insulated wires that suckled on her cranium like leeches. "You don't need those."

Inez frowned. "It's just the two of us here. If anything goes wrong . . ."

"I can handle myself. And you always have the Panic Button."

The prosecutor glanced at the red plastic circle on the control panel of the portable SoulScan unit she'd set up on the dresser. If pressed, it would send an electric charge into Natalie's brain, a power surge that would blow the inhabiting soul out of her neurons.

"That's fine, assuming I get a chance to push it," Inez said. "But you never know what these victims will do once they find themselves in a real body again."

"I realize that."

"I'd feel better if we took precautions."

Natalie was about to repeat her refusal when she remembered her mother speaking with the reptilian inflection of the Thresher.

Let's get to know each other. . . .

"Maybe you're right. Better safe than sorry."

Inez nodded and knelt beside her, binding Natalie's wrists and ankles to the arms and legs of the chair with the plastic cuffs. "Just like old times, eh?" she chuckled as the last band clicked to snugness.

"Too much so." Natalie wriggled her arms and legs to make sure the bonds were tight.

"This shouldn't take long." Returning to the briefcase, Inez took out two packages wrapped in white butcher paper. "These are the touchstones we plan to give Pearsall at the trial. They're not in the best condition, but . . . you understand."

Natalie did, and was not surprised when Inez unwrapped and unfolded the top half of a pair of men's pajamas, the expensive silk perforated with a starburst of buckshot holes and stained with a continent-shaped blotch the color of an old scab. Although any item touched by the deceased would do—a shoe, a car key, a box of breath mints—prosecutors inevitably chose items that would have maximum visual and emotional impact on the jury, objects that aroused sympathy for the victims and emphasized the violence of the crime committed against them.

Natalie disguised her sigh with a series of deep breaths. "Okay. Lay it on me."

Row, row, row your boat . . .

She looped the spectator mantra around in her brain as Inez draped the pajama top across the open palm of her right hand. An electric chill ran through Natalie as the silk touched her skin.

Life is but a dream . . .

Inez dragged a chair over to the dresser and sat beside the SoulScan unit, watching the tracery of green lines that scrolled across its small rectangular screen. The top three lines rolled with the regular brain waves of Natalie's conditioned thought pattern; the bottom three lines remained flat, awaiting the arrival of the summoned soul. The prosecutor glanced from the screen to Natalie and back again, her right hand resting near the Panic Button.

Natalie closed her eyes and allowed her mind to spiral into dormancy, waiting for Scott Hyland's father to knock. With the mesmerizing rhythm of the mantra, time collapsed into a motionless present, an eternal now. She was startled, therefore, when Inez jostled her out of the trance.

"Hey! You getting anything?"

"No." Natalie blinked at her, cranky as a nap-deprived toddler. "Why? How long has it been?"

"About an hour." Inez looked a bit bleary-eyed herself from staring at the SoulScan readout.

"An hour?" Some souls were difficult to summon, but Natalie couldn't recall one ever taking *that* long.

"You sure you didn't get anything?"

"Not even a nibble."

Inez harrumphed, as if her Subaru's engine had mysteriously refused to turn over. "Maybe we should try the wife."

She collected the pajama top from Natalie and set it aside, then tore the butcher paper from the second package. With a brusque snap of her wrists, Inez shook the folds out of Betsy Hyland's powder-blue nightie. Crusty black-red spatters clotted its sheer nylon weave.

Again, Natalie clutched the garment and concentrated while Inez eyed the SoulScan screen. This time even Natalie grew bored and restless, alone in her mind as she droned the mantra in pointless repetition.

After another hour, Inez stood and stretched, shrugging a kink out of her shoulders. "Maybe we should break for a while. Try again after lunch."

"Okay." Natalie noted her friend's cross expression when Inez knelt to cut off the plastic bands with a box cutter. "Sorry."

"Hey, we all have our off days." Though she tried to sound nonchalant, the prosecutor frowned. "I'm going for takeout. Get you anything?"

Massaging circulation back into her freed hands and feet, Natalie put in an order for a turkey breast sub—dry, no cheese, all the veggies—and Inez left. Natalie unplugged the electrode cable from its jack on the SoulScan and paced the room with the hydra of wires still winding from her head.

When Inez returned with their food, the two friends ate their sandwiches in desultory fashion, slurping their fountain drinks during the yawning silences in the conversation. Natalie inquired about the prosecutor's three grown sons and received terse updates on their progress in college and grad school. Inez gave perfunctory compliments about what a bright, pretty girl Callie was, which Natalie acknowledged with modest thanks. Then they threw away their empty cups and wrappers, and Natalie let Inez bind her to the chair again.

As before, Natalie took hold of the pajama top and the nightie in turn and opened herself to inhabitation. A perverse performance anxiety now rankled her, for even with her eyes shut, she could feel Inez staring.

Natalie had never failed to summon a soul. Never.

"It's three-thirty," the prosecutor announced at last. "You need to pick up Callie?"

"Pretty soon." Natalie glanced down at the powder-blue nightie. There couldn't have been a stronger touchstone for the woman who'd died wearing it. Why hadn't she come?

The prosecutor folded the victims' nightwear and laid it in her briefcase as if packing for a business trip. "What do you think happened?"

"I don't know. I've heard there are some souls that Violets can't summon, that go on to someplace we can't reach." She didn't mention that Dan had confirmed the existence of the place beyond.

I can feel it. It waits for all those who are ready for it. . . .

Inez plumbed her with a cross-examiner's glare. "I can see how your theory might apply to St. Peter or Mother Mary. But you really think the Hylands went on to this other place?"

"Maybe." Natalie didn't find the theory very convincing either.

"Here—try this one." Inez unwrapped a third paper bundle and handed her a black brassiere. "We found it tied around the neck of Samantha Winslow, Avram Ries' first victim."

Although already exhausted from futile effort, Natalie took the bra without argument and concentrated again, squeezing it in her hand as if to wring Samantha Winslow's soul out of the fabric like water. Nothing.

She sighed and gave the bra back. "I'm not getting anything."

Like a physician who has confirmed her worst diagnosis, Inez reacted with a kind of dismal satisfaction.

"This was the touchstone Lyman used to summon Winslow at Ries' trial," she said, putting the bra back into her briefcase. "I asked the Corps to have a different Violet summon her using this touchstone, but they refused. Now I know why."

"You think Lyman . . . *kept* the real Winslow from testifying?"

Inez cut Natalie loose again. "The possibility had occurred to me. Unless you think Samantha Winslow's joined the Hylands in the Great Beyond-the-Beyond."

"No. I don't." Natalie knew it was possible to imprison the electromagnetic energy of a person's soul by surrounding it with metal and insulation; in fact, the spirit of her old classmate Sondra Avebury, the Violet Killer's dead lover, still fumed inside a soul cage in the San Francisco Police Department headquarters. But the idea of someone consigning the soul of an innocent murder victim to an oubliette of perpetual isolation struck Natalie as such audacious cruelty that she wanted to reject it out of hand.

Her hands still prickling as blood flowed back into her fingers, she began peeling the electrodes off her head. "Suppose Lyman did cage her soul. How did he create the SoulScan readings in court? He couldn't fake those."

"You tell me," Inez retorted. "If Winslow didn't inhabit him, who did?"

Natalie remembered how Evan Markham, the Violet Killer, had repeatedly allowed Sondra to inhabit him. "Lyman must have an accomplice. A dead one."

"That's what I thought. But who? And how could he convince a ghost to help him? What could he offer it in return?"

"I don't know. Maybe a time-share in his body?"

The prosecutor threw up her hands. "Oh, great! How am I supposed to convince the jury of *that*?"

"You might be able to trip up the summoned soul somehow." Natalie rubbed her scalp where the skin stung from the adhesive tug of the surgical tape. "And I could come to the trial on the day Lyman takes the stand. See if I can spot any funny business."

Inez stopped picking tape off the SoulScan electrodes and looked at her. "You sure you want to do that?"

Like a parabolic mirror, the severity of her friend's expression magnified Natalie's own uneasiness. They both knew what was at stake.

We're going to get her anyway, you know, Arabella Madison had vowed. *All we need is a reason.*

Natalie nearly retracted her offer. She had to think about Callie. The problem was she couldn't keep herself from also thinking about Avram Ries hugging his attorney and about the soul of Marcy Owen, his second victim, keening for her baby boy.

"I want to help," she said at last.

Inez thanked her with a sober nod, then put on a grin to brighten the mood. "With any luck, Lathrop is only blowing smoke up our heinies. He may figure that Pearsall's inability to summon the Hylands will lay the foundation for reasonable doubt. He may think we can't convict his client if the victims aren't able to testify. But he's wrong."

She patted Natalie's bare temple playfully. "Sorry if you shaved your head for nothing."

"Me, too." Natalie chuckled, but told herself that a few years' growth of hair would be a small price to pay if all went well.

That night, for the first time in years, she dreamed of the Thresher again.

In the vision, she was seated in the art therapy room at the Institute wearing a shapeless hospital robe and a pair of shabby blue slippers. Although she couldn't see it, she knew that a giant SoulScan unit sat behind her, broadcasting her brain waves to the room. She could feel its electrodes suckling at her cranium like the pads on a squid's tentacles. It seemed to leech volition from her, immobilizing her with apathy.

The door opened, and Andy Sakei led Callie to a chair next to hers. He beamed with professional joviality. "Look who's here, Natalie! It's your little girl."

She didn't respond. The effort to speak seemed impossible.

Callie pushed herself onto the chair, her feet dangling an inch above the floor. Shiny with worry, her violet eyes kept looking past Natalie, as if watching the SoulScan screen. "Mommy? You okay?"

Natalie ached to cry out, to leap from the chair and clamp her daughter in her arms, but the dream-paralysis permitted her merely to bob her mouth open like a beached fish.

Callie's mouth shrank as she took a thin hardcover book from under her arm. It was *Horton Hears a Who*. "I learned to read it. Would you like to hear?"

She waited for an answer. When none came, Callie opened the book on her lap anyway. Stopping to sound out some of the words, she only made it through the first couple of pages.

She glanced up for her mother's reaction, and her gaze fixed on a point past Natalie's shoulder. Face crinkling, Callie shook her head. "No, Mommy—*don't let him in!*"

Exerting her entire will, Natalie slowly rotated herself to glance behind her. In the place where she expected the SoulScan monitor with its wavy green lines, a face shaped like the head of a gravedigger's spade leered at her with black angry slashes for eyes and mouth. The metallic prods that she took for electrodes were actually the needles of the Thresher's fingers, injecting its essence into her head.

Natalie gagged but could not scream. The Thresher thinned to vanishing as it siphoned itself into her, and suddenly Natalie *was* the Thresher, powerless to stop herself as she turned and extended her tendril arms and hypodermic fingers toward her shrieking daughter . . .

She flailed awake in her sheets, abdominal muscles hiccuping as she gasped.

"He's not real," Natalie hissed to the dark bedroom, repeating the words as if they were a protective mantra. "He's *not* real."

8

Discipline and Patience

IT WAS AROUND 1 A.M. WHEN THE CHEVY BLAZER WITH the Arizona plates crept back to Cabin 7 at the Shady Pines Resort near Lucerne. A clean-shaven gray-haired man with thick glasses got out on the driver's side, the elevator soles of his boots sinking in the muck of mud and pine needles left by the recent storms. He pressed on the sides of his large hooked nose as if making sure it hadn't slipped to one side, and tramped over to unlock the cabin door.

He then went around to open the SUV's side door and hefted a large canvas laundry sack from inside, which he slung over his shoulder with a grunt and lugged into the cabin. His chest thudding, he set down the limp bundle and shut the door. "What'd I tell you, buddy?" he panted, slapping his potbelly. "You gotta keep in shape for this stuff."

A muffled groan rose from the laundry bag.

With the curtains drawn on the windows, the only light source was a dying artificial log in the fireplace grate, which flickered orange like a blacksmith's forge. In the murky glow, the bag looked too solid and angular to contain clothing. The canvas stirred, a cocoon ready to break open.

Seeing the bag's movement seemed to restore the man's energy, and he pulled off his gray toupee and latex nose. He spat out the dentures that gave him his overbite and took off his thick glasses, revealing the face of Lyman Pearsall, minus its bushy mustache. The clean shave wasn't the only difference in the visage. Its usual doughy impotence had given way to a new vigor, its features sharp with cunning and hunger.

Dropping the elements of his disguise into a suitcase that lay open on the modular sofa by the fireplace, he stripped nude and grabbed a woman's florid robe from the suitcase, wrapped himself in it and tied the sash, then plopped onto the couch. He shut the case and set up a makeup mirror on its lid, flicking a switch that illuminated the mirror's circumference. His face leered back at him in the glass, its age makeup running and smearing with sweat.

A couple scoops of cold cream and a dirty hand towel cleared the old cosmetics from his skin. A new layer of foundation turned his ruddy complexion pale and delicate, and he painted his lips with red lipstick, his cheeks with rouge, his eyes with mascara and blue eye shadow that matched his contact lenses. His bald head he covered with a long curly wig the color of crow's feathers.

See what a pretty girl you are!

He smiled at the feminine visage in the mirror. Lyman's face was too lumpy to be beautiful, but he'd done a passable job of dolling it up. Mama would be proud of how pretty he could make himself. She'd taught him everything he needed to know to imitate the enemy.

He stood and modeled for the man propped up in the easy chair next to the couch. "What do you think, honey?"

The man in the easy chair faced the twenty-inch television in the corner of the room as if engrossed in a program on the dark screen, but his eyes had rolled up to gaze at the ceiling without blinking. He was James Alton Henderson, the former owner of the Chevy Blazer with the Arizona plates, and the birth date on his driver's license put him at just past forty. A gummy sheen of drying blood ran from the curling gash at his throat down to his genitals, pasting the black hair between his nipples flat against his chest. Rigor mortis had caused his fingers to tighten on the remote control that had been placed in his right hand. The smoke from the fireplace couldn't quite hide the odor of ripening meat.

The man in the robe and makeup put his hands on his hips and shook his head at the silent corpse. "Men!"

Another soft moan drew his attention back to the canvas bag. With unhurried efficiency, he set aside his cosmetics and dug a fresh hypodermic out of his suitcase. He wasn't sure if she needed another dose yet or not; too much phenobarbital might kill her, and that would never do. Best to be prepared, regardless. He'd use it sooner or later.

Sliding the syringe behind his ear like a Lucky Strike cigarette, he half carried, half dragged the wriggling sack through a connecting door into the cabin's bedroom. The room's sole occupant awoke when he entered, wheezing like a reedless wind instrument and rattling the headboard as he took the unconscious blond girl from the sack and lashed her to the other side of the queen-size bed with nylon rope.

The new girl was about nineteen, with a long, plain face and stringy hair. The emaciation of crack addiction made her look older, however, her cheeks sunken, her skin parched. She hadn't been picky about the johns she chose to entertain—even a portly, gray-haired man with thick glasses and a goofy overbite.

Lifting the lid of each eye, he checked the dilation of her pupils and decided another injection wasn't necessary at this point. Instead, he plugged in the soldering iron that lay on the nightstand and waited for it to warm up. When its metal tip glowed orange, he pulled a chair up beside the bed and took the open jackknife from the nightstand.

The woman on the other side of the bed squirmed and hissed again, tugging at her bonds and pantomiming panic. He smiled at her and tilted the chin of the unconscious girl until the tube of her trachea bulged upward, its ridges straining against the skin.

With tools in hand, he meticulously carved a small circle in her windpipe, cauterizing every point of incision with the hot soldering iron so she wouldn't choke on her own blood. Each drop of crimson vanished with a sizzle and a wisp of iron-scented smoke. Soon he'd created a burn-blackened porthole through which he could see the glistening, mucous-lined trachea's rear wall. Air leaked in and out of her lungs without ever passing through the larynx.

Ah, blessed silence! he thought, listening to the dog-whistle duet of the two women in the bed. The only day in his mother's life that she actually shut up was the day he opened her throat.

Stepping into the adjoining bathroom for a moment, he washed his hands and checked his wig and makeup. The confusion of gender, he knew, would make it harder for his artworks to identify him if the police summoned them later. But this face—older than the one he used to have, with deep furrows and a small, cross mouth . . .

Aren't you precious? he could almost hear Aunt Pearl dote. *You look just like your mama!*

Of its own will, his hand grabbed the half-full water glass on the basin and hurled it at his reflection. It exploded with a splash, and the mirror fractured, blurred with spattered liquid.

Killing his mother hadn't been enough. Some perverse magnetic attraction—between parent and child, between killer and victim—had drawn him to her even in death; she welcomed him into the void with outstretched claws, her contempt squeezing his spirit like the jaws of a nutcracker. No matter how many times he wrested himself free of her, she'd sucked him back into the crushing maw of her black-hole soul.

But now Lyman had provided him with a refuge in the world of the living—a willing vessel who, unlike his prior receptacle, wouldn't resist his inhabitation. He was on this side, his mother was on that, and he was never going back. He'd make sure of that.

Smearing the lipstick on his mouth to dispel the family resemblance, he stalked out of the bathroom to the side of the bed where Marilyn Emmaline Henderson, widow of James Alton, writhed in desperation, the tapestry on her stomach billowing with each heaving breath. Grabbing the syringe from behind his ear, he flicked it with his index finger to dislodge any stray air bubbles. Since her hands were bound together above her head, the circulation in her arms tended to stall in her shoulders, which had turned a blotchy magenta color, and he had to wait almost a minute after tying off her left forearm before a vein bulged enough to inject the sedative. He then had difficulty holding his hand steady so as not to let the needle slip.

Discipline and patience, Vanessa, his mother always admonished him. *With discipline and patience you can do anything you put your mind to.*

As Marilyn Henderson lost consciousness, he threaded his embroidery needle and surveyed the areas of his canvas that still needed to be filled in. The palette of colors available to him was inevitably limited, for only red and black threads preserved their hue when he dipped them below the skin.

Nevertheless, his latest sampler was a breathtaking creation. Marilyn's midriff bore a pyre of scarlet flames from which rose a winged ebony figure, phoenixlike, arms raised in triumph. The fire licked up onto the undersides of her breasts, with one tear-shaped outline left to fill.

He pricked the needle under a small bridge of skin in the blank patch, pulled the thread taut, and looped it over for the next stitch. Prick, pull. Prick, pull. Every once in a while, he paused to blot the oozing blood with a stained Shady Pines towel.

Needlepoint is an excellent pastime for a young lady, Vanessa. It promotes both discipline and patience.

He'd bought the needles and embroidery thread for only a few dollars at a Michaels art supply store. They weren't intended for surgical use and hadn't been sterilized, but the risk of infection didn't concern him. Like Native American sand paintings or Buddhist mandalas, his art was ephemeral, its beauty all the more resplendent for the fact that it would not survive.

The blond girl came around as he worked on Mrs. Henderson. When he heard her perforated windpipe sputter, he couldn't resist glancing up every now and then to grin at her twisting tear-streaked face. It was so much more satisfying to have an audience. His excitement increased, and it was all he could do to keep his hands feverishly stitching.

When the picture was at last complete, he returned to the living room, relaxed and refreshed. "If you don't mind," he said to James Alton Henderson, and pushed a button on the remote in the cadaver's hand.

The television's screen filled with snow. A VCR sat on the TV, and on top of that towered a haphazard stack of VHS cassettes. He picked up one labeled "XMAS" and shoved it in the recorder.

The tape rolled, and the shaky image of a Christmas tree freckled with fairy lights appeared on the screen. A Solomon hoard of gold and silver foil-wrapped gifts surrounded the tree in small pyramids. Outshining all of these, a 2003 hundred-year-anniversary edition Harley-Davidson VRSC V-Rod leaned on its kickstand with the careless attitude of a tuxedoed dandy, its chrome gleaming, its leather seats buffed to a baby's-bottom sheen.

"Awesome!" exclaimed the amplified voice of the camera-man. He panned back and forth over the motorcycle, the auto-focus alternately blurring and refining the image. "I can't believe you actually found one."

"Finding it was the easy part," a flat male voice retorted from offscreen. "Outbidding everyone on eBay took the work."

"You sure you're ready for this, Scotty?" a woman asked.

The camera swung over to where she sat in an overstuffed Victorian chair. "Relax, Mom! It's easier than riding a bike."

She did not seem convinced. "I just want you to be careful is all."

Moving away from James Henderson, the man in the robe mimicked the woman's posture as he seated himself on the sofa: hands folded, knees together, ankles crossed and tucked back under her chair. Her hair was cut short, dyed brown yet obviously going to gray, and her face was just be-ginning to fall into wattles.

"You *better* be careful," the other male voice added. "I'm spending a fortune on insurance as it is."

Another swish pan, and the camera came to rest on a bored-looking man in a matching Victorian chair. He wore a three-piece suit and power tie, the collar of his shirt so tight it doubled his chin.

"Christ, Dad, it's not like you can't afford it."

"If you got a job, you'd realize how much you have to bust your ass to get a bike like that," the father shot back. He spread himself out in the chair, legs apart, forcing you to look at his crotch. A cigar smoldered in his right hand, but he never took a puff. He smoked a fifty-dollar cigar to show you he could, daring you to challenge his right to cloud the air with its tea-scented fog. Shifting out of his feminine pose, the man in the robe adopted the father's body language, mouthing the words he spoke.

"Press, honey, he's only sixteen," the mother said.

"Yeah, and I was helping my dad paint houses when I was eight. But Einstein here couldn't even file papers for one summer without screwing up."

"Give it a rest, Dad! That job sucked, and you know it."

The camera zoomed in on the father's wide-eyed look of affront. "Oh, you think that job sucked, do you? Maybe you'd like to stock kitty litter and tampons at Safeway to pay your way through college."

"Honey, you promised," the mother pleaded. "It's Christmas."

"So? Every day's a damn holiday for this kid."

"Whatever, Dad. Screw you." The camera jiggled, tilted toward the floor.

"I can sell that bike as easily as I bought it!" the father's voice shouted. "You hear me, Scott? Listen to me when I'm talking—"

The camera shut off, and the picture dissolved into static. An Eminem concert taped off cable TV filled the rest of the cassette.

The man in the robe languidly scanned through some of

the other VHS tapes, viewing birthday celebrations, catered Fourth of July barbecues, and Thanksgiving dinners, until he grew bored. Soon he would need to make his exit. Close the chimney flue, squirt a little lighter fluid here and there, and bow out with the flick of a match. But before he destroyed, he would create.

Humming to himself, he strolled back into the bedroom, where a fresh canvas awaited the attention of his needle and thread.

9

Opening Statements

NATALIE SAW THE OPENING OF THE HYLAND MURDER trial on Court TV, along with ten million other legal-system rubberneckers. Inez had told her that Lyman Pearsall wouldn't be taking the stand until the second day at the earliest, and Natalie didn't want to risk having the Corps see her at the courthouse before then. She spent the morning giving Callie her home-schooling lessons instead.

Her daughter sprawled tummy-down on the living-room floor, her chin resting on the edge of a math workbook as she doodled on the open page with a thick pencil. "After this, can we watch SpongeBob?"

"No. Not until after your writing exercises." Seated cross-legged on the sofa, Natalie monitored Callie with her peripheral vision while keeping her gaze fixed on the TV. "And sit up while you're working. It's not good to have your eyes so close to the paper."

Callie groaned and got up onto her knees, hunching over her homework as if it were a sweatshop sewing machine.

On the television, the camera centered on Inez, who stood before the jury delivering the opening statement for the prosecution. "As an only child, Prescott Hyland Jr. was the sole recipient of his parents' attention and affection," she informed them. "He grew up enjoying everything a son could ask for. But that wasn't enough for Scott Hyland. When Elizabeth and Prescott Hyland Sr. refused to satisfy his growing greed, Scott turned on them, ruthlessly destroying the very lives that conceived his own.

"The prosecution intends to show that the clean-cut, soft-spoken young man you see here"—she pointed to the defense table behind her, where Scott Hyland sat wearing a suit and an expression of puritanical solemnity—"systematically and cold-bloodedly plotted and carried out his parents' murders, then attempted to disguise his horrid crime as the work of a common burglar in order to escape justice."

She went on to tout the damning testimony and evidence she would present against Scott, striking poses of iron certitude as she looked each and every juror in the eye. Natalie smiled when the camera caught the silver twinkle of the cross that hung from a chain around the prosecutor's neck. A good Catholic, Inez always wore her crucifix, but never displayed it so prominently as when she appeared in court.

Callie picked up her workbook by one corner; it flopped down from her tiny fist like a prize rabbit pelt. "Finished! Could you check it to see how I did?"

"Later, honey. Start on your writing."

With languid confidence, Malcolm Lathrop stood to give the opening statement for the defense, giving Scott Hyland's shoulder a commiserating squeeze as he did so. "First of all, I want to thank all of you for taking time from your jobs and families to be here." He bowed his head before the jurors, abashed, as if he'd interrupted them during dinner. "Without people like you, Scott might never get a chance to defend himself against these charges.

"As the prosecution has told you, Prescott Hyland Sr. and Elizabeth Hyland were the victims of a brutal, calculated, and premeditated murder. That much is certain. But was Scott Hyland the killer?" He waved a hand toward his client, who gaped at the jury like a startled fawn. "That's not certain at all."

Lathrop raised his hands in a world-weary shrug. "Of course, he is the *obvious* suspect. I mean, isn't it *obvious* that the person who stood to gain the most by the Hylands' death was their only son and sole heir? And isn't it *obvious* that Scott had discipline problems and repeatedly fought with his parents? What teenager doesn't?" He smiled, and several of the jurors chuckled. "No doubt the police were delighted that the case seemed to have such an *obvious* solution."

Lathrop's expression grew severe. "But the obvious solution isn't always the right one. Prescott and Elizabeth Hyland were wealthy, powerful people, and wealthy, powerful people make enemies. Any one of these enemies might have committed the murders for which Scott Hyland stands accused." Lathrop pointed at the jurors. "It's your duty to find the truth. Not a bunch of hasty assumptions and blatant prejudices— the *truth*. An innocent young boy's life depends on it."

He scanned the jurors again, allowing his final sentence to hover like smoke, then maneuvered back behind the defense table. His speech had been brief, and it gave virtually no clue to the defense strategy.

"Mommy, I'm hungry. Can we have lunch now?"

"Sure, honey." Natalie hustled to the kitchen and slapped together a couple of peanut butter and jelly sandwiches for the two of them, all the while listening to the scattered mumbling from the TV. With their sandwiches on paper plates and cups of milk in hand, she and Callie returned to the living room as Inez began to question LAPD officer Eric Tanaka, the prosecution's first witness.

The polished shield of his badge gleaming against the dark navy of his uniform, Tanaka answered the prosecutor's questions with glib military precision. He related how he and his partner, Officer Jordan Hooper, had been dispatched to the Hyland residence in Bel Air after 911 received a call from the family's Vietnamese housekeeper, Mai Phan, at 8:32 A.M. on Monday, August twenty-third, of the previous year.

Mrs. Phan met them upon their arrival at the scene and told them how she had arrived for work that morning only to find the front door locked. After ringing the doorbell several times and calling into the house on her cell phone without a response, she said, she walked around to the backyard to see if a rear door might be unlocked. That was when she discovered that the window of the study stood open and saw broken glass scattered on the ground beneath it. Fearing an intruder might be in the house, she phoned the police.

"She showed you the broken window here?" Inez asked Tanaka, indicating the appropriate spot on a large floor-plan diagram of the Hyland mansion.

"That's correct."

"And was the whole window broken?"

"No. One pane near the window latch had been knocked out and the sash lifted open."

Inez displayed blown-up photos of the window and the glass fragments below it. "In your experience, does this seem consistent with other cases of forced entry you've seen?"

"No. The fact that the glass shards were outside the window implies that the blow which shattered the pane came from inside."

Because of this fact, Tanaka said, he suspected that the damage might have been accidental and not deliberate. When he shone his flashlight through the open window, however, he saw that the front of Prescott Hyland Sr.'s gun cabinet had also been smashed. At that point, he and his partner took the threat of a possible intruder more seriously. They called for backup and drew their guns. Believing they had probable cause to suspect that a crime was in progress and that the Hylands' lives might be in immediate danger, they decided to enter the house and shouted a warning to the occupants.

With a battering ram, the two officers pounded open the rear entrance to the laundry room, thereby activating the mansion's security system. As the alarm began to blare, they moved cautiously through each of the downstairs rooms, calling out for Mr. and Mrs. Hyland.

"Did you find any objects disturbed in the downstairs rooms?" Inez asked.

"Only the gun cabinet," Tanaka replied.

The prosecutor placed a poster-size blowup photo of the cabinet on her easel. "Was this how you found it?"

"Yes, ma'am."

A converted Victorian china cabinet, it consisted of a cherrywood frame and a glass front with a central door and rounded corners. Inside, a vertical rack in the middle propped up a half-dozen rifles of various calibers, while brackets on the rear wall held twenty-eight different handguns, ranging in style from a classic Colt revolver to a German Luger to a Desert Eagle .44 Magnum. Jagged glass fragments still fringed the cabinet door, and one notch in the rifle rack was vacant.

Inez held a hand toward the photo. "What would you estimate is the current street value of the guns in this cabinet?"

Tanaka considered Prescott Hyland's arsenal. "Fifteen thousand dollars. At least."

"Did you see any signs that the person who broke into the cabinet tried to take any of the guns we see here?"

"No, ma'am."

Confident that the ground floor was secure, the officers proceeded up the marble staircase. With Hooper covering the hallway, Tanaka checked each of the upstairs rooms in turn.

"Do you remember this room?" Inez placed another photo enlargement on the easel: Scott Hyland's bedroom. Posters of Eminem and swimsuit models frescoed the walls and crumpled clothing littered the floor and bed.

"Yes, ma'am."

"Did it appear that anything in this room had been disturbed or taken?"

"It was a little hard to tell." Tanaka broke into a smile, cracking up the courtroom audience. "But, no, I don't think the room had been ransacked. As you can see, none of the dresser drawers were pulled out."

"Did you find anything out of order in any of the other upstairs rooms?"

The police officer's expression turned grim. "Only in the master bedroom."

A few of the jurors gasped as Inez placed another placard on the easel. "Is this how you found the master bedroom?"

"Yes, ma'am."

This placard featured two enlargements. In the wide-angle shot, Prescott Hyland Sr. lay on the king-size bed, propped awkwardly against the headboard, open eyes vacant, his skin tinged with green. He wore the pajama top that

Natalie had used as a touchstone, and the periwinkle percale sheets beneath him bore a magenta stain where his wounds had leaked into the mattress. The shotgun that had killed him lay on the floor beside the bed among some scattered papers and documents.

Betsy Hyland couldn't be seen in that photo. A close-up of the floor on the right side of the bed showed that she'd fallen off, a Danielle Steel hardback flopped facedown beside her, covers spread like the wings of a dead bird. The hem of her blue nightie had scrunched up around her waist, leaving her livid legs splayed and exposed. Her left eye still stared upward; the other one had disappeared along with much of the right half of her head. The remaining hemisphere of her brain had slid out into a puddinglike lump on the carpet.

Tanaka stated that as soon as he and his partner were sure the perpetrator was no longer on the premises, they called in the murders and secured the house until the investigative team arrived. Their initial examination of the scene prompted them to report the crime as a double homicide and attempted burglary, for the drawers of the master bedroom's dresser and nightstand were pulled out, tongues of disheveled clothing lolling out of them as if someone had rifled through their contents. The fact that the murder weapon was taken from the victims' own collection and then left at the scene also suggested that the killings were opportunistic rather than premeditated.

When he had finished, Inez thanked Tanaka for his testimony and glanced toward the presiding judge. "No further questions, Your Honor."

That's a piece of luck, Natalie thought, recognizing the justice's patrician, Arabic features and gray-flecked beard. A seasoned and scrupulously fair jurist, Tony Shaheen also happened to be a longtime friend of Inez's outside the courtroom.

Inez returned to the prosecution table and Judge Shaheen nodded toward the defense. "Your witness, Mr. Lathrop."

The attorney looked up from his notes as if interrupted while reading his morning paper. "No questions, Your Honor."

Judge Shaheen arched his salt-and-pepper eyebrows in mild surprise. "Very well. You may step down, Officer Tanaka."

Officer Hooper took the stand next and essentially reiterated Tanaka's version of how they discovered the Hylands' bodies. Then Morris Eckhardt, a firearms expert, testified that the buckshot and wadding recovered from the bodies fit the type associated with the shells found in the shotgun discovered at the crime scene. Although buckshot pellets could not provide a positive ballistics match the way bullets could, Eckhardt said the "overwhelming" evidence indicated that the lethal shots had been fired from that gun, which was registered to Prescott Hyland Sr. Since the cabinet from which it had been taken contained no shotgun shells, the intruder who'd used the gun would have to have brought the proper gauge shells with him—or have known that Mr. Hyland kept his guns loaded for "home security."

With the nonchalance of Mighty Casey rejecting one perfect pitch after another, Malcolm Lathrop allowed these witnesses to pass virtually unchallenged. He did not attempt to contest the physical evidence or the manner in which it was collected, as most attorneys would in such a case. Granted, nothing Inez had presented so far automatically implicated Scott Hyland . . . but she was clearly digging the hole in which to bury him. Yet Lathrop smiled like a poker player who doesn't have even a pair of jacks showing yet smugly refuses to fold. Was he bluffing, Natalie wondered, or did he possess the aces he pretended to hold?

The only glimpse he gave of the defense strategy came when he cross-examined Dr. Ardath Cox, the coroner who'd performed the Hylands' autopsies. "You estimated the time of death as being between ten P.M. on Saturday, August twenty-first, and two A.M. on Sunday, August twenty-second," he said. "Is that correct?"

"Yes. It couldn't have been much later than that," the medical examiner replied, attempting to head off the attorney's next question. "Rigor mortis was completely resolved by the time we collected the bodies. That generally takes about thirty hours. Also, the bedside lamps were left on in the Hylands' bedroom, indicating that the couple had prepared for bed but had not yet gone to sleep."

"Could it have been earlier than you estimated? Say, between nine and ten on Saturday evening?"

"Yes, it's possible that death could have occurred before ten that night," Cox said, her words slow with suspicion. "Time of death can be difficult to establish after the first twenty-four hours. The onset and resolution of rigor mortis may vary due to environmental conditions or to the physiology of the deceased individual.

"However, the fact that the Hylands were dressed for bed makes it dubious that they were killed much before nine, unless they were in the habit of going to bed *much* earlier than most people. Also, the lack of blistering on the cadavers' skin due to bacterial gas formation indicates that they hadn't been dead more than two days. It's my considered opinion that the Hylands died thirty to thirty-five hours before their bodies were discovered by the police."

Lathrop smiled. "Give or take a couple hours?"

The M.E.'s mouth tightened. "Yes. Give or take a couple hours."

"Thank you for clarifying that, Dr. Cox. Now, in your medical opinion, having examined the wounds suffered by Mr. and Mrs. Hyland . . . would you say that either of them could have retained consciousness for any length of time after the fatal shots had been fired? Even a few moments?"

Natalie sat forward in her chair.

"Possibly," the coroner replied, "at least in Mr. Hyland's case. We know that neural activity in the brain continues even after the cessation of autonomic functions, sometimes for several minutes."

"And his body was discovered with its eyes open, was it not?"

"Yes. Yes, it was."

Lathrop gave another gratified smile. "Thank you, Dr. Cox. No further questions."

And that was it. Lathrop had paved the way for the defense to put Lyman Pearsall on the stand. As with most attorneys who called for Violet testimony, he'd taken pains to assure the jury that the summoned victims had been able to bear witness to their killer's actions at the time they were murdered. The cross-examination itself didn't bother Natalie—but Lathrop's confidence did. "Never ask a question that you don't already know the answer to," Inez had once said of grilling witnesses in court. Lathrop acted like a man who already knew all the answers.

Which means he knows *what the Hylands will say,* Natalie thought. *He knows that they can set Scott free.*

Beside Natalie's chair, Callie squirmed in an agony of impatience. "Pleeeeeeeeease can we watch SpongeBob now?"

Natalie considered the proceedings onscreen a moment

more, then aimed the remote at the VCR above the TV. "Yeah. Let's."

Cheery cartoon colors filled the screen, and the pressure in Natalie's chest relaxed. No point in fretting about the trial now. There would be plenty of time for that tomorrow, when she took her seat in the courtroom gallery.

10

Showtime

MALCOLM LATHROP SLUNG HIMSELF INTO THE SECOND-run movie theater seat beside Pearsall's just before the last of the preview trailers ended. Dressed casually in a denim shirt and jeans, his hair pomaded to perfection, the lawyer looked like a CEO vacationing at a dude ranch.

"I've got a busy day tomorrow, Mr. Pearsall," he murmured as the legend SILENCE IS GOLDEN flashed on the screen. "What can I do for you?"

"I want a down payment." The spirit gum holding Lyman's false mustache had started to dissolve in his sweat, and he held it in place under the pretense of smoothing it. "Five hundred thousand. Now."

Lathrop chortled. "Couldn't find an ATM, eh?"

Lyman's jaw screwed shut like a vise. The main feature started: an Eddie Murphy buddy movie that had bombed at the box office. Seated in the back row at the final showing on a weeknight, Pearsall and Lathrop constituted more than half the audience.

"You don't have a chance without me," the Violet reminded the attorney.

"Exactly. And that's why I can't have you running off to South America with your 'down payment.' " He gave Pearsall a good-humored smile. "But not to worry, my friend. You'll have your money soon enough. Always assuming you can deliver what you claim, of course."

His expression darkened, and Lyman looked down at his own pudgy hands. "Oh, I *can*, all right. Remember what I told you about Avram Ries. But what if I *choose* not to?"

The lawyer shrugged. "You know the Corps better than I do. What do you think they would do if you failed to produce the testimony you promised?"

Lyman said nothing. His toupee felt as if it floated on sweat.

"Something bothering you, Mr. Pearsall? There a problem?"

"No. No problem." Lyman's fingers knotted around one another like copulating worms. His memories of the past few days screened in his mind like outtakes from a much longer film. He had left the house in Lakeport, headed north on Route 29. He stopped for gas in Lucerne. There was a resort across the street, a Lincoln Log assemblage of cabins . . . and then he was here in L.A., searching for a pay phone to call Lathrop to set up this meeting.

The gaps in his recollection were deliberate; he didn't *want* to know what had happened in the interim.

Lathrop chuckled. "Good. If you pull it off tomorrow, we could have our verdict by the end of next week. I'll wire the money to your offshore account, and then you can go to Rio or Bali or Mars, for all I care."

With a fraternal slap on Pearsall's shoulder, he rose to leave. "Don't forget, showtime's at nine sharp."

"Yeah."

The lawyer pushed his way out the exit door, leaving Lyman in darkness.

The Violet put a hand on the breast pocket of his rumpled sports coat, where the jackknife weighed like an anchor on his heart. Tomorrow he'd tape it to his chest, underneath his shirt. If the metal detectors at the courthouse picked it up, he'd tell them it was his pacemaker.

You don't need that rusty ol' knife to call me, Lyman, said a voice inside his head, as if replying to his thoughts. *I'll be here for you, buddy.*

"What the—*what are you doing here?*" The only other person in the theater, a punk kid wearing a backward baseball cap, turned to stare at him, and Pearsall hushed his words to a whisper. "I told you not to knock! Do you want to ruin everything?"

Relax, my friend. I know when to take a powder.

"But the trial! If you show up too soon on the SoulScan—"

Fear not. I have . . . an old friend I can visit until you summon me. You won't mind my company in the meantime, will you, Lyman?

"No. Of course not." But Pearsall knew his words didn't fool the loathsome guest in his brain, who could feel his fear. Tomorrow, when he got the money, he could sever himself from this Siamese twin forever, Lyman reminded himself. After their performance in court.

Showtime, indeed.

11

The People v. Scott Hyland

ON THE MORNING SHE WAS DUE TO ATTEND THE trial, Natalie stuffed a change of clothes, an extra purse, and her auburn wig in a canvas book bag, which she took with her when she dropped Callie off at day care. Keeping a close watch on the tan LeBaron that shadowed her Volvo, she drove to Brea Mall and parked in the lot near Nordstrom.

George pulled up beside her, and she waved at him as she got out. He gave her an offhand salute and fed a cassette into his car stereo. Good thing he had the day shift; Madison or Rendell would probably have followed her as she headed into the department store, book bag in hand.

Slipping into a stall in the women's restroom on the second floor, Natalie shed her T-shirt and jeans and put on the skirt, blouse, and pantyhose she took from her bag. She also traded her Doc Marten boots for pumps and her blond wig for the red one. The straight copper locks accentuated the pallor of her skin, sharpened the edges of her cheeks and chin. Checking her look in the restroom mirror, she barely recognized herself, for it had been six years since she'd worn the hairpiece. The day she met Dan.

Anyone ever tell you you look good as a redhead?

The memory of Dan's clumsy icebreaker line made her smile, then frown. It became a running gag he'd repeated every time she put on a different wig, and the joke turned from irritating to endearing the more he said it. She'd never had a man who wasn't a Violet try to hit on her before that. A few had tried since then, but . . . she couldn't think about them. Not while she still had Dan in her life.

Natalie smoothed the wrinkles in her outfit as best she could and put on a pair of dark glasses with tortoiseshell frames. When she left the lavatory and headed downstairs, Natalie scanned the shoppers around her but didn't see George among them. She proceeded to stroll out of the mall to the parking lot near the Embassy Suites hotel. As scheduled, an Enterprise car-rental delivery truck arrived shortly after 10 A.M., bearing on its back the hunter-green Toyota Corolla that Inez had ordered for her.

After more than an hour of wading through traffic and hunting for parking, Natalie arrived at the L.A. Criminal Justice Center. A riptide of nostalgia engulfed her as she entered the building. The whole place was one giant touchstone for Dan; it was here that he first approached her for help with the Violet Killer case. He didn't knock, but he might as well have, for his presence permeated her as thoroughly as if he'd inhabited her.

In his nerdy navy suit, FBI Special Agent Atwater had seemed such a typical Fed flunky that at first she treated him with the same contempt she currently reserved for the likes of Arabella Madison. She could almost see him now, griping as he gamely lugged her suitcases down nine flights of emergency stairs.

What have you got against elevators, anyway?

Maybe Dan *had* possessed her, for Natalie crossed the courthouse's marble-lined lobby to an alcove lined with sets of sliding steel safety doors and pressed a call button as if she'd been doing it her whole life. Once she would rather have climbed a hundred flights of stairs than set foot in one of these coffins on cables, but Dan had prodded her into taking chances on elevators . . . and so much more.

A cancerous melancholy metastasized in Natalie's mind, and she recited her protective mantra to crowd out the memories causing it. As if the mantra alone could ever erase Dan from her thoughts.

More than an hour late, Natalie crept into Courtroom 9–101 like a tardy churchgoer. Fortunately, Inez had instructed Avery Park, one of the prosecution's key witnesses, to save a seat for Natalie in the front row of the packed gallery. Unfortunately, Mr. Park's corpulent body sagged over the edge of his own chair and onto hers, and she had to cross her legs and fold her arms to keep from rubbing up against him.

On the witness stand, LAPD homicide detective Dennis Raines related how he had obtained Scott Hyland's cell phone number from the cellular service provider in order to notify him of his parents' murders.

"Could you describe your initial phone conversation with the defendant?" Inez asked.

Raines gave a gruff nod. "Once I'd confirmed that I was actually speaking to Prescott Hyland Jr., I informed him that his parents were dead. He expressed shock at the news and asked if we had any idea who killed them. 'What makes you think someone killed them?' I asked. 'I only said they were dead.' "

Inez looked toward the jurors. "And how did the defendant respond?"

"He hemmed and hawed a bit, then said that since I was a detective, he figured his parents must've been murdered. I didn't question him further about the crimes until we met later at the Hyland residence."

"Can you describe the defendant's demeanor at that time?" Inez asked.

"Almost from the moment we met outside the house, he started shaking his head and saying 'I can't believe it' over and over."

"In your experience, is that an unusual reaction for the relative of a murder victim?"

"A little. Usually people are numb with shock by the time we walk them through the crime scene. Real quiet. But everyone's different."

"Did anything about the defendant's behavior arouse your suspicion?"

"He kept covering his face like he was crying, but his eyes were dry." The stocky detective cast a disparaging glance at Scott Hyland. "I think he was overplaying the part of the bereaved son."

Malcolm Lathrop snapped to his feet. "Objection! With all due respect, Your Honor, Detective Raines is neither a mind reader nor a drama critic. He couldn't possibly know the grief my client was enduring at that moment, and any suggestion to the contrary is outrageous speculation."

Judge Shaheen acceded with a nod. "Sustained. The jury should disregard Detective Raines' opinions about the defendant's mental state. Ms. Mendoza, please ask your witness for facts, not theatrical reviews."

Inez acknowledged the reprimand with stiff-lipped stoicism.

Lathrop smiled. "Thank you, Your Honor."

"And speaking of overacting, Mr. Lathrop . . . in future, I'd appreciate it if you stated your objections as succinctly as possible and spared me the melodrama."

"Yes, sir." The defense attorney seated himself, looking a bit less cocky.

Natalie saw the corners of Inez's mouth rise. The prosecutor turned back toward Raines. "Could the defendant account for his whereabouts on the night of Saturday, August twenty-first, and the morning of Sunday the twenty-second?"

"In a manner of speaking," the detective replied. "He claimed to have spent the first part of the evening having dinner with his girlfriend, Danielle Larchmont, and her parents at their home, leaving there with Ms. Larchmont at around nine P.M. and proceeding to Chez Ray, a dance club in Westwood. The doorman and bartender from the club both remembered seeing him there that night, and he paid the bar tab with his Visa, confirming that he was there to sign the receipt at the end of the night. After that, he spent the rest of the weekend with several witnesses at a beach house owned by the parents of his friend Troy McDonnell. Ms. Larchmont has assured us that he was with her the whole time."

Inez shook her head in mock consternation. "That seems a pretty convincing alibi. Did you consider the possibility that the Hylands really were killed by an intruder?"

"Of course. But we found several problems with the burglary theory. To begin with, the window that presumably served as the assailant's mode of entry was broken from the inside, indicating that the individual who broke it was already in the house. All the other windows were undamaged and latched, so the perpetrator must have entered through a door.

"But the doors to the Hyland residence are all wired to a central security system that requires one to punch in a deactivation code within thirty seconds of entering the house. We checked with the security firm that operates the system, and their records showed that no alarm went off at the Hyland residence that night. Whoever entered the house that evening would have to have known that code.

"What's more, the security system also features alarm buttons in all the bedrooms that automatically summon police or ambulance services in the event of emergencies. It seems unlikely that the Hylands would not have heard the sound of breaking glass as the intruder broke the window and then smashed into the gun cabinet in the downstairs study, and yet they never activated the alarm. That strongly suggests the window and gun cabinet weren't broken until after the Hylands were dead."

"Was anything actually stolen?" Inez asked.

"As near as we can determine from insurance company records and other sources, a box of Mrs. Hyland's jewelry is missing, as well as her purse and Mr. Hyland's wallet. As yet, no retailers have reported any attempted use of the couple's credit cards."

"Does this fit the pattern of other burglaries you've seen in the past?"

"Hardly. First of all, it's highly unusual for a thief to break into a house when the residents are obviously at home, with lights on and cars in the driveway. Second, the average burglar wouldn't pass up the valuables in plain sight downstairs—the handguns in the cabinet, the stereo and video equipment in the living room—to go rummaging through drawers upstairs. Burglars want to get in and out with as many big-ticket items as fast as possible, and searching for stuff wastes time.

"Burglary is all about keeping risk to a minimum. Most

burglars would flee the scene even if caught in the act, but this perpetrator went out of his way to kill the Hylands. That tells me the primary objective of the crime was murder, not theft. I believe the perpetrator deliberately staged the crime scene to resemble a burglary in order to disguise the fact that his true goal was the death of Mr. and Mrs. Hyland."

"And what conclusions can you draw about the perpetrator's identity from the facts as you've presented them?"

"I would say the killer is someone who knew the Hylands, their habits, and their home intimately."

"I see." Inez aimed her glare at the gangly figure of Scott Hyland, who brooded at the defense table like a class clown in detention. "Thank you, Detective."

The prosecutor took her seat and Judge Shaheen inclined his head toward the defense. "Your witness, Mr. Lathrop."

"No questions, Your Honor."

A few of the jurors exchanged puzzled looks, and for the first time, Natalie saw Scott Hyland whisper to his attorney with peevish anxiety. Lathrop lifted a hand to hush him.

Judge Shaheen stroked his beard with his forefinger and scowled at the lawyer over the flat tops of his reading glasses. "You do plan to mount a defense for your client at some point, don't you, Mr. Lathrop?"

The attorney smiled with an I've-got-a-secret smugness. "So far, Your Honor, the prosecution has done an excellent job of presenting our case for us."

Glowering, the judge dismissed Raines, who stepped down to be replaced by Ben "Buzzer" Blish, the doorman and bouncer for Chez Ray. A bodybuilder whose Herculean stature made the witness stand look like a child's playpen, he confirmed that Scott Hyland had indeed visited the club on the night of August 21. "He tipped me a fifty," Blish said. "You remember a guy like that." When asked why he let a couple of seventeen-year-olds like Scott Hyland and Danielle Larchmont into a club that served alcohol, he merely shrugged. "Their IDs looked legit to me."

As Inez questioned him further, the bouncer revealed that Scott had reentered the club shortly before midnight. He seemed sweaty and out of breath, and he told Blish he'd just run to his car to fetch his girlfriend's sweater. Scott even showed the doorman the sweater "as if I cared," Blish recalled.

Trish Sanders, the club's bartender, also remembered Scott coming to the club that night, in large part because of the fifty he tipped her. When Inez pressed her, however, Sanders admitted that, although she was sure Scott had set up the bar tab and signed the credit slip at the end of the night, she couldn't recall seeing him between those times. Instead, Danielle Larchmont would come alone to the bar occasionally, order two cocktails, and carry them back into the club's crowd of undulating dancers.

Inez next called Danielle Larchmont herself to testify. Natalie was darkly amused to see the teen in a knee-length skirt and cream-colored business jacket buttoned to the chin, her black hair wound into a prim bun. The paparazzi shot on the cover of the latest *National Enquirer* showed Danielle in a black corset top, belly chain, and low-rise jeans that exposed the side straps of her thong.

"How long have you and the defendant been in a committed relationship?" Inez asked the girl once the bailiff had sworn her in.

"About a year." Her eyes half lidded, Larchmont betrayed a trace of jaded annoyance, like a C student pretending to listen to a physics lecture.

"And during that time, have you ever known Scott Hyland to become angry with his parents?"

The girl rolled her eyes. "Like, who doesn't?"

Several people chuckled.

"Answer yes or no, please."

"Yeah, he got mad at them. But it was no big deal."

"Did he ever threaten to kill them?"

"No."

"Did they ever get mad at him?"

"Yeah. Once in a while."

"Do you know what they were mad about?"

"No. Scott didn't want to go into it."

"Were the defendant and his parents angry with one another at the time of the murders?"

Larchmont's eyes flicked toward the defense table, where both Malcolm Lathrop and Scott Hyland stared at the girl as if trying to prompt her telepathically. "No. Not that I know of."

Inez nodded, but her expression made clear that she only agreed in order to humor the witness. "When questioned by police about the night of August twenty-first, you said that Scott Hyland spent the early part of the evening with you and your parents at their house, and that you and Scott went directly from there to Chez Ray, where you stayed from about ten P.M. until two A.M. Is that correct?"

"Yes."

"Did you stop anywhere between your parents' house and Chez Ray?"

"No."

"And Scott Hyland was with you the entire time?"

"Yeah."

"Think carefully, Ms. Larchmont. He didn't leave you at all that Saturday night?"

The girl gave a crooked smile and shrugged. "He might've gone to the bathroom or something."

The audience in the gallery laughed, and Larchmont giggled with them.

Inez did not share their levity. She sauntered over to the prosecution table and picked up a sheaf of computer-printed papers, which she flipped through with a casual air. "I have here the cell phone records for both you and Scott Hyland for last August. They say he made a two-minute call to you at eleven twenty-two P.M. on the night of the twenty-first, which would have been during the time you claim to have spent together at the club. Tell me, Ms. Larchmont, why would he call you on his cell phone if you were right next to him the whole time?"

The teen's mouth shrunk to a pout as the whole courtroom hushed for her answer. Most of the spectators focused on the prosecutor and witness, but Natalie, always keeping a wary eye on Malcolm Lathrop at the defense table, saw him bow his head slightly and deliberately. Larchmont evidently saw the bow, too, for she pressed her hands over her eyes and let out a small cry.

That was it, Natalie realized, her stomach fluttering. *That was the cue she'd been waiting for.* She wanted to shout a warning to Inez, as if seeing a cinematic villain reach for her friend's throat.

The prosecutor and judge both looked at the girl on the witness stand. "Ms. Larchmont?" Inez asked, her tone softer than before.

The teen held her head and sniveled. "I'm sorry. I lied."

Inez studied Larchmont the way one might examine an unexploded grenade. "Exactly *how* did you lie?"

"We did stop somewhere on the way to the club that night. We stopped at Scott's house."

Chairs squeaked as people sat up for a better view. Inez didn't blink. "You mean the Hyland residence?"

Larchmont nodded, her brash tone crumbling into a brittle whine. "He wanted to run in and get some towels and stuff for the beach the next day. But when he came out . . . he said someone had killed his parents."

Nothing on Inez's face registered shock, but an intensity of concentration flared in her gaze—a chess player who suddenly discovers her king in check. "He told you his parents had been killed. But you didn't actually see the bodies, did you?"

"No, thank God. I was waiting in the car. Oh, my God." The girl bent almost double, shuddering, but the timbre of her weeping sounded flat. Natalie noted, too, that the teen never took her hands from her face, and remembered that Detective Raines said Scott Hyland had done the same thing.

"All right," Inez said in an indulgent tone, "what did you do after Scott discovered his parents' bodies?"

"Scott said we couldn't be seen there. He said people would never believe that he just found his mom and dad that way. He knew they'd say *he* did it. That's why we went to the club."

"If you went to the club to establish an alibi, why did he leave you there?"

"He said he was going to sneak back into the house and make it look like someone else did it. A burglar."

"You realize that's a crime, don't you, Ms. Larchmont? It's called obstruction of justice."

"I know! I know! But we were both so scared!" The teen rubbed her eyes with her wrists. "Could I get a Kleenex or something?"

Prepared for such outbursts, Judge Shaheen proffered a box of tissues to her. She took one and dabbed at her face, sniffling.

Inez didn't let the girl's histrionics put her off. "A minute ago you admitted lying to this court. Why should we believe you now?"

"Because it's the *truth!* I swear it!" Larchmont pleaded, pitiful as a whipped puppy.

"Isn't it also the truth that Scott Hyland bought you a lot of nice things? Clothes, jewelry, trips to Hawaii and Tahiti. Isn't it true that he could buy you a whole lot more than that with his parents' fortune?"

"No! I'd never hurt anyone. Not for all the money in the world."

"Really? I hope that statement is more accurate than everything else you've told us." The prosecutor cocked her head toward Malcolm Lathrop. "*Your* witness."

As she took her seat, Lathrop stood and addressed the judge with paternal protectiveness. "Your Honor, I think Ms. Larchmont has endured enough for one day. Her courageous confession supports what the defense has maintained from the beginning: Scott Hyland's innocence. Therefore, we have no questions for her at this time."

Judge Shaheen looked like he'd taken a bite of something rotten but was too polite to spit it out. "Very well. The witness may step down. Court is adjourned for a brief recess. I'd like to remind the jurors not to discuss the case or formulate any opinions about it during the break. We'll reconvene in fifteen minutes." He brought his gavel down with a single dismissive rap.

As she rose to leave, Natalie noticed that the secretive smile had returned to Malcolm Lathrop's face.

* * *

During the break, she managed to catch up with Inez at the basins in the women's restroom. Natalie rinsed her hands while waiting for a third woman to exit, then bent close to her friend's ear. "Our buddy Malcolm threw you a curve in there. You still on track?"

"Oh, yeah." Inez checked her hair in the mirror, dabbed powder from a compact onto the shine on her nose and forehead. "I knew he'd give Danielle some fish story to tell. I'm going to hang him with it later."

"And Lyman?"

The prosecutor's iron mask slipped a bit as she snapped her compact shut. "We'll have to wait and see, won't we?"

She left Natalie to towel her hands dry.

Troy McDonnell was a skinny scarecrow of a boy, doomed by his gawky features and pale, freckled skin to serve as perpetual lackey to a handsome jock like Scott Hyland. Another son of wealthy parents, McDonnell had evidently purchased some secondhand popularity by hosting a series of notorious parties for his high-school cronies, much like the impromptu beach-house bash he now described to the court.

"It was Scott's idea," he began. "He called me up Thursday night and asked if I could throw something together that weekend at my dad's place in Malibu."

"He called you on the night of Thursday, August nineteenth—two days before the murders," Inez emphasized for the jury's benefit. "Out of the blue, he asked you to plan a party in two days. Didn't you find that a little unusual?"

McDonnell snickered. "Nah. Scott was always up for partying."

"Did *anything* about it surprise you?"

"Only the fact that his parents let him go. I thought they'd grounded him, even taken the keys to his Cherokee."

"Do you know why they grounded him?"

"Scott said there'd been trouble at work, but he never said what. His dad was always on his case for something."

"We'll get back to that in a minute. What do you remember about Scott's behavior at the beach house that weekend?"

"For starters, he and Danni didn't even get there till almost three in the morning, which kinda ticked me off since he's the one who asked for the party in the first place. Then he spent the whole next day fondling his cell phone and checking his voice mail, like, every fifteen minutes."

"Did he tell you why he kept checking his messages?"

"Said he was expecting an important call."

"What happened when it came time for you to vacate the beach house on Monday morning?"

"Scott asked me if we could all stay another night. 'Why bother?' I asked him. 'You can play with your phone at home.' I told him my dad only let me have the house for the weekend—and getting him to do that was like pulling teeth—but Scott gave me this sob story about how he and his folks had this big fight and he didn't want to go back until they had a chance to cool off."

"What happened then?"

"Everyone else left. It was just me, Scott, and Danni, sitting around watching DVDs. I was wondering if they'd ever leave, when Scott got the call from the cops."

"You mean the call from Detective Raines, notifying him of his parents' death."

"Yeah."

"How did he take the news?"

"Objection," Lathrop snapped before McDonnell could

open his mouth. "Once again, the prosecution is asking the witness to make blatant assumptions about the mental state of my client during this time of tragedy."

Inez raised her hands in conciliation. "I'll withdraw the question. Mr. McDonnell, you've mentioned that Scott Hyland's parents were angry with him. Do you know why?"

The boy gave a sophomoric snigger. "The usual stuff. His old man expected him to work, like, twenty hours a day or something. You know parents."

"And was Scott ever mad at his mom and dad?"

"Sure."

"Did he ever express a desire to kill them?"

Until that moment, McDonnell had not looked at the high-school buddy who glowered at him from the defense table. Natalie now saw Troy throw a stool-pigeon glance at Scott, as if to say *Sorry, dude—wasn't my idea.*

"Please answer the question, Mr. McDonnell."

His cheeks puffed out as he exhaled. "Yeah. But I didn't think he was serious."

"Could you describe that conversation for us?"

McDonnell scratched the back of his head. "His dad had really blown his top the day before. Took a driver from his golf bag and whaled on Scott's Harley. Scott kept that bike immaculate, and his dad totally trashed it.

"Scott's telling me about the whole thing when he kind of laughs and asks me how much I think it would cost to have his folks whacked. I laugh and say, 'More than you got!' 'Cause I think he's joking, acting like he's on *The Sopranos,* y'know?

"But then he gets all serious and asks me if Richard knows anybody who'd do it."

"That would be your classmate Richard Parkhurst, correct?"

"Yeah. He helped Scott and Danni get their fake IDs and

he hangs with some scary people, gangbangers and stuff. But I told Scott he'd be making a huge mistake, 'cause I've seen those true-crime shows on Discovery, y'know? I told him how all these guys who tried hiring hit men ended up getting busted by undercover cops."

"What did he say to that?"

"He laughed and said that with his allowance, he probably couldn't afford it anyway."

"And when did you have this conversation?"

"Beginning of last August."

Inez faced the jury. "Only two weeks before the murders of Prescott and Betsy Hyland. Thank you, Mr. McDonnell."

She gave the floor to Lathrop, who strolled over to the witness with a slight shake of his head.

"Mr. McDonnell, would you say you're a *good* friend of my client?"

The boy's gaze flicked to Scott, but only for an instant. "Yeah."

"I mean, you'd have to be a *good* friend for him to confide a murder plan to you. In fact, you'd have to be the best friend Scott ever had for him to tell you something like that. Would you say you're the *best* friend Scott ever had?"

McDonnell squirmed like a paramecium caught on a glass slide. "I don't know."

"I see. Then maybe you can tell us whether Richard Parkhurst is a *good* friend of yours."

"I wouldn't call him a *friend*. . . ."

Lathrop put a finger to his lips. "No, 'friend' probably isn't the right word. Wouldn't it be more accurate to say Mr. Parkhurst is your *dealer*?" Lathrop snatched a police report off his stack of documents and brandished it before the jury. "In fact, weren't you and Mr. Parkhurst both arrested while you were in the act of purchasing five ounces of cocaine from him?"

McDonnell's voice dropped to a croak. "Yes, sir."

"And isn't it true that the prosecution has agreed to drop the drug-possession charge against you in exchange for your testimony here today?"

"Yes, sir."

Natalie heard Avery Park grunt with disgust beside her. She watched Inez to see if she flinched as the credibility of one of her key witnesses crumbled, but, true to form, the prosecutor monitored the proceedings with stony resolve.

Lathrop smiled. But he'd barely returned to his chair before Inez raised her hand. "Permission to redirect?"

"Proceed," Judge Shaheen said.

Inez stood but did not bother to come out from behind the table. "Mr. McDonnell, was Scott Hyland also a customer of Richard Parkhurst's?"

"Oh, yeah." The boy grinned, obviously relishing the chance to stick it to Lathrop.

"And what products did he purchase?"

"Mostly pot and coke. A few 'shrooms."

"How much money did you see the defendant spend on drugs?"

"Thousands. He went through cash so fast, his old man cut off his allowance a bunch of times." McDonnell's expression blackened with envy. "It's a miracle he never got busted."

"Were his parents aware of his drug use?"

"You bet. Especially after he ran up a few grand in cash advances on his Visa."

"Did they do anything to stop his drug use?"

"They tried taking away his plastic, but he'd already applied for a bunch of new cards they didn't know about. But you know what his folks were like—they'd rather die than have people know their kid was in juvie hall or rehab." He grimaced again, recognizing his poor choice of words. "I mean, they'd be really embarrassed—"

"We know what you mean, Mr. McDonnell. Thank you. No further questions."

She took her seat. Judge Shaheen gave the defense an opportunity to re-cross, but Lathrop quietly declined. Delving further into his client's substance abuse wouldn't improve Scott's image with the jury.

The prosecution next called Avery Park to the stand, and Natalie had to scrunch sideways to let the corpulent businessman sidle out of the row of chairs. His jowls hanging in a perpetual frown, Park seemed incapable of registering any emotion other than impatience, which grew more intense as he recounted Scott Hyland's tenure at the construction firm of Hyland & Park.

"The kid's a slacker and a delinquent," he declared. "If he hadn't been Press' son, I'd have kicked his fanny to the curb the day we hired him. Come to think of it, Press would've done the same."

"Please refrain from expressing your opinions when answering counsel's questions, Mr. Park," Judge Shaheen interjected. "You may continue, Ms. Mendoza."

"Thank you. When did the defendant first begin working for your company, Mr. Park?"

"Three summers ago. Press thought it'd be good for Scotty to take an interest in the family business. Help him straighten up and fly right. Like there was any chance of that."

The judge leaned forward again. "Mr. Park . . ."

"Sorry, Your Honor."

"What positions did the defendant hold at the firm?" Inez continued.

"Name it. Press made him a file clerk at the main office until our accounts became so disorganized that we needed a half-dozen temps to sort 'em out. Then we tried him in construction and warehouse positions, but our managers told us the kid would disappear for three-hour lunch breaks and come back reeking of marijuana. He's the boss's son, though, so who's gonna fire him?"

"How did he end up in the accounting department?"

Park shook his head with Cassandra-like exasperation. "I told him, but Press insisted, God rest his poor, deluded soul. Scotty was going to graduate from high school this year, and Press wanted to groom him for a regular job with the company since he didn't have the grades to get into a decent college. He also figured he could keep Scotty on a short leash if he was right there, looking over the kid's shoulder."

"What happened then?"

"He robbed us blind, that's what happened. Right away I noticed that the margins on our jobs dropped by about ten percent, due almost entirely to a spike in our materials cost. Now, the price of wood and such always goes up and down, but you don't generally see a jump like that inside of two months, so I start going back over the invoices to find out what the devil's going on.

"What do I find? We've been billed for thousands of board-feet of lumber and hundreds of bags of cement that never showed up at our warehouses. I call the suppliers about it, but they don't have a clue what I'm talking about; they never even submitted these invoices. Then I compare the invoices with earlier ones from the same companies and find that they're all bogus—printed on different-colored paper with different fonts and such. Scotty must've done 'em all with his home computer.

"I check with our bank and find that Scotty's been drawing cash from the company account. He then covered the withdrawals with his phony invoices and copies of forged checks that he never issued to our suppliers."

"How much cash had he withdrawn?"

"Over twenty-four thousand dollars."

"And what was Prescott Hyland Sr.'s reaction when you informed him of his son's embezzlement?"

"How would you feel? He nearly had a coronary. Threatened to call the cops and let Scotty rot in jail for what he did. Betsy talked him out of it, though—she was always soft on the kid. So we kept the whole thing quiet and let the lost profit go. But Press vowed that the minute Scotty turned eighteen, he'd send him packing without a penny."

"Did the defendant know of his father's intention to 'send him packing,' as you put it?"

"I don't doubt it. Press Hyland always spoke his mind."

"And when did the defendant's embezzlement come to light?"

"Last August third. I know, because I filled out Scotty's termination papers myself."

"August third." Inez angled toward the jury. "The same week Scott Hyland asked Troy McConnell about hiring a hit man to kill his parents. Thank you, Mr. Park."

She deferred to Malcolm Lathrop with a curt nod. He rubbed his hands together like a diner salivating over a favorite meal as he rose to cross-examine.

"Mr. Park, you helped design and build the Hyland mansion, didn't you?"

"Yeah. So?"

"Then you were familiar with the security system installed in the residence?"

Lathrop was so genial that it took a moment for the outrage to surface on Park's face. "What the hell are you trying to—"

"I only wanted to point out that you're one of the only people outside the Hyland family who could've deactivated that alarm."

Inez cut off Park's boiling outburst with one of her own. "Objection! It's the defendant who's on trial here, not Mr. Park."

"Your Honor," Lathrop said, "the defense intends to show that the police did not adequately pursue the investigation of other potential suspects before arbitrarily and unjustly accusing my client of the crime."

Judge Shaheen studied both attorneys. "Overruled. But this had better be leading somewhere, Mr. Lathrop."

The lawyer gave a slight bow. "It is, I assure you. Now, then, Mr. Park . . . can you account for your whereabouts on the night of last August twenty-first?"

The businessman jerked his head left and right, chins quivering, as if searching the courtroom for a referee to reverse the call. "As I told the police at the time, I worked late that night and went home, relaxed in front of the TV awhile, and went to bed. End of story."

"I see. Do you know of anyone who can attest to your actions that night?"

"No."

"Really? Not even your wife?"

Park seethed. "I'm not married."

Lathrop slapped a hand to his forehead. "Oh, that's right! Your wife divorced you last year, didn't she?"

The witness threw his hands up in disbelief. "What the devil does that have to do with anything?"

"Didn't the former Mrs. Park get your custom-built, three-million-dollar home as part of your divorce settlement? Isn't that why there was no one around to verify that you spent the night of August twenty-first at your one-bedroom apartment in Canoga Park?"

"Objection!" Inez snapped again. "Counsel has no right to delve into the witness's private life with this pointless fishing expedition."

Judge Shaheen's eyes shifted like a tilting balance. "I'll allow it. Please answer the question, Mr. Park."

The businessman let out a huff, the pop of air from a punctured tire. "Yes, she got the house."

Lathrop strolled back to the defense table, picked a page off the pile there. "You also had to give the former Bernice Hudson Park the cash value of half your interest in Hyland & Park. Is that correct?"

"Yessss."

"You didn't have that much cash, did you? Isn't that why you tried to convince Prescott Hyland Sr. to put the firm on the auction block, as outlined in this internal memo dated February twenty-sixth of last year?" The lawyer waved the paper in his hand.

A vein pulsed on Park's forehead. "With the housing boom, it was a seller's market. We could've made a fortune."

"But Mr. Hyland didn't agree, did he? Instead, he offered to buy you out at a fraction of the market value. But you had to accept, didn't you?"

"I *chose* to accept, yes."

"Press Hyland wasn't entirely unsympathetic, though. He let you stay on in a managerial capacity, after all. Still, I can't help but think that must've been a blow to your pride—to end up as an employee in a company that has your name on it. Wasn't that a bit . . . well, *humiliating*, Mr. Park?"

The businessman's expression settled into a threatening calm, like a tsunami still miles from shore. "There are worse things."

"Still, it must have bothered you that your longtime friend and business partner took advantage of your misfortune to buy your stake at a fire-sale price. So, where are these forged invoices and checks you claim my client made?"

"I shredded them."

Lathrop gave an incredulous chuckle. "You *shredded* them? They were evidence of a crime and you destroyed them?"

"It wasn't my idea. Press said to bury the whole thing, so I did."

"Of course, you realize that means we only have your word that these forged documents even existed."

"What do you mean?"

"I mean, what if *you* were really the one Prescott Hyland caught cooking the books?"

The tsunami broke. Park slapped his hands on the railing of the witness box as if about to launch himself at Lathrop, but the beige-shirted bailiff put a heavy hand on the businessman's shoulder until he sat back down.

An anxious murmur ran through the gallery, and Inez sprang up like an overcranked jack-in-the-box. *"Objection!* Your Honor, this isn't just speculation, it's science fiction!"

"Sustained," Judge Shaheen responded. "Mr. Lathrop, I advise you to withhold such accusations unless you have the evidence to support them."

"I assure you, Your Honor, I would never make such a

charge unless I could prove it." The lawyer regarded Park with the righteous sobriety of an executioner. "No further questions."

"Permission to redirect?" Inez demanded before he'd even seated himself.

Judge Shaheen gave a nod. "Granted."

"Mr. Park, have you ever been accused of a crime before?"

The businessman lifted his head so high it almost gave him a single chin. "Never."

"Really? You've never had any trouble with the police, ever?"

"Maybe a speeding ticket."

Inez shot the jury a wry look. "Me, too."

The jurors chuckled.

"Doesn't sound like much of a criminal record, does it?" the prosecutor observed. "Particularly compared with a young man with a known history of drug abuse, delinquency, and embezzlement. Thank you, Mr. Park."

The judge turned to the defense. "Mr. Lathrop?"

"No further questions at this time, although we reserve the right to call this witness for future cross-examination."

"Noted. Ms. Mendoza, your next witness?"

Inez remained standing. "Your Honor, the People rest."

"In that case, let's adjourn for lunch." He repeated his warning to the jury not to consider the evidence outside the courtroom and excused the gathering with another rap of his gavel.

Natalie lingered while the people around her dispersed, hoping she might have another chance to talk with Inez. But when she inched toward her friend, she caught sight of another loiterer in the courtroom—a man seated in the back of the gallery who wore a New York Yankees baseball cap and

jawed a wad of gum with casual disrespect for his surroundings. When she met his gaze, he eyed her intently and jotted
some note to himself on the legal pad in his lap.

Something about him jarred Natalie's memory. Was he
with Corps Security?

She shied back from Inez, and Avery Park hustled up to
the prosecutor instead, cheeks quivering as he harangued her
in hushed tones. Inez bobbed her head to placate him and
scooped the papers on the table into her briefcase. Natalie
slunk out of the courtroom, bowing her head to the floor to
avoid the temptation to glance at the man in the baseball cap.

She sat on the concrete wall of a planter box in the square
behind the courthouse to eat her lunch, but the turkey sandwich she bought weighted her stomach like wet cement. The
hour's ticking boredom only escalated the dread of what
would follow: Lyman Pearsall's appearance on the witness
stand.

The rest of the courtroom audience seemed to share her
unease, for Judge Shaheen had to call them to order several
times before they settled into silence. The justice let the quiet
coalesce into cold severity before beginning his mandatory
admonition to the jury.

"You are about to hear the testimony of Elizabeth Hyland
and Prescott Hyland Sr. Such testimony is often of a disturbing and deeply emotional nature."

A pallid young juror with rumpled hair dabbed perspiration from his forehead with his sleeve, and Judge Shaheen
directed the subsequent warning at him. "*Do not allow the
intensity of these emotions to cloud your judgment.* The statements of the victims should be considered as carefully, and
with as much skepticism, as that of any other witnesses when
you decide your verdict. You must weigh the testimony of the

deceased against the other evidence presented by both the prosecution and the defense in order to determine the truth for yourselves. Do you understand your responsibilities as I have described them to you?"

Some of the jurors hesitated, but all agreed. The judge waited for the last of them—the pallid young man—to nod before continuing. "Mr. Lathrop, you may call your first witness."

"Thank you, sir." Lathrop stood and faced the jury. "As His Honor has indicated, the defense wishes to summon Elizabeth Hyland. Bailiff, would you show the conduit to the stand?"

The heavyset black officer opened a side door and gestured to the unseen occupant of the room beyond. He held the door as Lyman Pearsall strode into court as if greeted by his own coronation march.

Without his shaggy toupee, Lyman's freshly shaved pate became shiny and skeletal, gleaming with cerebral authority, the tattooed node points a brand of phrenological superiority. When the bailiff swore him in, Pearsall surveyed the jurors as if reviewing troops for battle, making sure they all saw his deep-set violet eyes.

During the lunch recess, courthouse personnel had replaced the witness stand's wooden chair with a padded reclining chair that belonged in the office of a sadistic dentist. Pearsall made it look as comfy as a hammock, though, as he draped himself onto its curved back and headrest.

Malcolm Lathrop approached the stand. "Please state your name for the record."

"Lyman Pearsall."

"Are you a licensed conduit of the North American Afterlife Communications Corps?"

"I am."

"And do you intend to serve the court today with complete honesty and to the best of your abilities?"

"Of course." Pearsall made a face, as if he found the very question an insult.

"Thank you. Mr. Burton?"

Lathrop stood to one side while a portly man with glasses entered the witness box. Joe Burton had been the L.A. Criminal Court's resident SoulScan expert for as long as Natalie could remember, and he performed the ritual with quiet efficiency: inspecting the Violet's eyes with a penlight to make sure he wasn't wearing colored contact lenses, then taping electrodes to the node spots on the crown of Pearsall's head.

When Burton switched on the SoulScan unit beside the witness box, Lathrop pointed to the large green monitor on the wall behind Lyman. "The top three lines represent Mr. Pearsall's consciousness," he told the jury. "When the lines at the bottom of the screen begin spiking like those on top, you'll know that the victim's soul has inhabited the conduit's mind."

All the jurors and spectators fixated on the SoulScan screen as if afraid they might miss the big moment if they blinked. Without saying a word, Joe Burton fastened the witness chair's thick nylon straps across Pearsall's legs and chest and bound the Violet's wrists together with a ratcheted plastic band.

"Are you ready to proceed, Mr. Pearsall?" Malcolm Lathrop asked when Burton withdrew.

"Yes." The Violet shut his eyes, his lips barely visible beneath his frizzy mustache as he mouthed the words of his spectator mantra. Above him, the glowing green alpha waves on the top half of the SoulScan screen rolled with greater regularity, frenetic crags smoothing into gentle hills and valleys. The lines on the bottom half of the monitor remained flat, lifeless. Pearsall opened his hands.

Lathrop strolled over to the prosecution's table. "Ms. Mendoza, may I have the first touchstone?"

She passed him a thick plastic bag, and even before Lathrop removed the contents, Natalie recognized Betsy Hyland's blue, brain-spattered nightie. Inez had already displayed the garment for the jury while questioning the coroner and the ballistics expert about the victims' wounds. Lathrop unfolded the negligee and put it in Pearsall's grasp.

For the next several minutes, the only sound in the courtroom was the Violet's unintelligible whisper. Burton took his customary position by the SoulScan control panel, his hand poised near the Panic Button, just in case.

When the SoulScan registered no inhabitation, Natalie scrutinized Malcolm Lathrop's reaction. He peered at the flat green lines on the screen with his palms pressed together in front of his lips. Scott Hyland adopted much the same pose, his elbows propped on the defense table. Was that a bit of uncertainty shading their faces? Even fear, perhaps?

Then a blip, like the beat of a resuscitated heart, jumped along the screen's bottom three lines.

Who? Natalie thought, as Lyman Pearsall's face shuddered and changed.

The blip became a scribble of panic, and Pearsall bulged against the straps of his chair. He let out a series of falsetto gasps and popped his eyes wide and white, as if waking from a prolonged nightmare into a more ghastly reality. Jerking his head left and right, he tried to sit up, but the straps held him fast to the chair. The regal arrogance of his expression had dissolved into frightened befuddlement. "Where—where am I?"

His gaze lit upon the defense table, and a frantic hope rose in his voice. "Scotty?"

Scott Hyland sat up straight for the first time during the trial. He didn't seem to be faking the tremors of awe in his watery eyes or open mouth.

"Scotty, is that you? Please, honey, tell me . . . *where have I been?*"

Malcolm Lathrop, the only person in the room who now looked relaxed, leaned over the railing of the witness box, his face bearing the gentle concern of a father confessor. "We don't mean to scare you. Can you tell us who you are?"

Pearsall gaped at the lawyer, uncomprehending. "What? You want to know my name?"

Natalie's stomach shrank. *No . . .*

"Why, I'm Betsy," Pearsall said. "Betsy Hyland."

12

Surprise Witnesses

MALCOLM LATHROP DID A STAGE TURN TOWARD THE jury. "Let the record show that the witness has identified herself as Elizabeth Hyland."

Pearsall dropped the stained nightie and pulled at the nylon straps that held him down, face pleading. "Scotty? What's happening?"

Scott Hyland turned a whiter shade of pale. "Mom, I didn't—"

Lathrop interposed himself between the witness stand and the defense table. "Betsy, I know this is difficult for you, but we need your help. *Scott* needs your help."

Like a little girl trying to be brave at the doctor's office, Pearsall drew a deep breath and nodded.

"Now, Betsy, I want you to think back." The lawyer spoke with the lullaby lilt of a hypnotist. "Think back to the night you and your husband were shot."

Lyman's mouth opened, lips quivering, and he stared straight ahead as though the scene replayed itself before him. "Oh, oh, God . . . *Press!*"

"Easy, Betsy. Tell us what happened."

The Violet swallowed, moistened his lips. "Press and I had just climbed into bed. He was looking over some papers for work and I was reading my book, like we usually do before we go to sleep. Then a man threw the bedroom door open and burst into the room. Press sat up and started to ask what's going on, but the man, he lifted a gun and he . . . he . . ." Pearsall balled his fists in front of his mouth, squelching a sob.

Lathrop laid a comforting hand on the Violet's forearm. "Yes. Go on."

Lyman gulped air to continue. ". . . he shot Press in the chest. I screamed, tried to get up, but the man aimed his gun right at my face, and the shot—so loud, I thought my head would explode . . ."

A soft gasp from the jury box drew the room's attention. The pallid young man looked a bit green and was bent forward in his chair with a hand over his mouth. The woman next to him whispered something to him, but he shooed her back.

Lathrop raised his voice to regain the audience. "Who was the man with the gun? Can you describe him?"

Pearsall shook his head, his expression crinkled like wadded foil. "He wore all black clothes, with gloves and a ski mask that only showed his eyes."

"And yet you're sure it was a man?"

"Yes."

"What made you so sure? What can you tell us about him?"

The Violet sniffled. "Well, you know, he had a man's body. He was kind of short—shorter than Press—but he was big, with a big, fat belly and real thick legs."

Like everyone else in the room, Natalie looked at Scott Hyland. The boy stood at least six two, with a lean, toned musculature.

"I see." Malcolm Lathrop stepped aside to allow the witness to see the defendant again. "Then the gunman was *not* your son, Prescott Hyland Jr.?"

"*Scotty?* Don't be ridiculous!"

Scott Hyland seemed as startled as everyone else to hear his mother exonerate him.

Lathrop gestured to the boy. "But didn't you and Mr. Hyland have repeated fights with Scott?"

"Well, of course. Scotty could be a troublemaker sometimes, but he's a good boy and wouldn't think of hurting us."

"Did he ever threaten you?"

"Never!"

"Not even when your husband discovered that Scott had been siphoning money from his company?"

"*What?* How dare you say such a thing!" The witness acted as if this were a more serious accusation than her own murder.

Lathrop raised his hands. "Wait a minute. Didn't your husband find that Scott had embezzled several thousand dollars from the family firm?"

"He found no such thing!"

Murmurs of surprise rippled through the gallery. Beside Natalie, Avery Park hissed, "*That's not possible.*"

The defense attorney registered his own astonishment with the jury. "Then why on earth did your husband smash up your son's motorcycle?"

"Because he found out that Scotty had been experimenting with drugs. I guess that awful McDonnell kid put him up to it." Pearsall shook his head sadly. "Press always did have such a temper. He felt bad about Scotty's bike and had already promised him a new one."

"Did Mr. Hyland ever threaten to kick your son out of the house as soon as he turned eighteen?"

"Heavens, no! What kind of people do you think we are?"

"So there was no bad blood between you and your son at the time of the shootings?"

"Absolutely not."

"Betsy, did you know of anyone who had anything against you or your husband? Anyone who might want to hurt you?"

Pearsall shook his head, but without conviction. "Sometimes Press rubbed people the wrong way . . . but I don't see how anyone could . . . could . . ."

"I know—it's hard to believe. But think carefully. Had your husband argued with anyone recently?"

"Well, he was furious with Avery about the business—" Horror dawned on Lyman's face. *"Avery."*

Natalie cast a sidelong look at the man next to her. Avery Park put his hands to his temples and muttered, "No, this is wrong. This can't be happening."

Lathrop inclined an ear toward the Violet. "Yes? What about Mr. Park?"

"It was him!" Pearsall's voice rose with certainty. "It was him! It *had* to have been him—"

Inez cut him off. "Objection! The witness is speculating."

"Sustained," Judge Shaheen responded. "The jury should disregard the witness's assumptions."

Malcolm Lathrop held up a hand, eyes shut, as if to say *I'm way ahead of you, Judge.* "Betsy, tell us exactly what the dispute between Mr. Park and your husband was."

"Press was about to *fire* the bastard, that's what. Called him the biggest ingrate since Judas." Pearsall hyperventilated like an incensed matron. "He bailed Avery out of his divorce mess, let him keep a good job with the firm, and the man ends up stealing from him!"

"Wait! You say Mr. Park stole from your husband?"

"That's right. Those papers Press was reading in bed—he

was looking for evidence to fire Avery. He even talked about filing charges."

"THAT'S A LIE!" Avery Park pushed himself to his feet, his head as red as a wine grape ready to burst. "IT'S A GOD-DAMN LIE!"

"Sit *down*," Inez hissed over her shoulder.

The bailiff rushed to restrain Park, and Judge Shaheen hammered his gavel to quell the anxious babble in the courtroom. "Take your seat, Mr. Park," he commanded. "Another outburst like that, and I'll have you escorted from the building."

"I have a right to defend my name!" Park bellowed.

"This is not an invitation to discussion, Mr. Park. Take your seat. Mr. Lathrop, your next question."

The defense attorney patted Pearsall's arm. "It's all right, Betsy. We'll find the truth."

"You can't let them hurt my boy," Lyman begged the courtroom audience. "You can't let them hurt Scotty. He had nothing to do with this."

Natalie watched Inez to see if she would object to this blatant play on the jury's sympathy, but the prosecutor merely stewed in silence. It was a no-win situation. If she let the remarks slide, the victim's plea would no doubt pull some jurors' heartstrings; if she protested, she would make herself seem a callous, nitpicking bully.

Malcolm Lathrop, on the other hand, came off looking like Superman—defender of the defenseless, champion of Truth, Justice, and the American Way. "We'll find out what really happened, Betsy. I promise you," he said, squeezing Pearsall's hand in solidarity. "No further questions, Your Honor."

Judge Shaheen gave a dour nod. "Ms. Mendoza?"

Inez stood, her face a furnace door, immobile as iron yet

searing with the heat of the fire behind it. "Mrs. Hyland . . . when is your wedding anniversary?"

That's it, Natalie thought, scrutinizing Lyman's reaction. *Let's see if you're really who you say you are.*

Pearsall's eyes narrowed, an unmistakable glimmer of shrewdness in them. "April twenty-third. Why?"

"What was your maiden name?"

The Violet's gaze searched the air momentarily, hesitating a split second too long. "Vandenburg."

"And what was your mother's birthday?"

"I don't see what this has to do with anything—"

Lathrop cut in. "The witness is right, Your Honor. The prosecution evidently has no pertinent questions to ask, so it's stalling for time. I suggest we waste neither the court's nor Mrs. Hyland's time with this senseless trivia quiz."

"I'm afraid I agree." Judge Shaheen said it with real regret. "Unless you can somehow justify this line of questioning, Ms. Mendoza, you should stick to the case at hand."

Inez remained standing, and Natalie could almost feel how her friend ached with the urge to tell the court about their experiments in the room at Motel 6. But Natalie's attempt to summon the Hylands had been illegal, and, as far as Judge Shaheen or anyone else knew, falsified Violet testimony was unprecedented—unthinkable, even.

The prosecutor swallowed any arguments she may have had. "No further questions, Your Honor."

"Very well. Mr. Lathrop?"

The defense attorney returned to the witness stand to take hold of Pearsall's hands. "Betsy . . . we need to talk to your husband now."

"I see." Lyman gawked at the people in the gallery and the

jury box, guileless as a newborn once more. "Please help Scotty. Please help my son."

When his gaze came to rest on the defendant himself, the Violet half smiled in adoration. Then his face slipped into slackness, and the bottom three lines of the SoulScan monitor went flat.

For an instant, real tears moistened Scott Hyland's eyes, and the boy bowed his head into his hands.

"How could she do this to me?" Avery Park muttered to himself over and over, lost in the solipsism of self-pity.

Malcolm Lathrop bent to collect the fallen nightie. As the lawyer folded it back into a neat bundle, Lyman Pearsall groaned back to consciousness.

Lathrop fawned over him, a manager with his punch-drunk boxing champ. "Mr. Pearsall? Can you hear me? Are you all right?"

Lyman waggled his cheeks like a groggy hound. "Yeah . . . I'm okay."

"Are you ready to continue? Do you need a recess to rest?"

"No. I'll be fine. Just gimme a minute." But he panted and massaged his forehead with his banded hands to make sure everyone knew what a strain this ordeal was on him.

"Take as much time as you need." The attorney gave the nightie back to Inez and demanded Prescott Hyland Sr.'s tattered pajama top in exchange. He brought it back to the witness stand and waited for Pearsall to catch his breath.

At last, the Violet held out his hands again. "Give it to me."

Lathrop draped the shirt over Lyman's hands and stepped back. Natalie watched the SoulScan monitor, praying that Prescott Hyland Sr. might prove a no-show. A moment later she knew her hope was in vain.

While Betsy Hyland apparently needed to be coaxed out

of the void like a rabbit from its burrow, her husband sprang out with the clawing ferocity of a badger. The inhabitation lines on the SoulScan screen blurred with skittering thought-waves, and Pearsall lurched forward, the nylon straps snapping him back against the seat like a slingshot. Snarling, he threw his weight against them again, causing the entire chair to shudder, and twisted his wrists to try to break the plastic band. *"Get me out of here!"*

Stationed at the SoulScan console, Joe Burton flagged the attention of the judge and indicated the Panic Button, awaiting authorization, but Malcolm Lathrop raised a hand to stop him.

The attorney approached the frantic figure in the witness stand. "Who are you?"

Pearsall glared at him as if he'd asked what that glowing yellow ball in the sky was. "Press Hyland, you idiot! Now get me the hell out of here!" He scowled toward the defense table. "Scotty? Don't just sit there, boy—help me!"

"I'm afraid your son can't help you right now," Lathrop said. "He's on trial for your murder."

"My *what?*" As the implications of the lawyer's words sank in, Pearsall became blank-faced with shock. "Oh, sweet Jesus . . ."

Natalie evaluated his reaction. If it was a performance, it was a good one. Many souls were in denial about their own demise, preferring to believe that their imprisonment in the limbo of the afterlife was merely some anesthesia-induced fever-dream and that they would soon wake up in a hospital, alive and well.

Natalie wasn't the only one who found the inhabitation convincing, for Avery Park stood to shout at the witness stand. "Press, it's me! You've got to tell them I didn't do it!"

Judge Shaheen brought the gavel down again. "Mr. Park, I warned you—"

Pearsall stared at Park, and his features curled up like burning paper. "You son of a bitch! Thought you'd finished me off, did you? I'm gonna—"

Lathrop held him back as the Violet pushed forward again, seething. "Tell us exactly what you saw at the time you were murdered."

"I'll tell you what I saw! *That* fat slob with my own shotgun in his hands."

"But your wife said the killer wore a ski mask . . ."

"He did, but the arrogant bastard assumed I was dead after he shot me. I saw just fine, though—saw what he did to Betsy. Then he pulled his mask off and *smiled* at me. Said 'I guess you're the one who got fired, eh, Press?' and laughed."

Lathrop faced the jury. "Let the record show the victim has identified Mr. Park as the gunman—"

"*NO!*" Park struggled against the bailiff, who tried to push him back toward his seat. "It's not true! Press, how can you do this to me?"

"You got a lot of nerve saying that after what you did to us," Pearsall growled.

The shouting nearly drowned out Judge Shaheen's gavel. "Order! Order! Bailiff, escort Mr. Park from the room."

Brows lowered, Pearsall shook his head. "Oh, no. He's not getting away that easy."

Thrusting his bound hands out toward Park, the Violet rocked his weight so violently that he tipped the chair until it crashed against the rail of the witness box. Spectators shrieked and Lathrop jumped back as Pearsall tried to worm out of the straps, howling hatred, fingers clawing for Park's throat. Park still protested his innocence while the bailiff wavered, unsure whether to lead him from the room or to subdue the crazed conduit on the stand.

The judge stood and raised his arms, the black sleeves of his robe like raven's wings. "Please! Everyone remain calm. Burton—"

That was all Joe Burton needed to hear. The electrode wires taped to Pearsall's scalp had dragged the SoulScan console to the edge of its cart, threatening to send it tumbling to the floor, but Burton caught hold of it and slapped his hand on the Panic Button.

Pinned between the upset chair and the witness-stand rail, Lyman Pearsall flopped like a dying flounder as current coursed through his brain, banishing the inhabiting soul to oblivion. When the green waves on the lower half of the SoulScan screen had flatlined, Burton stooped to check the Violet's vital signs and to free him from the chair.

"Everything's okay," Judge Shaheen assured the assembly and took his seat. "I suggest we adjourn until ten A.M. tomorrow morning—"

"Your Honor," Inez broke in, "the prosecution did not have the opportunity to cross-examine this last witness."

"I don't think that will be necessary. Do you?" The justice cast a pointed glance at the prone form of Lyman Pearsall, who moaned softly as Burton attended to some minor scrapes and bruises on the Violet.

Inez took several measured breaths. "If you say so, sir."

"In that case, court is adjourned." Shaheen repeated his caution to the jurors and dismissed them. The closing gavel sounded, and Malcolm Lathrop clapped a stunned Scott Hyland on the shoulder before loading his papers into his briefcase. Burton helped an unsteady Lyman Pearsall limp out a side door.

As the people in the gallery around him dispersed, Avery Park still quivered with rage, gaping in disbelief at both the prosecutor and judge. "What? That's *it*? I *demand* a chance to clear my name!"

"You've got it."

Park turned to confront the speaker and found Detective Dennis Raines and a uniformed LAPD officer standing behind him. "I'm afraid we're going to have to detain you for questioning regarding the Hyland murders," Raines said. "Please come with us."

"I don't *believe* this." The irritation in Park's voice edged into hysteria, and tears of fear glistened in his gaze. "This can't be happening."

So intent was Natalie on watching Raines and the cop lead Park away that she nearly missed seeing Inez head up the courtroom's center aisle. The prosecutor sneezed loudly as she passed, however, and Natalie glanced over in time to see her drop a tightly folded rectangle of paper on the floor.

Natalie sidled down to the end of the row where Inez had been and pretended to fumble with her dark glasses, which she let fall to the floor. After scooping up the paper along with the glasses, she donned the shades and made her way out of the courtroom.

Through the thinning crowd in the gallery, she saw the man in the Yankees baseball cap follow her with his eyes.

She waited until she'd locked herself in a ladies' room stall before unfolding the note clutched in her fist. MEET ME ON EMERGENCY STAIRS, SIXTH FLOOR, it read in hasty block letters. NOW.

13

In Case of Emergency

NATALIE KNEW THE EMERGENCY STAIRS OF THE L.A. Criminal Justice Center well from past experience, and she found it comforting to stand on the sixth-floor landing, sealed off from the clamor surrounding the Hyland trial. Quiet and cavernous as a cathedral, the empty stairwell offered sanctuary, a place to stop and sort out her jabbering thoughts.

The respite didn't last. Inez blustered down the stairs from above. "Sorry to keep you waiting," she muttered. "Damn reporters."

"Understood. By the way . . . I do elevators now."

Inez gave a tired smile. "Thanks for coming. And for putting up with the cloak-and-dagger stuff."

"I can't stay long. Have to pick up Callie." Natalie hugged herself, working up the courage to look her friend in the eye. "Sorry things didn't go according to plan."

"They never do." The prosecutor propped herself against the wall, the ice in her voice starting to crack. "Did we make a mistake?"

"I don't think so. It was a good plan to summon the Hylands before the trial. I'm sorry I couldn't—"

"No, I mean, did *I* make a mistake? Is Scott really innocent?"

Natalie was no longer sure how to answer that question.

Was Scott innocent? Was Avery Park guilty? Malcolm Lathrop had clouded even Inez's mind with doubt, and doubt would set Scott Hyland free.

But that cunning gleam in Pearsall's eyes—Natalie hadn't imagined that. Had she?

"There's *something* wrong here," Natalie said slowly. "I can't point to anything definite. But I know it wasn't the Hylands who inhabited Lyman in there."

"If that's true, how can I *prove* it?"

"You came close when you asked Betsy Hyland those personal questions. If you'd found one she couldn't answer, Pearsall would've had some serious explaining to do. He definitely seemed to be stonewalling, waiting for Lathrop to lodge his objection. I think that's why Prescott Hyland—or whoever it was—turned violent there at the end, knowing Joe Burton would push the Panic Button if things got hairy. That way Hyland could point the finger at Avery Park without ever exposing himself to cross-examination . . ."

". . . so we'd never find out who he really was. Yeah." The prosecutor's face firmed with renewed purpose. "But what do we do now?"

What do you mean, "we"? Natalie wanted to ask but didn't. "Maybe I can look into Lyman's background," she offered. "See if there's anything hinky about his past, anyone he knew who died recently."

"Good. I'll do what I can to stall for time. Given what a mess things are, Tony Shaheen ought to give me at least until Monday or Tuesday to rework my case. I'll see what I can squeeze out of Park and try to get you some files on Pearsall."

"Thanks . . ." *but no thanks,* Natalie thought. "And what if we can't find anything?"

"Then Scott Hyland deserves to go free." The determination in Inez's eyes turned desperate. "But I'm not going to be able to sleep at night unless I convince *myself* he didn't do it."

Natalie held her sigh until her friend had said good-bye and left her alone on the landing. *I'm not going to be able to sleep at night regardless,* she thought, and started down the stairs.

14

Bursting Bubbles

NATALIE EXITED THE COURTHOUSE BUT COULDN'T escape it. She'd hoped this would be the last day she would ever come back to this place, but now it clung to her with webs of obligation. Should she have stayed out of the case, left Inez to fend for herself? Why risk her own future with Callie to keep Scott Hyland off the streets?

Because he's a killer, she told herself as she crossed the courtyard outside. *Because if you let him get away with it, you're inviting every angry kid to blow his parents away. There were times when even you were tempted to do that, weren't you?*

But she also couldn't ignore another possibility—one she hadn't even admitted to herself, much less Inez: some Violets who suffered brain damage from either a head injury or a degenerative neural condition lost their ability to summon. If Lyman Pearsall really *had* summoned the Hylands today, it not only meant that Scott Hyland was simply a troubled boy who made a convenient patsy for Avery Park. It meant that Natalie might have a brain disease, perhaps a fatal tumor. And if she died, what would happen to Callie? Arabella Madison would become her wicked stepmother, that's what.

However, a darker concern scuttled ratlike underneath all these legitimate fears: the prospect of losing her ability to summon souls terrified Natalie.

She almost laughed at the irony of it. She'd spent most of her life wishing she were deaf to the dead, but now that she confronted the prospect of being "normal," it struck her as a sort of death in itself. Being a Violet had defined her entire existence—her career, her family, her friends. How she looked and how she lived. If she was no longer a Violet, who was she?

And there was Dan to think about. Summoning him was not the same as holding him in her arms, but it was something. At least she could feel his love inside her, enfold his spirit in her mind's embrace. If she didn't even have that . . .

"Ms. Lindstrom!"

The sound of her name jerked her out of the free fall into despair like a bungee cord. The voice was male and gravelly, as from too many cigarettes. She didn't recognize it, and that scared her. No one but Inez should have known who she was. Could she have heard wrong?

Natalie stepped to the curb of Los Angeles Street and glanced to the left, as if awaiting an opportunity to jaywalk. Her eyes hidden behind her dark glasses, she scanned the sidewalk behind her and saw the man who'd eyed her in the courtroom—the one in the Yankees baseball cap. He hurried to catch up, waving to flag her attention.

"Hey! You're Ms. Lindstrom, aren't you? Natalie Lindstrom?"

She pretended not to notice him and crossed the street.

"Wait!" He trotted after her, sidestepping as a Lexus squeal-stopped to keep from hitting him. "We haven't been properly introduced. Sid Preston, *New York Post.*"

Circling around, he walked backward in front of her, hand extended. The name prodded Natalie's memory: the baseball cap, the gum, the yellow legal pad under his arm—this was the reporter who'd blown her cover during the Violet Killer investigation six years ago.

Preston dropped his hand when she didn't accept it. "It *is* Natalie Lindstrom, isn't it? I made a point of memorizing that face, no matter what color hair or eyes you had."

Natalie paused on the sidewalk, checking to see whether any of the surrounding pedestrians took notice of her conversation with the reporter. If it ever got back to the Corps that she was here . . .

"What do you want, Mr. Preston?" she asked, to pacify him.

"Just curious about your interest in the Hyland trial. That was some show in there, wasn't it? You think the D.A.'s gonna drop Scott Hyland and go after that Park guy?"

"It's not my place to say."

She resumed walking toward the lot where she'd parked her rented Toyota, and he paced her. "I saw you with Mendoza. You an advisor to the prosecution?"

"No. Inez is a friend. We were going to do lunch, but she didn't have time."

"But you've worked with the D.A.'s department before. How do you think they'll save face?"

"I don't think they'll have to save face."

"Can I quote you on that?"

"No."

Preston rubbed his stubble-covered cheek. "You're still working freelance these days, right?"

"If I'm not mistaken, that's *my* business, Mr. Preston."

"Oh, sure! I know that. But I had a proposal I wanted to bounce off you."

"In that case, I'm *not* freelancing."

"Ha! That's funny. Anyway, here's what I was thinking: once the trial's wrapped up, I figured maybe you could give me an exclusive interview with the victims." He grinned encouragement at her, still chomping his gum.

"I'm afraid I can't do that," she said. Little did Preston know she was telling the literal truth.

"You know, my paper would pay handsomely for a piece like that. We're talking six figures handsomely. And we might swing a book deal on top of that."

"Sorry."

"You have a kid, right? One payday like this could go a long way toward funding her education."

Her education. Natalie pictured Callie at the School and stopped to regard the reporter. Did Preston realize the trouble he could cause by reporting Natalie to the Corps? Would he use it to blackmail her?

"You have a card?" She let a lilt of interest lift her tone.

Preston smirked and dug out his wallet. "You won't regret this."

He pulled a smog-colored rectangle from among the coupons and Bazooka Joe comic wrappers in the billfold, hastily smoothing out the card's creases before handing it to her. "You got both my cell and my voice mail there. Call anytime."

"I'll be in touch." Natalie made a show of filing the card in her purse. "You'll keep our contact confidential until then, won't you?"

"Of course. Wouldn't want to lose the exclusive, after all." Preston doffed his cap to her. "It was a pleasure, Ms. Lindstrom."

"I'm sure it was." She proceeded down the street, glancing over her shoulder only when she was sure he no longer followed her.

Sid Preston still stood where she'd left him, scribbling on his yellow notepad. When he saw her watching, he winked and blew a happy pink gum bubble for her benefit.

15

Separation Anxiety

WHEN SHE GOT BACK TO THE MALL IN BREA, NATALIE hastily purchased a pair of blue jeans she didn't need so she could flash both a smile and a big Nordstrom bag at George as she returned to her Volvo. Despite this precaution, he shot her an incredulous look through the LeBaron's window. It was nearly five o'clock, which made her "shopping expedition" about eight hours long. Shaking his head, George started his car.

He tailed Natalie as far as the day-care center, where Arabella Madison leaned against the side of her Acura, flipping through a copy of *Vogue* and waiting to begin her shift. She, in turn, followed Natalie and Callie back to the condo. Stationing herself outside the kitchen window, Madison tapped on the pane and made goofy faces while they were eating dinner.

Callie giggled. Arabella's antics tickled her, despite her mother's repeated warnings. Natalie closed the curtains, but the Security Agent's gauzy silhouette lurked there throughout the evening, pulling at her peripheral vision.

"Read me a story?" Callie begged as Natalie carried her upstairs to bed. "Read me *Horton!* Pleeeeease?"

"Not tonight, honey. Mommy's really tired." She supervised her daughter's tooth brushing and tucked her in.

Although it was barely past eight, Natalie did her own dental hygiene and went straight to bed. She did not go to sleep, however, but instead undressed and lay on the sheets nude, her arms crossed over her breasts.

It was only a test, she told herself. She needed to summon someone to prove she still could, and he was the most convenient subject.

Truth was, she needed *him*. Dan was the only person she'd ever known who could lift the veil of death from her existence.

With the borders of the present erased by darkness, Natalie submerged herself in the past, calling to him with her longing.

"You all right?"

She opened her clamshell eyelids enough to peer through her dark glasses at Dan, who'd kindly offered to take the window seat for their flight. The last thing she wanted to see was thirty thousand feet of empty air beneath her. "Oh, yeah. Never better."

Another shockwave of turbulence hit their plane, making the fuselage buck like a spooked stallion. Natalie snapped her eyes shut again and pushed herself back into her seat, gagging on the air she gulped. She was grateful that she'd been too scared to eat anything while waiting for takeoff; now she had nothing in her stomach to puke.

"Hang in there, Natalie." Dan nudged her until she peeked at his wry smile. "It's the safest way to travel, after all."

"Says you." Natalie thought of the last pilot she'd summoned for a National Transportation Safety Board crash investigation—fighting to regain control even as the catastrophic depressurization burst the blood vessels in his brain, the altimeter needle dropping as the green hills below rushed up to slam him . . .

She stared at the FASTEN SEAT BELT *sign, willing it to shut off.*

Only a job as important as the Violet Killer investigation could have persuaded her to get on a plane, a device she considered nothing more than an elevator without cables.

Dan's face pinched with hesitation until he looked almost as anxious as she was. Then, without speaking another word, he gently pried Natalie's left hand loose from the armrest and clasped it between his trembling palms. Her hand squeezed his until the flesh whitened against the underlying bones, but he didn't complain.

She didn't find out until later how much her touch terrified him. Dan had accidentally killed an innocent man in the line of duty, and he dreaded the possibility that she might summon the victim to confront him. But he let her hold his hand anyway, and she sensed, even then, that he cared for her in a way no one else had before.

They sat like that for most of the rest of the flight, their hands fused together as the plane shuddered and dipped, perversely united by their fears, inextricably bound by the trust they shared . . .

Spreading herself across the sheets, Natalie let her mind drift on the rolling syllables of her spectator mantra, her head so full of Dan that she thought he must be knocking already.

He wasn't.

She curled up and concentrated harder. Minutes passed, yet he refused to come. Perhaps he couldn't come . . . or perhaps she had lost the ability to receive him.

Tears pressed on the insides of her closed eyelids, but she repeated the mantra faster and faster, unwilling to admit the possibility that he was lost to her.

Things must be bad, he abruptly commented in her head. *You haven't called me back this quickly since Callie was born.*

Her muscles relaxed, and the salt liquid remained pooled

in her eyes as she opened them. "I . . . I didn't know if you'd come."

Why would you think that? He sounded genuinely surprised by the statement. *What's worrying you, Natalie?*

"I'm not sure how much longer I'll be able to speak to you."

The pause that followed stretched even longer.

If you want me to leave you alone, you only have to ask . . .

"No! It's not that. My brain is changing as I get older—I could lose my ability to summon." She didn't mention that such a change might be fatal.

The crushing pressure of his sadness threatened to implode her heart. *Maybe it's for the best.*

"I don't want to lose you. Ever."

But what if she already *had* lost him?

The thought jolted her like the electric fire from a Panic Button, and she snapped up in bed. During the six years since she had left the Corps, she'd never had a SoulScan confirm any of her inhabitations. What if she'd lost her ability to summon long ago and had simply imagined every soul that entered her since then? Hysterical summonings, just like her mom's. Her Dan might be no more real than Nora's Thresher.

I am real, he insisted.

She tore off her wig and massaged her bare scalp, her chest heaving. In her distraction, she'd forgotten that her thoughts became his in the head they shared.

"Is that really you, Dan?" she breathed, not wanting to believe that she was merely talking to herself.

Yes, it's me. Give me your hands and I'll prove it to you.

Natalie did as he asked, her arms tingling as she relinquished control to him. She lay back on the bed, and he guided her hands over her body, gliding her fingertips along the undersides of her breasts, down the gentle convexity of her midriff, in between the softness of her thighs. He touched her in ways that only he had, that only he could.

Afterward, they nested together, united in mind, body, and spirit, enfolded in the fleeting peace given to lovers who forget the world exists.

Without taking his eyes from the darkened windows of Natalie Lindstrom's condo, Horace Rendell popped a Vivarin, a Sudafed caplet, and an echinacea supplement in sequence, washing each down with cold coffee from a travel mug in his Hyundai's cup holder. Another sneezing fit hit him while he still had liquid in his mouth, and he sprayed the steering wheel with a mist of coffee and spit.

Coughing curses, he grabbed a wad of grease-stained fast food napkins to wipe up the mess. This was the third cold he'd had this year, and it had lasted six weeks and counting. In a truly just universe, he could've sued Corps Security for workman's comp for putting him on the godforsaken grave-yard shift. He'd never adjusted to sleeping during the day and felt lucky when he managed a few hours' light doze each morning; consequently, he was always run-down and caught every virus that happened to drift his way. Add that to the perpetual hemorrhoids and constipation he suffered from sitting in this stupid car every night, not to mention his utter lack of any social life, and he ought to be able to squeeze the N-double-A-C-C for a couple million in punitive damages. In a just universe.

But the universe sucked, so here he sat in the dead hours of the morning, hacking up phlegm and watching the condo for any glimmer of an opportunity. Hope alone kept him vigilant.

He rubbed his face until it hurt, the pale skin red with capillaries bursting from high blood pressure. That witch Madison had ended her shift as she always did, by blowing him a kiss as she sashayed from the Lindstrom's doorstep to her car. Cocky slut thought she had the bonus in the bag: four hundred thousand, tax-free, for snagging the Violet kid.

Well, she'd be using that smirk of a mouth to kiss certain portions of his anatomy before he was done. That money was his golden parachute, and he'd do anything necessary to get it. Even if it meant working some unpaid overtime.

Rendell wiped his runny nose with a damp napkin and glowered at the quiet condo. The Lindstrom woman would slip up sooner or later. He'd make sure of that, and he'd make sure that he was around to get the girl when it happened.

It was only a matter of time.

16

Work to Do

A FEDEX PACKAGE ARRIVED AT NATALIE'S DOOR FIRST thing the following morning. As she signed for it, she saw the mailing label bore the return address for "Libra Enterprises," and she accepted it as if receiving a letter bomb. She carried the rectangular cardboard box to the kitchen, where Callie sat at the table eating her morning cereal.

"Is it a present?" her daughter asked.

"Not exactly, honey." Natalie grabbed a knife from the butcher block and sliced through the packing tape that held the lid shut. Inside the box, she found a thick sheaf of faxed and photocopied documents and newspaper articles to which a handwritten note had been paper-clipped:

> Pulled strings to get these. Look them over and meet me at the Motel 6, Rm. 308, on Sunday, 9 a.m.
>
> I.

Natalie rolled her eyes but picked up the files and paged through them. Inez had evidently begged, borrowed, or stolen every scrap of information about Lyman Pearsall she could find—articles about each of the cases he'd worked on as well as supposedly confidential Corps personnel files, even Lyman's transcript from his boyhood days at the School. (According to this, he'd been a C student at best.)

She assigned Callie a lengthy phonics assignment, brewed herself a cup of herbal tea, and plunked down on the living-room couch to see if she could uncover an incriminating needle in this biographical haystack. Lyman August Pearsall, born May 28, 1957, in Lake County, California, third son of Herbert Ryan Pearsall and Lydia May Strickert. His parents put him up for adoption by the School at age four. (No doubt the Corps paid them handsomely for that selfless sacrifice, Natalie thought.) Never married. Two drunk driving convictions, but otherwise no criminal record.

Natalie skimmed Pearsall's history of Corps service, but found it unremarkable. The Ries case notwithstanding, he'd always done an adequate, if not stellar, job as a conduit. He went AWOL once in the late eighties, but the Corps brought him back within three months. He'd never gone missing since.

Only Lyman's medical history caught Natalie's attention. Throughout his life, Corps doctors had treated him several times for bouts of anxiety and depression and once for addiction to a prescription sleep medication. It also said that Pearsall had twice received mandatory psychiatric counseling, although Inez evidently hadn't managed to get her hands on *those* files.

Psychological problems were common among Violets, of course. Occupational hazard, so to speak. Even if he were somehow delusional, though, it didn't explain how he faked the SoulScan readout or how he created credible testimony for dead witnesses. He needed a shill on the Other Side.

Natalie scanned Pearsall's personal data again. His parents and brothers were all still alive, apparently, and he barely had any contact with them. He seemed to have few friends either inside or outside the conduit community. Natalie knew of some Violets who'd passed over during the last few years, but none who would agree to lie in court. Did Lyman somehow convince the soul of a total stranger to be his confederate? Who would do such a thing? And why?

Callie flopped an open storybook on top of the stack of papers in Natalie's lap. "Can you tell me what this word is?"

Grateful for the interruption, Natalie put aside the Lyman files. "Sure, honey. Let's try and sound it out."

She looked at the page where Callie pointed. The word was "danger."

Like a seed crystal, it froze the swirling uneasiness in her mind into a jewel of ice. Natalie shivered and stared at Callie, watching for telltale signs of inhabitation. Was someone inside her, someone who wanted to give Natalie a warning?

Callie merely gazed up at her with polite expectation.

"As I said—let's sound it out. What sound does *d* make?"

Her smile a bit unsteady, Natalie forced herself to forget about Pearsall and the Hyland trial and spent the rest of the morning teaching her daughter. Later, she thought, she could go online and see what a Web search turned up. She didn't have much hope, however. So far, it seemed that the only person Lyman Pearsall had ever hurt was himself.

No one at the Home Depot in Hollywood paid much attention to the pudgy little man with the sunglasses and bad toupee as he loaded his orange shopping cart with rolls of chicken wire and rubber padding. The enormous store's echoing acoustics amplified the rattle and clatter of hardware and two-by-fours, burying the man's mumbling in noise.

Only the woman in front of him at the checkout line gave him an odd glare as she placed her potted plants on the conveyor belt. She must have drawn close enough to make out the words:

One penny, two penny, three penny, four,
Five penny, six penny, seven penny, more . . .

Lyman paid for his goods and pushed the cart out of the store's dim, lumber-scented interior into the gray haze of an overcast L.A. afternoon. He tossed the chicken wire and insulation into the back of his Bronco, where several bags of aluminum foil already lay in a heap. He'd decided it would be easier to buy the stuff down here and take it with him rather than to try to find it all up in Lakeport.

After climbing into the driver's seat, Pearsall rubbed his temples with the heels of his palms, his hands a vise around his head. Reciting the mantra had already given him a headache, and he still had a ten-hour drive ahead of him. But he didn't stop repeating the refrain. He didn't dare stop.

Lathrop had blown him off again. Big surprise. *Patience, Lyman! You'll get your money as soon as I get my verdict.* Insert patronizing smile here. *Until then I want you to wait around. You may need to testify again.*

Pearsall couldn't wait. Not while *he* was here. Lyman knew what *he* was thinking, had seen it all in his mind while they were together on the witness stand. It would be worse than before—worse than whatever had happened in that cabin in Lucerne. That's why Lyman needed to build another soul cage *now*.

One penny, two penny . . .

He took a lungful of breath to continue his mantra and started the engine.

What do you think you're doing, Lyman?

That familiar voice in his brain, its tone half annoyance, half pity.

"What're you doing here?" Startled by the panic in his own voice, Pearsall threw the Bronco's transmission from reverse into neutral. "I didn't call for you!"

You didn't need to call. I've been here all along.

Pearsall shook his head. He couldn't have—and yet Lyman never even felt him knock.

He resumed reciting his protective mantra, but it came out of his mouth a childish sneer.

One penny, two penny, three penny, four,
Isn't Lyman a big, fat bore?

He heard himself laugh, though he wanted to scream. "Boy, you are *way* out of your league," his own voice said. "First you want me to be your best friend, then you want to shove me in one of those metal boxes of yours. Well, I got news for you. I've tilted with your type before, and I know your little tricks. Now, if you don't mind, we've got work to do."

But we made a deal! Lyman bawled, his words now merely an echo in a head no longer his. *I gave you what you wanted! I PAID you!*

"You haven't even begun to pay."

Lyman saw his hands put the car in gear. Then a black door slammed on his perceptions, entombing him in the darkness of his skull.

17

A Bad Night for Nora

"WAKE UP, HONEY! TIME TO GO HOME."

Seated on a chair in the locked ward's hallway, Andy Sakei blinked weariness out of his eyes and looked up at the nurse who'd come to relieve him: a plump, whimsical woman with curly orange hair and heavy makeup. He didn't recognize her, but by that time, he didn't really care.

"What happened to Roger?" he asked.

"Down with the flu, poor thing. They had to borrow me from Metropolitan State. Every place is short-staffed these days, you know."

"Tell me about it." It was Andy's first day back at the Institute since the baby was born, and he'd had about five hours' sleep in the last three days. Little Sarah was a gift from heaven, but she screamed like a holy terror and seemed to nap in fifteen-minute increments between crying fits. He rubbed his eyes and glanced at his replacement's ID badge and the beaming photo on it. "Glad to see you . . . Bridget."

"Call me Bridge, hon." She extended a fat-fingered hand with stubby nails polished in silver, and he shook it. "Tell me what I need to know."

Andy got up with a groan. "It's been a beast of a day. Seven's been manic and Sixteen refused to take his meds, so we had to go intravenous," he said, referring to the patients by room number so she'd know whom to keep an eye on. Andy's side and leg still ached from the bruises Mr. Johnson had given him while he restrained him for medication. "You sure you can cope with the violent cases?"

The nurse laughed. "Honey, I've manhandled patients twice my size. I'll be fine."

Andy sized her up. She was short but stout, breasts drooping over a broad belly beneath the white knit shirt of her uniform. Her fleshy, hairless arms looked strong enough, though—she could probably take care of herself. Nevertheless, Andy passed her his walkie-talkie. "Don't hesitate to buzz Harry upstairs if you need help."

"Thanks. Now get yourself home to bed."

She nudged him in the ribs in camaraderie, not realizing that she was jabbing one of his sore spots. He winced but smiled in gratitude. Starting down the corridor toward the ward's exit, he slowed when he passed Room 9 and put a hand to his forehead. He'd forgotten about Nora.

"Oh! By the way, I should probably tell you . . ." He turned back toward the nurse, pointing to the door. "Nine's a paranoid, and she's been getting worse lately. She might scream during the night. Don't let it rattle you. Just peek in to make sure she hasn't hurt herself."

"Don't worry, hon." The nurse smiled. "I'll take good care of her."

After Andy was gone, his replacement took the orderly's chair and pulled an emery board from the pocket of the nurse's uniform to file the silver-painted nails. They added a nice touch, if he did say so himself. But, then, his mother had taught him to be detail-oriented. Nothing overlooked: the nails, the wig, the makeup, the shaved arms, the support hose, the bra filled out by balloons stuffed with birdseed. "It's the little things that count, Vanessa," Mama always said, and, oh, she was soooooo right.

The ID badge, for example. He'd carefully slit its lamination with a razor blade and replaced the original nurse's photo with the picture of himself in drag, gluing it shut with hardly a trace of tampering. Bridget Mahoney, the Metropolitan State Hospital nurse who'd provided both the ID and the uniform, now lay folded, naked, in the trunk of her stolen Thunderbird along with Roger, the night-shift orderly who'd come down with something far worse than the flu. Roger had kindly given him the keys to the ward, which he now wore on the white belt at his waist.

When at last he felt sure that Andy would not come back to question him further or to fetch a forgotten belonging, he sauntered down the ward and opened the door to Room 9.

Mumbling to herself, the room's occupant ceased her abstracted shuffle around the small space. She wasn't screaming. Not yet. Her violet gaze meandered toward her visitor. "Who are you?"

"Only an old friend, honey." He grinned and shut the door behind him. Of course she didn't recognize his buddy Lyman under all that makeup.

Nora Lindstrom ran broken-twig fingers through fog-thin hair. "He's coming. He's coming."

The man in the nurse's uniform approached and put an arm around her shoulders, as if to comfort her. "I know, dear."

Nora's hands fretted the air while she wagged her head in frantic indecision. "I've got to tell Natalie."

"Don't worry, hon. I'll tell her." His hands a blur, he

yanked the handcuffs from his pocket and wrenched Nora's arms behind her back to manacle her wrists.

She cried out, and he heaved her onto the room's small cot. Dodging her kicking feet, he ripped the cotton hospital gown from her body and used it to tie her ankles together.

"Did you miss me, Nora?" He took out the jackknife and pulled open the blade as if calibrating a precision instrument. "You must have, since you imagined that I visited you even when Mama wouldn't let me come. How touching!"

Nora stopped shrieking, her violet irises seeming to shrink in the widening whites of her eyes. He could see the haze of her psychosis clear as cold daggers of comprehension pierced her brain.

She *knew*.

"I must say," he continued, "despite your lack of hospitality, I appreciate your providing me with occasional shelter from the Old Lady all these years. But, as you can see, I'm looking for a more permanent residence, so I won't be needing your services anymore." He smiled and gently drew the flat of the knife down the entire length of her bare, withered body. "You know, if it wasn't for those tacky wigs she wears, Natalie'd look just like you."

Then Nora did scream, even before he set to work. The shrill wail resounded throughout the ward, but the other patients didn't let it rattle them. They'd heard it many times before.

18

Flesh and Blood

THE PHONE RANG AT 5:37 ON SATURDAY MORNING. Natalie let the machine get it.

It rang again a minute later. She rolled over in bed and let the machine answer again.

The third time the phone's chime twittered, she swept the sheets off her. "Oh, for the love of—"

Although she could have grabbed the extension on her nightstand, she stomped downstairs to check her messages, refusing to give the gadfly caller the satisfaction of an immediate reply. By the time she reached the kitchen, the machine had already picked up, and Inez's voice trolled the air for her.

"Natalie? Natalie? If you're there, please pick up. It's urgent."

Shivering in her T-shirt and panties, Natalie snatched up the receiver, her eyes only half open because of the sleep dust in them. "Honestly, Inez, do you have any idea what time it is?"

"Yes. I do." Her tone flat as a collapsed paper lantern.

"Look, if this is about the . . . *project*, I haven't found anything yet. I'll let you know tomorrow."

"Forget about that. How soon can you meet me at the Institute?"

"Institute? What Institute?"

"You know which one."

Adrenaline clarity evaporated the remaining fog of sleep. "What's going on?"

The line was silent. Inez must have sought a more delicate way to deliver the news. She didn't find one. "Someone killed your mom last night."

The world around Natalie shrank to the size of the receiver in her hands. *"What?"*

"I'm sorry."

"One of the other patients . . . ?"

"No. I think you'd better come down here before I explain."

"Yeah." She paced away from the phone, almost forgetting she still held the cordless receiver, but doubled back in distraction. "Callie . . . I need to find someone to watch her."

"Do what you need to," Inez said. "See you when you get here."

"Yeah. Thanks." Her hand quavering over the phone's keypad, Natalie pushed the flash button.

She'll never meet her grandmother.

Natalie tamped the emotions down like dynamite and dialed the babysitter's number.

The perversity of L.A. traffic is that it gives you all the more time to dwell on the business it's keeping you from. An accident had blocked two lanes of the freeway, and with nothing to occupy her mind but the fitful roll-stop-roll of the jam's progress, Natalie couldn't help but visualize one horrific tableau after another. The vagueness of Inez's comments served only to increase the variety of terrors.

Someone killed your mom last night . . . I think you'd better come down here before I explain.

A gangrenous self-loathing spread out from the pit of her stomach, until she merged into the far-right lane in case she had to pull the car over and retch on the shoulder of the freeway. She wasn't crying. Her mother had just been murdered, and she wasn't crying. Why wasn't she crying? Because she barely knew the woman. But the woman was her mother, so she ought to be crying . . .

Over and over again.

Natalie had often imagined receiving a grim phone call from the Institute. She now admitted that a small, dark part of her had *wished* the call would come. Relief for Nora, absolution for Natalie. The best thing for all concerned.

But not like this. She'd never wanted this. In fact, she realized that she'd never wanted her mother's death at all. What Natalie really longed for was an end to her *own* suffering, the crushing cycle of futile hope and inevitable disappointment each year her mother grew older with no sign of recovery.

But, no, that wasn't it, either. What she truly wanted was the one thing she could never have: her mother, restored to her, ready to make up for all the blank years of Natalie's childhood.

I'll never get to know her now.

Blinking to focus on the road, Natalie started to weep, and once she started she didn't want to stop. It felt so *right*. She was finally acting like a real daughter.

I'll never get to know her now.

But that wasn't necessarily true, was it? Natalie happened to be one of the few people in the world who *could* renew a relationship with her dead mother . . . if she chose to do so. What would Nora be like now? Had death freed her from the chains of her mind as well as the burdens of the flesh? If so, what would a lucid Nora think of her child—the grown woman who seldom came to see her, the stranger who pretended familiarity when she visited at all?

Natalie's cheeks turned cold as the tear-trails dried, and a sickening anxiety akin to stage fright gripped her. By the time she stepped into the Institute's foyer, she was compulsively circulating her protective mantra in her mind.

An LAPD officer had taken Marisa's place at the front desk, and the door to the locked ward was propped wide open to allow white-coated crime-scene technicians to hustle in and out. Natalie assumed that they had moved the surviving residents to another location while the police did their work. As she entered the ward, though, a keening wail resounded in the corridor, making her wonder if one of the patients still huddled in some corner, plagued by unseen tormentors.

A second door stood open about halfway down the hallway, another cop posted beside it. Natalie stalked toward it, but Inez spotted her from the other end of the corridor and hurried to interpose herself between Natalie and the doorway.

"Hey! You okay?" The prosecutor wore a Saturday-morning sweat suit and no makeup; without foundation, her eyes and cheeks bore the shadows of total exhaustion. "Come with me," she said, and herded Natalie down the hallway.

They passed the entrance to Room 9, and Natalie glimpsed a group of crime-scene techs inside, clustered about the room's cot like medical students at a dissection table. Their curtain of white coats parted momentarily, revealing a splash of red. The ward's usual ammonia scent became heavy with the added smell of iron.

Numbness prickled in Natalie's fingers, in the soles of her

feet. Her mother was already knocking. Natalie concentrated on the mantra. *The Lord is my shepherd; I shall not want . . .*

Inez led her into the same group-therapy room where she'd last visited her mother. There, Natalie found Andy Sakei hunched on one of the plastic chairs, sobbing into his hands, as a slender, middle-aged black woman in a business suit sat across from him, nodding sympathetically. The woman rose as they entered, causing Andy to glance up and see Natalie. She was about to greet him, but the orderly hid his face behind thick fingers.

"Oh, God, I'm sorry! I can't believe I let this happen." His cheeks plumped in a grimace, and he let out another racking sob worthy of one of his charges.

"Don't blame yourself." The woman in the suit touched his shoulder. "We'll catch whoever did this."

The gesture failed to console him. The woman withdrew a few steps to confer with Inez and Natalie. "You get anything from him?" the prosecutor asked in hushed tones.

The woman shook her head. "Not much. Someone posing as a nurse. Caucasian female, chunky, fiftyish. I'll try again when he calms down a bit."

Inez indicated her colleague. "Natalie, this is Marianne Williams, the detective assigned to your mother's case. She's the one who called me—she knew we'd worked together and figured you'd rather get the news from me."

Natalie gave Williams a limp handshake. "I appreciate it."

"I understand how hard this must be for you, Ms. Lindstrom," the detective responded with downcast eyes, as if ashamed to be the bearer of bad tidings. "But we felt you should see the crime scene for yourself, painful as it may be."

"I don't understand."

Inez and Detective Williams exchanged a glance. "Marianne was hoping you might be able to aid the investigation," the prosecutor said.

Natalie heaved a sigh. "I'll do what I can."

"Do you know of anyone who'd want to hurt your mother?" the detective asked.

"No. She was completely harmless. Hardly anyone even remembers her anymore."

The prosecutor and detective held a silent debate between themselves as to who should speak next. "What do you know about Vincent Thresher?" Inez asked at last.

The name plunged into Natalie like a stone into a well, churning the silt of her subconscious. *He maketh me to lie down in green pastures,* she repeated, *he leadeth me beside the still waters* . . .

"You mean *the* Thresher?" She swayed on her feet as the blood drained from her head, starburst shimmers obliterating her vision. "What does *he* have to do with this?"

Inez frowned and folded her hands. "Nothing, probably."

"The circumstances of the crime suggest a connection," Detective Williams added. "As you may know, Vincent Thresher was better known as the Needlepoint Killer, and your mother's murder . . . shares elements of his M.O."

Natalie struggled to jam this information into the jigsaw picture she'd constructed of her mom's past. Having shunned the case as if it were plutonium, she actually knew almost nothing about the real Thresher—not even his true name. Given the maiming and mutilation Nora had described during her fits, Natalie had always assumed "Thresher" was one of those awful epithets invented by the press—a reference to what the killer did, not who he was.

"But I thought they executed this Thresher back in eighty-two," she protested. "What can he have to do with my mom's death?"

Inez drew a long breath and beckoned her. "I suppose you'll have to see this for yourself."

Natalie followed her back out into the corridor. Andy's low moan trailed after them, and Detective Williams stayed behind with him. Ahead of them, a member of the coroner's crew emerged from Room 9, her nose and mouth covered with a surgical mask, her hair underneath what looked like a shower cap. Her latex-gloved hands stained with stickiness, she carried a clear, labeled plastic bag that contained something dark and glistening. A deep burgundy tube with clumps of meat still clinging . . . then the coroner's assistant was gone, down the hall and out of the ward.

An image, disconnected from thought, scanned across Natalie's mind like the flash from a photocopier: a white sock puppet with jiggly eyes, red lips puckering comically with the curling of unseen fingers.

Yo-Yo . . .

Nora was knocking again, signaling her presence with the one memory she knew her daughter would recognize. Natalie's pulse quickened. She feared her mother's judgment almost as much as she feared the Thresher, so she accelerated her mantra to repel them both. *He restoreth my soul; he leadeth me in the paths of righteousness for his name's sake* . . .

Inez blocked the doorway. "This is bad, Nat. I for one won't blame you if you don't want to see it."

"No . . . I have to," Natalie said without conviction. The option to cop out tempted her more than it should have.

Her friend's face registered neither admiration nor disapproval. Like Virgil, she was only there to lead the way.

As they entered the room, the last of the crime-scene techs crouched beside the cot, snapping close-ups. Inez touched his shoulder. "Would you excuse us for a minute?"

The photographer evaluated the two women with a glance, decided they wouldn't ruin his crime scene, and edged past Natalie out the door. She now had no choice but to look at the thing on the bed.

This can't be my mother, she thought.

Only the open violet eyes, now dry and dull, distinguished the corpse as Nora Lindstrom. Blood slicked the exposed bone of her cranium where the killer had peeled away the skin. The murderer had evidently scraped the remains of Nora's thinning hair from the scalp, for he—or she—had appliquéd the bare patch of skin to her naked torso with thick black thread. The concentric ellipses of tattooed node points served as a sewing pattern for an elongated needlepoint web in which a large red spider devoured a small black fly. The stitches still looked wet.

"I think that was the trachea they just took away," Inez remarked, referring to the contents of the plastic bag in the assistant M.E.'s hand. "They didn't find the ears."

So much blood coated Nora's head that Natalie hadn't noticed that the ears were missing from her mother's temples. Like a victorious matador, the killer had cropped them as trophies.

Natalie barely considered these atrocities, however. She couldn't tear her gaze from her mother's mouth.

Inez put a hand behind Natalie's back, as if to keep her from collapsing. "Is it too much? We can go—"

Mute, Natalie shook her head and stepped up to the cot for a closer look. *I will fear no evil . . .*

Only a raw, empty trench remained in Nora's throat

between her lower jaw and her clavicle, the loose tongue lolling down through the cavity with hideous length. With only a ragged fringe of flesh left on the chin, the killer had taken Nora's withered right hand and forced it up under the jaw and into the open mouth so that the fingers poked out from between her teeth.

The image of Yo-Yo, the sock puppet, flared in Natalie's mind again, its grins and grimaces manipulated by the hidden hand behind the face. Her mother hadn't simply been nostalgic when she called up that memory; she was giving her daughter a message—a warning.

"He's the puppeteer," Natalie murmured, unaware that she'd spoken aloud.

"What?"

She turned to Inez. "Nothing. How did it happen?"

"All we know is what the orderly's told us. When it came time to change shifts, his usual replacement didn't show. Instead, it was some person posing as a nurse from Metropolitan State Hospital. Sakei said her ID looked legit, but he can't remember the name she gave him. The orderly who was supposed to be on duty last night is missing, and they're still checking with the hospital to see which nurse it might have been. Of course, we can't be sure the killer was really a woman."

The comment distracted Natalie from the corpse. "What?"

"Thresher was notorious for playing both sexes."

"Oh."

She stared at the vandalized corpse again, pushing down her panic by detaching herself from the victim. That wasn't her mother on the bed—it was another crime to solve.

"It's a copycat," she muttered. "It *has* to be."

"If it is, he did his homework. See this?" Inez extended a

finger toward the embroidered spider on Nora's belly. The cursive letters *V* and *T* curled among the black markings on its red abdomen. "Vincent Thresher signed all his 'artworks' like this. Your mom was the first to discover the hidden initials, and it became the key clue that eventually led the cops to Thresher."

Natalie shook her head. "That doesn't mean anything. There must be a dozen books about those murders by now. A copycat could have learned Thresher's M.O. from any one of them."

You're the daughter, aren't you? the crocodile voice repeated in her head. *Let's get to know each other. . . .*

She stifled the memory. *He's DEAD,* she reminded herself.

Inez frowned. "You're right, of course—it's got to be the work of a copycat. But he's as dangerous as the original. That's why Marianne and I brought you down here. If this psycho is trying to avenge Thresher, he might start hunting other Lindstroms."

"I see." A childish belief in bogeymen eroded Natalie's investigative detachment. She remembered how Nora had grinned at her with the Thresher's hunger.

I look forward to meeting every member of the Lindstrom family. . . .

"Are they bringing a Violet in on this case?" Natalie asked.

"Yeah. The current conduit for the L.A. Crime Division— Lyman Pearsall."

Natalie made a face. "Joy."

"That's the other reason I asked you to come. I wanted to give you first shot at summoning her."

You knew this was coming. Natalie glanced from her friend to the ruin of her mother. She felt like telling Inez that she didn't need to summon her mother. In fact, she'd been trying to keep Nora out of her head for the last twenty minutes.

But you always said you wanted to be closer to Mom, she sneered to herself. *Here's your big chance!*

Natalie moved toward the door, away from the corpse on the cot. "I can't . . . not today. I've got to get Callie."

Inez kept pace as they exited into the hallway. "I understand."

"I'm sorry. About the trial, I mean. I really wanted to help—"

The prosecutor cut her off with a *tsk-tsk* wave of her hand. "Don't fret about that. I've still got a few tricks up my sleeve." She gave a tight smile. "Anything I can do for you? You want to talk?"

"No." Natalie paused at the entrance to the locked ward. "Maybe later."

"You know where to find me." Inez hugged her. "Take care of yourself, Nat. In every way."

"I will. Thanks."

Natalie said good-bye and left the hospital, the Twenty-third Psalm still twining around her brain in music-box repetition. She knew the mantra was futile, though, for her mother would eventually get through. You can never really escape your family.

The LAPD had erected a barricade at the Institute's entrance to control foot traffic in and out of the building. By the time Natalie passed through the security checkpoint on her way back to the parking lot, a crowd of reporters and TV news vans had coalesced around the barriers, vying for the best shot of the body's removal and flinging questions at anyone official who happened to emerge. None of them paid much attention to Natalie in her sunglasses, baggy No Doubt

T-shirt, and black jeans—or so she thought until someone called from behind her as she unlocked the Volvo.

"Ms. Lindstrom! Wait!"

She recognized the voice but hoped she was wrong. Unfortunately, she looked around to find Sid Preston jogging to catch up with her, a Nikon camera swinging from the strap around his neck.

He shoved his gum into one cheek until he caught his breath. "Hey, I heard about your terrible loss. Want to let you know how sorry I am."

Natalie opened the car and swung into the driver's seat. "Is that so?"

"Absolutely." Preston glanced behind him and spoke sotto voce; he obviously didn't want to share this interview with any of his colleagues. "I wondered if you'd like to make a statement regarding the tragedy."

"Sure. Drop dead." She slammed the door.

Preston leaned down, shouted through the driver's side window: *"You still have my card?"*

She pulled away without looking at him.

As Natalie maneuvered out of the parking space, she passed a pale man standing beside a Hyundai, blowing his nose into a dirty handkerchief. He glared at her, and she recognized the red-rimmed gray eyes of Horace Rendell.

The dashboard clock read 9:22. Natalie glanced at her rearview mirror and saw George in his LeBaron swinging in behind her. What was Rendell doing up at this hour?

"All the vampires are out today." She sighed and drove off, already planning how she and Callie could hide.

19

Home Away from Home

NATALIE KNEW SHE COULDN'T GO HOME NOW. IF Preston had already found out about her mother, it wouldn't take long for other ambulance-chasers from the press to show up at her door. More than that, she worried that reporters might not be the only ones waiting for her and Callie.

I look forward to meeting every member of the Lindstrom family. . . .

When Natalie arrived to pick up her daughter, both Callie and Patti Murdoch still looked bleary-eyed from having been awakened at the crack of dawn on a Saturday.

"We've been eating cereal and watching cartoons mostly," the babysitter said as Callie collected her toys from the Murdochs' living-room floor.

"Thanks for watching her on such short notice." Natalie gave her sixty dollars, twice the normal fee and part of the three thousand in cash she had stopped to withdraw from her bank. "You're a lifesaver."

"I'm glad to help. Sorry I was such a space case on the phone this morning. Hey, I'm sorry about your mom—"

Natalie put a finger to her lips, glanced toward Callie.

"Oh, right! Well . . . you know. Will you be needing me again this week?"

"I'm not sure. Callie and I may be going away for a little

while." Natalie evaluated the babysitter a moment. "Patti, if anyone comes around here asking about us, could you just pretend you don't know us? It's hard to explain right now, but I'd really appreciate it."

The girl tugged her cashmere pullover down, as if suddenly aware of the vulnerable midriff above her low-rise jeans. "Sure. Whatever you want, Ms. Lindstrom."

Patti didn't ask any more questions. She sensed that the less she knew, the better.

Callie, of course, wanted to know everything.

"Where are we going, Mommy?" she asked when the Volvo headed into unfamiliar neighborhoods.

Natalie smiled as brightly as she could without glancing toward her daughter. "We're going on a little trip, sweetheart. It's going to be fun."

"But don't we need to go home and get some stuff? I don't have Horton or Mr. Teddy or anything."

"That's okay, honey. Horton and Mr. Teddy will be fine at home for a few days."

"But what about my clothes?" she wheedled. "Can't we get my clothes?"

"We'll get you some new clothes. Wouldn't you like some new ones?"

"No! I want *my* clothes. I want my tiger shirt."

"We can find an even better shirt. And we can eat at McDonald's tonight."

Callie considered the bribe, and Natalie prickled with the intensity of her gaze. "Mommy, why are you sad?"

Natalie's wax smile melted. The traffic ahead of her turned cloudy, wavering with the shifting water in her eyes, and she tilted her head down to peer over the tears without allowing them to flow. She'd never told Callie about Nora, had wanted to spare her child the trauma of those grim visits to the Institute. How could she tell Callie that her grandmother had been murdered—a grandmother Natalie had prevented her from ever knowing?

Visions of sock puppets and tea parties assaulted Natalie, but she wasn't sure whether her mother was knocking or her own conscience was tormenting her. *The Lord is my shepherd,* she recited, just in case. *I shall not want. . . .*

"I'm worried, honey," she told Callie, an evasive answer that happened to be true. "I'm worried that someone might try to hurt us."

"Why?"

"You know how we were talking about Horton? How some people were mean to him because he heard the Whos and they couldn't?"

"Uh-huh."

"I think someone like that wants to be mean to us."

Small face somber, Callie kicked the glove compartment. "Is that why we're going away?"

"Yes, honey."

Callie sucked on her lips thoughtfully. "Okay," she said.

She didn't complain after that. Not when Natalie took her to a local Target to get some new outfits. Not when Natalie made her wear a pair of Minnie Mouse sunglasses to hide her violet irises. Not when they checked into a budget motel on Beach Boulevard north of Knott's Berry Farm, where the pungent smell of curry from the manager's office seeped into their room.

Natalie made good on her promise of treating Callie to dinner at the Golden Arches, after which they played War and Crazy Eights in the motel room with a pack of playing cards they bought at a neighboring convenience store. For a while, it felt like they really were on vacation.

Then bedtime came, and the reality of their situation hit Natalie like a cold draft. She double-checked to make sure the door was locked and all the windows latched while Callie put on her new PJs. The precautions gave her the illusion that she had some control over their safety, but she knew, deep down, that the safeguards were futile.

The people she feared most couldn't be shut out. Not that way.

She tucked Callie into one of the room's twin beds and kissed her good night, then crawled into the other bed, leaving a light on for Callie's sake as usual. Though Natalie verged on total exhaustion, sleep eluded her. The morning's visit to the Institute already seemed a decade ago, and yet it replayed in her head with the infuriating resilience of a commercial jingle. Eventually Natalie slipped into a shallow doze, mumbling the Twenty-third Psalm as if counting sheep.

She awoke in darkness—or, more precisely, the darkness itself awakened her. The light should have been on. Was there a blackout?

Catapulting upright, Natalie looked over at Callie's bed. Her daughter was also sitting up, her black silhouette outlined in the bluish light that leaked through the crack between the drawn shades of the window.

"I don't really like dolls," Callie said in a slumber-party whisper, "but I've got lots of teddy bears. There's Mr. Teddy, and Eddie the Panda, and a koala named Jenny—"

"Callie?"

The girl broke off her conversation, answered in a voice

that already apologized for what she'd been caught doing. "Yes, Mommy?"

Natalie squinted, but couldn't make out her daughter's face. "Did you turn off the light?"

"Yes, Mommy. We didn't want to wake you up."

This didn't surprise Natalie. Callie often hid in closets to talk to her dad when she knew she wasn't supposed to. She'd never been as afraid of the dark as her mother was.

Relaxing a bit, Natalie rubbed her eye and yawned. "Are you talking to Daddy?"

"No, Mommy. It's Grandma."

Natalie's breath caught in her throat, as if her little girl, in all innocence, had brought a pit bull home for a pet. *"Who?"*

"Grandma. She wants to talk to you." Callie said it so matter-of-factly that she might as well have been prattling on a telephone.

Natalie steadied her voice, but couldn't keep her body from shivering. "Callie, you know what I've said about talking to people like your daddy without permission."

"But it's important, Natalie." Her daughter's voice had dropped in pitch to a serrated alto.

Natalie reached for the switch on the lamp beside her bed, but pulled back her hand. Callie's face remained a Rorschach blot of blackness. Did Natalie really want to see the expression on that face? Would Nora be furious with her for all those years of neglect and perfunctory affection?

It's important. Natalie knew it was important—essential— for her to talk to her mother about the murder as soon as possible. But, as it had at the Institute, cowardice got the better of her.

"Callie, tell your grandma we need to sleep now. We

can—" Natalie moistened her lips. "You can talk to her another time."

The child's silhouette appeared to ripple, and her voice
recovered its wistful wind-chime tone. "Okay."

Her outline shrank as she retreated under her bedcovers.

Natalie exhaled and turned the lights back on. "Good
night, sweetheart."

"Night, Mommy."

Sliding back between her own sheets, Natalie lay on her
side, watching her daughter's placid face and even, easy
breathing. *Rest for both of us, little one,* she thought, giving up
hope of getting any sleep that night.

20

Foregone Conclusion

OVER THE NEXT COUPLE OF DAYS, NATALIE MADE THE necessary calls to the mortuary and to her father, whose home number hadn't changed since she used to phone him collect from the School to hear his latest excuse for not visiting her. In between, she watched the end of the Hyland murder trial on the motel TV out of a sense of obligation to Inez, but it brightened her day about as much as a rainstorm on a sinking ship.

Although Inez had claimed to have a few surprises in store, she ended with a whimper, not a bang. Franklin Jaffe, the Hylands' next-door neighbor, had been low on the prosecution's original witness list, and Inez hadn't bothered to call him before, indicating her lack of confidence in his testimony. The fact that she did now indicated how desperate she was.

With a widow's peak and receding chin, Frank Jaffe hardly cut a charismatic figure. A CPA with several big-name Hollywood clients, he described the night the Hylands were murdered as if itemizing deductions on a tax return.

At 10:55 P.M. on that Saturday, he recalled, he stepped out onto the patio of his home for a cigarette. He'd been standing there in his silk robe and slippers for about four minutes when he heard two loud bangs come from the direction of the Hyland residence. While they sounded like gunshots, Jaffe didn't feel confident enough in that assumption to call the police. When no further noise came from next door, he figured the bangs must have been something innocuous and went back inside.

"Ten fifty-five P.M. That's pretty exact, Mr. Jaffe," Inez said. "What makes you so certain that was the time?"

"Because *Law and Order: Special Victims Unit* had just ended, and I wanted to finish my smoke before the eleven o'clock news started," he replied.

"Ten fifty-five. You're sure about that?"

"Positive."

"And you didn't hear any other bangs earlier in the evening?"

"No."

"So you heard what you believe to have been two gunshots coming from the Hyland residence at close to eleven o'clock—over an hour *after* Scott Hyland and Danielle Larchmont claimed to have discovered the bodies of Mr. and Mrs. Hyland. Is that correct?"

"Yes."

"Thank you, Mr. Jaffe."

While this contradiction could have been devastating to the defense, Inez's resigned expression showed that she knew the testimony wouldn't hold up. She surrendered the floor to Lathrop, who made short work of the accountant.

"Mr. Jaffe," he asked with a pleasant smile, "how much do you know about guns?"

The accountant shrugged. "I don't know. Just what I see on TV."

"Could you, say, tell *at a distance* the difference between a shotgun blast and the discharge of a .45 automatic pistol?"

Jaffe considered a moment. "I'm not sure."

"What about the difference between a shotgun blast and a car backfiring?"

"Um . . . probably."

"A shotgun blast and an M-80 firecracker?"

Jaffe paused longer this time. "I don't know."

"How about the difference between a real shotgun blast and one from a DVD soundtrack played on a high-fidelity home entertainment system?"

Jaffe let out an embarrassed laugh. "I guess not."

"So, what you actually heard shortly after ten fifty-five on the night of Saturday, August twenty-first, was either a pair of shotgun blasts . . . or a pair of shots from a .45 automatic . . . or a car backfiring . . . or a couple of firecrackers . . . or a DVD action movie?"

The accountant smiled weakly. "Yeah. I suppose so."

"In fact, wasn't it your own uncertainty as to whether these sounds were actually gunshots that kept you from calling the police?"

"Yes."

"And isn't it possible that, while you were indoors watching TV, you might *not* have heard real gunshots that occurred earlier in the evening?"

"That's certainly possible, yes."

Lathrop still smiled, genial and polite. "Thank you, Mr. Jaffe."

Inez quietly declined Judge Shaheen's invitation to redirect, and Jaffe left the stand with a bemused awkwardness.

The prosecutor never dared to question Lyman Pearsall's

credibility. Without proof of the Violet's deception, she couldn't air her suspicions in court; even her friend Tony Shaheen would have forbidden such blatant speculation.

Inez might have poked some holes in Scott Hyland's story if she ever had the opportunity to grill the defendant himself, but Malcolm Lathrop wisely advised his client against testifying in his own defense. As it was, Inez relied mostly on her closing arguments to salvage her case. She reminded the jury of how Scott Hyland and Danielle Larchmont had both lied about their actions on the night of the murders, and she suggested that the Hylands might have misidentified the masked gunman who shot them "due to emotional stress from their recent dispute with Avery Park." Natalie could tell that her friend didn't put her heart into it, though. The ferocity had faded from her eyes.

When it came time for Malcolm Lathrop's closing statement, all he had to do was summon the image of Lyman Pearsall pointing his finger at Avery Park, his face clenched with Press Hyland's hatred.

Perhaps as a personal favor to Inez, Judge Shaheen gave instructions to the jurors that again exhorted them to "consider the statements of the victims as carefully, and with as much skepticism," as those of any other witnesses. It didn't matter. The jury deliberated a little more than an hour and probably stalled a bit so they didn't seem too flippant in their decision.

Natalie didn't even need to wait for the bailiff to read the statement from the jury foreman, for all the jurors broadcast the verdict with their faces. Inez had once said that she always knew she'd won a capital case when none of the jurors would look at the defendant. But these people seemed only too glad to look at Scott Hyland. Even the pale young man smiled with relief.

They let him go.

Scott Hyland hugged Malcolm Lathrop the way Avram Ries had embraced his attorney, and Natalie punched the OFF button on the TV's remote control.

Callie stopped scribbling in the coloring books she'd sulked over all morning. "Could we go somewhere?" she suggested timidly. "Like for a walk or something?"

Yes, Natalie thought, *that's exactly what I'd like to do. Go for a walk and forget all about it*. She remembered how Dan had cajoled her into riding a carousel at one of the worst times of her life, coaxing smiles from her even as she grieved for the friends murdered by the Violet Killer. *How ironic that our appetite for fun is least when we need it most*.

"You've never been to Disneyland, have you, honey?" she asked with a genuine smile.

Callie shook her head.

Natalie swung herself off the motel bed, feeling lighter already. "Neither have I."

They had a marvelous time that evening walking around the Magic Kingdom and watching the Disney-designed spectacles, although Callie perversely gravitated toward any ride that resembled a roller coaster.

"Ooh, Mommy, let's go on this one!" she bubbled as the runaway steam engine of Big Thunder Mountain Railroad clattered past, whipsawing the screaming passengers in its rattlesnake tail of rickety cars.

Natalie, who'd never ridden anything riskier than a merry-go-round, felt her stomach undulate. "Maybe when you're older," she said, and dragged her daughter toward the gentler attractions of Fantasyland.

If it hadn't been for Dan, Natalie might never have set foot on a carousel. She'd been so afraid of carnival rides at the time that he practically had to bind and blindfold her to get her to mount one of the fiberglass horses. She had so much fun she asked to ride it five more times that night.

She had no such difficulty persuading her daughter to try King Arthur's Carrousel in Fantasyland. Natalie was grateful that, in addition to inheriting her father's smile and love of junk food, Callie also shared Dan's carefree joie de vivre. It was a precious gift, and as they seesawed up and down on their charging steeds, Natalie stared at the vacant saddle of the horse in front of her and thought: *he should be here.*

She tried to dismiss the idea. After all, hadn't she brought Callie here so the two of them could enjoy life and the living and forget about death and the dead, at least for now?

As her little girl whooped and spurred her fiberglass horse with the heels of her tennis shoes, though, Natalie remembered Dan's increasing reluctance to come when summoned, the growing eagerness with which he spoke of the place where souls go and never return. She would have other chances to come to Disneyland with their daughter; he might not.

Natalie shut her eyes, whispering the words of her spectator mantra.

Dan settled into her body while the ride was still in motion, and the abrupt disorientation nearly caused him to lose his balance. He grabbed the pole with her hands and pinched her thighs tighter on the horse's flanks, grinning when he saw where they were. "It's like old times," he murmured, Natalie's voice warm with his amusement.

I thought we should have some time together, she replied in the head they shared. *As a family.*

Their throat tightened as they looked toward Callie with two eyes and one mind. "Yes," Dan said, as the carousel started to slow. "Thank you."

Their daughter beamed at them, shouting over the din of the crowd and the calliope music. "Did you see me, Mommy? Did you see me?"

Dan beamed back at her. "We sure did, honey. And it's Daddy, not Mommy."

Callie gaped at him as if he were the Easter Bunny. *"Daddy?"*

He nodded, and her face lit with the wonder of a wish fulfilled.

"Can we ride some more, Daddy? Pleeeeeeeease!"

"Well . . . if it's okay with your mother."

Go ahead, Natalie said. *But no roller coasters.*

Dan laughed and helped Callie dismount so they could get back in line for the merry-go-round. Natalie watched with quiet delight, content to lend herself to Dan for the night. But the happiness she felt at having him with her only increased her anxiety as the park's closing time drew closer.

Too soon the rides began shutting down for the night, and costumed personnel herded them into the crowd heading down Main Street toward the front gate. Natalie delayed their inevitable good-bye by encouraging Dan to eat a fat- and carb-filled ice-cream cone with Callie, but she couldn't prevent the evening from ending.

Will you come back? she asked just before he ceded control of her body.

He took so long to respond that she feared he might

already have departed. "As long as you need me," he answered at last.

When they walked out of the Magic Kingdom back into the real world, Dan was gone.

Callie squeezed Natalie's hand more tightly as they headed for the trams to the parking garage. "Daddy?"

"No, honey." Her mother sighed, an aching vacuum in the chambers of her heart. "It's just me."

By the time they got back to their motel, Callie was so tired that Natalie had to carry her into the room. She wasn't asleep, however, for she murmured into Natalie's ear, "Who is Grandma Nora?"

Natalie's smile fled. She set Callie on the edge of the bed and sat beside her. "She was my mother—*is* my mother."

"So Grandma Sheila isn't your mommy?"

"Definitely not."

"So she's not really my grandma."

"No, baby girl. She's not."

Callie's lips pouted as she puzzled over some insoluble paradox. "How come we never used to visit Grandma Nora?"

Natalie exhaled a half-truth. "Callie, Grandma Nora was really sick for a long time before she died. I didn't take you to see her because I was afraid—afraid you might catch her sickness."

"Oh." She still seemed dubious, unable to reconcile her child's instinctive recognition of falsehood with her naive, unquestioning belief in her mother. "She seems really nice. Why won't you talk to her?"

Because you're a coward, Natalie's internal voice jeered.

192 ○ **Stephen Woodworth**

"I will," she vowed, both to Callie and herself. "When the time is right."

She probed her daughter's eyes, shared the longing in them. *She wants a family. Just like I did.*

"Would you like to see Grandma Nora?" she asked.

Callie radiated desperate hope. "Can we?"

Natalie hugged her and sighed. "I'll see what I can do."

21

First and Last Respects

IT WAS A SAD FACT THAT NORA LINDSTROM LOOKED better at her funeral than she had during her last years alive.

For obvious reasons, Natalie had originally planned for it to be a closed-casket service. After talking to Callie, though, she decided that she owed it to her daughter to show her grandmother as she once was ... if possible. Natalie asked her father to dig an old photo of Nora out of a family album, and he faxed it to the mortician for reference. The undertaker told her that cosmetic restoration would be possible "at a substantial extra charge."

"Do your best," she said. "Whatever it takes."

The mortician gave her her money's worth. Nora lay in her coffin with a repose that Violets never knew in sleep. A wig of blond hair, highlighted with gray, flowed down to her shoulders, discreetly arranged to cover the red barrenness on the scalp and the sides of her head where her ears should have been. The shrunken apple of her face, drained of fluid by blood loss and embalming, was now puffed to freshness and fullness with some polymer formula, the blush of health painted over the hardened skin's pallor. A latex prosthesis tented the empty cavern of her throat, so lifelike that one expected the tiny gold cross on the chain around her neck to rise and fall with respiration. She wore a flattering blue dress,

194 o Stephen Woodworth

her meticulously manicured hands folded just above her waist, her legs and shoeless feet hidden underneath the casket's closed half-lid.

This is the mother I should have had, Natalie thought as she and her daughter peered down at the attractive older woman displayed on the folding bier. Instead, she got the frantic wraith she visited at the Institute . . . and the defiled corpse found in Room 9.

"She's pretty, Mommy," Callie whispered.

"Yes, honey. She is." Natalie set her daughter back on the chapel floor and took hold of her hand. "Let's sit down. We can look at Grandma again after the service."

They stepped off the low platform and took one of the two padded pews in the front row. The tiny chapel was otherwise vacant. Natalie had deliberately avoided publicizing the funeral so as not to alert the press to its location; she'd even booked the funeral parlor for "Nora Fontaine"—her mother's maiden name—to keep the deceased's identity a secret. Fortunately, the mortician who'd camouflaged Nora's wounds was either too ethical or too ignorant to realize how much money he could have made by leaking the news to the tabloids.

Natalie and Callie remained alone, listening to maudlin prerecorded organ music, until Wade Lindstrom strode into the chapel, wearing a crisp charcoal suit. Sheila wasn't with him. When he reached the front, he wavered an instant, as if tempted to share their pew, but instead took a seat across the aisle. Their eyes met, and he gave Natalie a somber nod. Callie waved at him, and Wade held up a hand for her, eyes crinkling in amusement.

Another quarter hour passed, and no one else showed up. Natalie wasn't surprised, for she hadn't known whom else to invite. The Violet Killer had taken the lives of most of her mother's closest friends. Of course, there was still one, but—

"It's eleven-thirty." The funeral director bent to show her his open pocket watch. "Shall we begin?"

"Yes. I don't think anyone else is coming."

The mortician cleared his throat. "Actually, there *is* another mourner here. He says he knew the deceased and would like to deliver the eulogy." His eyes flicked toward the rear of the chapel. "Since you expressed some reluctance about speaking, I thought you might want to consider his offer."

Natalie swiveled her head toward the man who waited at the rear of the aisle. *"Simon."*

The man wore a floor-length white cassock and clasped his hands in front of him in a pose of monastic placidity. Oversized ears stuck straight out from the sides of his shaved scalp. He smiled and bowed his head.

"It's up to you, Ms. Lindstrom," the funeral director said. "You may lead the service, if you'd rather."

Natalie contemplated the figure of her former schoolmaster. Simon McCord's egotistic self-righteousness had always grated on her, but he was one of the few people who still remembered Nora the woman as opposed to Nora the mental patient. Not to mention the fact that Natalie also owed Simon her life. If he hadn't assigned his disciple Serena Mfume to be her bodyguard, Natalie would probably have been disemboweled by the Violet Killer.

"Okay," she told the mortician. "Let him speak."

He nodded, unsmiling, and hastened up the aisle to exchange hushed words with Simon. The latter bowed his head again in acknowledgment and proceeded toward the three mourners in the front row.

"I regret that we only meet under such unpleasant circumstances, Ms. Lindstrom. I can't tell you how distressed I was to hear of your mother's death—she was truly a credit to our kind."

Natalie managed not to roll her eyes at Simon's usual Violet bigotry.

"And you must be Callie!" Keeping his back to Wade Lindstrom, Simon took hold of the girl's small hand, his violet eyes twinkling. "I can tell you've been blessed with all your family's gifts."

Callie gawked at him with the dubious awe children have for scary clowns.

Natalie hugged her daughter to her side. "Nice of you to come, *Simon*. Did the Corps invite you?"

"Since *you* did not—yes. And I would ask you to call me Master McCord."

" 'Master'? That's a new one. You get promoted, or was 'Professor' a little too plain for you?"

"While I find your wit as stimulating as ever, Ms. Lindstrom, I suggest you save it for another occasion." He indicated the podium to the left of the coffin. "Shall I?"

She refused to give him the satisfaction of affronting her. "By all means."

As he stepped up to the lectern, Simon finally spared a curt nod for Natalie's father. "Lindstrom. You're looking well."

"Mr. McCord," Wade murmured, mouth flat. "You haven't changed."

Simon resumed ignoring him, calling instead to the mortician at the rear of the room. "Mr. Abernathy, if you please."

Abernathy turned a knob on the wall, and the canned organ music faded out.

"As we know, death is not the end but the beginning of

the True Life," Simon began, projecting as if lecturing an auditorium of acolytes. "So it is with this woman we loved, Nora Fontaine Lindstrom. We should not weep for her. We should envy her and weep for ourselves that we cannot be with her.

"Nora was an exceptional and gifted human being, and more important, a *devoted* one. A devoted wife . . ."

He frowned at Wade Lindstrom, who uncrossed and recrossed his legs.

". . . a devoted mother . . ."

Natalie's gaze wandered to the casket, where only the tip of her mom's nose was visible over the coffin's side.

". . . a devoted friend. Above all, Nora devoted herself to her God-given mission on earth: to use her miraculous gift as a bridge between this life and the next. She recognized it as her duty and understood that duty calls for *sacrifice*."

Simon pierced Natalie with his glare. "She sacrificed her time. She sacrificed her freedom. She sacrificed her sanity. And now she has sacrificed her life. In doing so, Nora saved and enlightened countless other lives, and for that we should revere her as a hero, a saint, an avatar." He shifted his gaze to Callie. "May she serve as a radiant example to us all."

Natalie ground her teeth. She should've known Simon had a hidden agenda.

He left the podium and moved toward the open coffin, reaching toward Nora's face.

Natalie snapped to her feet. "Don't touch her."

Simon gave her a pitying look. "My dear, if I'd wanted to summon her, I would have done it by now." He touched the fingertips of his right hand to her mother's forehead. "Be free, Nora."

He stepped off the platform, Natalie hissing in his face. "Who put you up to this? The Corps? The School?"

"I'm here strictly as a friend of the family." He waved good-bye to Callie. "You know, your mother really was a remarkable woman. You ought to get to know her sometime." He left the chapel without looking back.

Wade grunted and got to his feet. "It's amazing. His manners haven't improved in thirty years. By the way, Sheila asked me to give you her condolences. She wanted to be here but—"

Natalie turned toward the casket on the bier. "Dad, could you watch Callie for a few minutes?"

"Uh . . . sure, honey." His own eyes flicked toward the coffin. "Can I come back later to . . . say my good-byes?"

Natalie smiled. "Of course. Actually, I was wondering if you'd represent us at the graveside ceremony. Callie and I don't do cemeteries."

"Understood. Be happy to." He went over and hoisted his granddaughter off the pew. "Hey, kiddo! Let's go for a walk."

"Okay." Callie let him carry her down the aisle. "Can *you* tell me about Grandma Nora?"

Wade darted a dark look back toward Natalie. "Well, she had your pretty eyes and cute little nose . . ."

When they were gone, Natalie stepped up to the coffin once more, put her lips to the idealized face that had never been Nora's. She didn't need a touchstone, of course—she *was* a touchstone—but it might be her last chance to kiss her mother, and she wanted the physical contact.

Row, row, row your boat, gently down the stream. . . .

She couldn't even think the mantra's second line. Touching her lips to the dry, unyielding skin of Nora's forehead was like sticking her tongue in a light socket. Her mother didn't knock—she splintered the door with a wrecking ball.

Natalie's legs folded and she collapsed against the casket, her weight throwing the bier off-balance. Mother, daughter, coffin, and bier all tipped over with a crash, but Natalie dropped too deep within her own mind to hear it.

There's too much to tell you, Natalie, and not enough time.

Natalie saw her mother lying in the coffin as before, but now Nora seemed spotlighted, the rest of the chapel dissolving in darkness around her. The lipsticked lips of her perfect face moved, but Natalie recognized the voice she heard as her own.

He's going to come for you. You and Callie. Don't let fear rule you the way I let it paralyze me.

Who, Mom? she implored. *Who did this to you?*

Awaking in the casket, Nora opened her eyes, and Natalie plummeted into the abyss of her dilating violet irises.

An instant later, she looked out through those same eyes, gaping up at a nurse with a lumpy female figure and curly orange hair. Face slathered with foundation, rouge, and eye shadow, the nurse spoke with a masculine huskiness.

Did you miss me, Nora? You must have, since you imagined that I visited you even when Mama wouldn't let me come.

The nurse pulled open a knife, brushed the edge of its blade along her nude breasts and belly. Natalie screamed and kicked, her arms pinned beneath her, the bracelets of handcuffs biting into her wrists.

I must say, I appreciate your giving me occasional shelter from the Old Lady all these years. But, as you can see, I'm looking for a more permanent residence, so I won't be needing your services anymore. The nurse smiled in fond commiseration.

You know, if it wasn't for those tacky wigs she wears, Natalie'd look just like you.

How does he know me? Natalie thought in the instant before the slitting, slicing, pricking, and piercing began.

The rest of the memory fragmented into a discordant suite of different forms of agony. When it ended, Natalie found herself staring straight up, the open lid of the satin-upholstered coffin on the left, her own downcast face on the right.

I'm sorry I wasn't there for you, Natalie. Her mother's voice this time, emanating from Natalie's lips. *I'm sorry I'm not with you now. I kept him from controlling my body, but I let him destroy my mind. Don't make the same mistake.*

Mom, wait! We can still—

But the lid of the casket fell shut with a deafening thud.

When light and vision returned, Natalie saw Mr. Abernathy bent over her, felt his hand lightly slapping her cheek. "Ms. Lindstrom? Ms. Lindstrom? Can you hear me?"

"Yes." Bruises smarted on her legs and side as she got to her feet.

The mortician braced her, peering behind her in dismay. "Are you all right? I came as soon as I heard the noise."

"He *did* come to her." The implications of Nora's memory crystallized in her mind. "And now he's in someone else. Another Violet."

"I heard you talking," Abernathy said. "Was someone here? Did a vandal do this?"

He held a hand toward the casket, and Natalie turned to see the coffin and bier lying askew on the platform. Nora Lindstrom lay twisted in her final berth as if troubled by unpleasant dreams. The tumble off the bier had shaken loose the latex prosthesis at her neck, exposing the ivory of her jaw and dried meat of her throat.

22

A Vivisection of Vincent

DRAPED ON AN ORANGE RETRO CHAIR THAT LOOKED like something out of a *Jetsons* cartoon, Natalie clicked on yet another blue-highlighted hyperlink on the Yahoo! search page and waited for Web site number 247 (out of 11,819 matching sites) to load. She'd been in this self-consciously hip Internet café for about ten hours now, and her eyes had become so dry and sticky from caffeine dehydration that she'd taken out her contacts. Coffee was a bad habit she'd developed over the past few years, and stress only weakened her resistance to it.

She blinked and scrolled through the archived news article on site number 247, but it didn't tell her anything more about Vincent Thresher than she'd learned from the stack of books on the table beside her, all bearing such lurid titles as *Tapestries of Flesh* and *Needle, Thread, and Blood*. In order to inhabit a Violet other than her mother, Thresher would have had to make that person a touchstone through some form of prior contact, but Nora Lindstrom seemed to be the only conduit associated with the Needlepoint Killer case.

Previously, Natalie had avoided learning anything about Thresher's crimes. She experienced enough victims' misery in her own work and had no desire to find out what horrors drove her mother beyond the brink of sanity, thank you very much. Even now, these true-crime books appalled her as they

Natalie looked away. "I'm sorry. Can you fix it?"

"Yes, but what—"

"Good. I have to go."

She left Abernathy stammering in the chapel and searched the funeral parlor's foyer for Callie and her father. When she didn't see them, she exited out the front door and found the two of them on a wrought-iron bench in the mortuary's formal rose garden. Wade wiggled his thumb in between the fingers of his left fist as he pretended to pull it off his right hand, performing the hoary trick as if he were the first grandparent ever to think of it. Skeptical, Callie slapped at his right hand until they both burst out in giggles.

Natalie hung back a moment, watching them, both joyous and jealous at seeing the happiness on her little girl's face. Witnessing the delight they took in one another made her next decision easier, however.

She moved toward the bench. "Dad, how long are you going to be in town?"

He glanced up. "My flight's scheduled for tomorrow morning."

"Could you push it back a couple days?"

"Sure. Why?"

"I have some work to do, and I was hoping you could watch Callie for a while. Would you like to spend the night with Grandpa, honey?" she asked her daughter.

The girl bounced with excitement. "Yes! Yes yes yes yes!"

"Is that all right with you, Dad?"

He chuckled. "All right? I'd love to! I'll call Sunny and let her know." Concern tempered his smile. "Did you find out anything?"

"Yes. That Mom wasn't crazy after all."

recounted atrocities with the avid tawdriness of Hollywood gossip.

"The medical examiner estimated that more than five thousand stitches composed the tiger figure on Eberhardt's torso," reported the author of *As Ye Sew: The Inside Story Behind the Needlepoint Murders*. "All of these stitches had been made while the victim was alive, most while she was conscious. It may have taken days for her to die."

Natalie wished the writer could *feel* that girl's five thousand stitches the way a Violet could: the relentless pinprick piercings and the loops of tender skin cinched tight by thread, followed by the delicate torment of oozing and itching as the tiny mouths of all those needle wounds sucked at the fiber strands that refused to let them heal. Maybe then the writer wouldn't describe a human being's agony like a third grader telling a campfire ghost story.

She wouldn't have had the nerve to wade through such muck if it hadn't been for Callie ... and Dan. When she left her dad and daughter at the mortuary that morning, Natalie had resolved to dig up every fact she could find about Vincent Thresher. By the time she got to the local bookstore, though, her urgency had turned to apprehension, and she dawdled. An agoraphobic fear made her queasy every time she got close to the true-crime section, and she drifted back to the front of the store, idly thumbing through fashion and entertainment magazines she ordinarily wouldn't have touched even in a doctor's waiting room. She was halfway through an issue of *Cosmo* before she threw the rag back on the rack, swearing at herself.

Ignoring the breathlessness that made her vision shimmer,

Natalie forced herself to go and grab the first paperback she could find on the Needlepoint Murders. She riffled the pages as if shuffling cards, but slowed when she came to the glossy photo pages in the center of the book. There, for the first time, she saw one of Vincent Thresher's "artworks": a woman's abdomen embroidered with a black horse rearing up in front of a setting sun.

On the facing page was the photo of a young woman who might have been beautiful if not for her bald scalp and the prematurely aged expression of her face. "Nora Lindstrom, an NAACC conduit who played an instrumental role in the Thresher investigation," the caption read.

An upsurge of revulsion made Natalie drop the book and run to the restroom, gagging uncontrollably.

Collapsed in the corner of one of the toilet stalls, she swallowed the acid in her throat and summoned Dan, thinking *Please come, please come, please come.*

"This is a bit of a comedown from Fantasyland," he murmured in her voice as he stood up and surveyed their surroundings.

Yes . . . sorry, she thought, suddenly embarrassed. *I didn't know who else I could talk to.*

She told him about her mom's murder and about the Thresher, the man who had been the monster in the closet of Natalie's mind since childhood. *I don't know if I can face him,* she said. *Maybe I should leave it to the cops. . . .*

"You can't run from this guy forever. If you don't find him, he'll find you. Or Callie."

Tell me something I don't know. The thought only added to the guilt she felt over her own cowardice. *But Thresher—my mom was one of the best Violets there was, and he got to her. What am I supposed to do?*

"Treat it like any other investigation. Forget that Thresher is the suspect and that your mom was the victim."

Easy for you to say.

"Not easy, but worth it. 'The truth will set you free.' Believe me."

She knew Dan was referring to his own posthumous reconciliation with the innocent man he'd mistakenly shot to death.

I'll try, she said, but the vow sounded feeble even to her.

"You won't try. You *will.*" Natalie found it reassuring to hear her own voice imbued with his calm. "You're not going to let him do to you what he did to your mom. You're stronger than your mom." She felt his smile play across her face. "You're stronger than anyone I know."

An afterglow of that smile remained as he left.

Disregarding the strange looks of the other women in the restroom, who no doubt wondered why she was talking to herself in a toilet stall, Natalie returned to the bookstore's true-crime section and picked out every book she could find on the Needlepoint Murders. She'd come to this café to supplement the literature with articles culled from the Web, sifting through the research for clues to how Thresher had returned from oblivion—and how to send him back there.

Vincent Thomas Thresher, she read, had been born in San Diego, California, on November 12, 1951, to Margaret Alice Thresher. Nothing was known of Thresher's father (the surname belonged to Margaret's family), but whatever relationship he'd had with the mother of his son left her with a vitriolic hatred of men that lasted the rest of her life. Some of the more sensational writers hinted that Margaret may have been an incest survivor, but no evidence existed to support this speculation.

According to numerous psychiatric interviews with Thresher conducted before and after his conviction, the killer spent the first dozen years of his life as a girl. Indeed, Thresher said that his first memory was of his mother brushing the tangles out of his shoulder-length black hair and calling him "Vanessa." Determined that she would never again have a man in her house, Margaret did everything she could to indoctrinate her "daughter" into femininity, including enrolling him as a girl in the local elementary school.

Despite her efforts, Thresher said, he always knew he "didn't belong in a dress." He wanted to wear jeans and roughhouse with the boys at recess, yet his teachers punished him and his mother beat him whenever he dared to get in a playground tussle. Although he possessed an IQ later estimated at more than 140, he never excelled in school and was considered a problem student and troublemaker.

Then came junior high and the gym class where "Vanessa" had to disrobe in front of "her" peers. The sight of him sent girls screaming from the locker room, and the resulting scandal earned Vincent expulsion from school. Shortly after that, he and his mother moved into a two-bedroom mobile home in Palmdale, north of L.A., where she home-schooled "Vanessa" to keep "her" out of the public school system.

Puberty, however, brought conflicts that Margaret Thresher couldn't circumvent. Now Vincent *knew* he wasn't a girl, a fact more apparent with each passing month. He got his first part-time job as a stock clerk at a Safeway supermarket and used the opportunity to be a boy for the first time. ("I didn't even know my real name till I tried to apply for a Social Security card," he told the state psychiatrist.) Each day when he left the house for work, he'd secretly swap his blouse and skirt for a T-shirt and jeans, tying his long hair back in a pony-tail and affecting a James Dean swagger.

One day his mother happened to stop by that Safeway to pick up some groceries for dinner and saw how much her son had grown to resemble his father. That night she pulled the largest carving knife from her kitchen's butcher block and told Vincent to take down his pants, muttering that this was "what she should've done in the first place." She'd made him do this many times in the past, and so he obeyed her. This time, however, she carried through on her threat. ("She flushed it down the toilet like a dead goldfish," Thresher recalled, laughing cigarette smoke from his nose.)

After nearly bleeding to death that night, Vincent became far more careful when wearing men's clothes. He quit Safe-way and took on a series of odd jobs, quickly acquiring skills in plumbing, electrical wiring, auto repair. Using what his mother had already taught him about wigs, makeup, and clothing, Vincent also refined a knack for changing his appearance and voice that would become infamous in his later avocation.

Eventually he grew so proficient and so bold that, disguised, he walked right into the salon where his mother worked as a hairdresser and asked her how to find the nearby movie theater. She gave him directions without showing the slightest glimmer of recognition. Emboldened, he began using his disguises to commit petty thefts . . . and to follow women. The handicap Margaret's knife had given him did not quell his growing desire for the opposite sex or the frustration it spawned.

Sometimes, he said, he would pick a girl he liked and fol-low her around all afternoon dressed as a man, until she started giving him dirty looks. The following day, he would dress as a woman and follow the same girl around town, accost her in a ladies' room, and exchange friendly words.

The more he teased himself this way, the more enraged he became with the impossibility of his lust. An idea formed in his head: if he couldn't penetrate a woman in the conventional fashion, he would find another means—a way to prick her again and again and again. Here, too, his mother's lessons served him well.

When a few prostitutes disappeared from West Hollywood in early 1978, no one had cause to suspect the grown son living with his mother in Palmdale. Nude bodies turned up in the Angeles National Forest, a mere fifteen miles away, the women's torsos embroidered like the samplers that covered the walls of Margaret Thresher's living room, and still no one considered seeking the killer in Palmdale, since the victims originated from L.A. Thresher was bright enough to know that you should never hunt in your own backyard.

Unable to find any leads, local police requested assistance from the FBI's Investigative Support Unit at Quantico, Virginia, where Nora Lindstrom worked as one of the primary Violets on serial murder cases. She summoned each of the Needlepoint Killer's victims in turn, yet what they revealed only confused authorities further. Depending on which woman's memories one believed, the murderer had been tall or short, thin or heavyset, old or young, male or female, blond or brunette, brown- or blue-eyed. There was a sole fact on which more than one victim agreed: the killer drove a white Volkswagen bus with a dented left front fender.

Working with the descriptions Nora Lindstrom gave them, forensic artists attempted to deduce the killer's underlying facial features based on those aspects he couldn't change with makeup, such as bone structure. They produced sketches of the hypothetical suspect drawn with different hair and eye colors and distributed them, along with the vehicle description, to local police departments throughout southern California. Based on the hidden leitmotif in the murderer's embroidery, the FBI also suggested that the initials "VT" might offer a clue to the killer's identity.

Within a few weeks, a pair of patrol officers in Lancaster spotted a white Volkswagen bus with a dented fender parked on the street in front of Margaret Thresher's rust-stained mobile home. They ran the license plate number and found that the VW was registered to Vincent Thresher, who'd bought it off an aging hippie for a thousand bucks. Their suspicion piqued by the coincidence of the owner's initials, the patrol officers knocked on the door of the mobile home.

According to the report they filed later, a young woman answered the door—tall, plain, and "big-boned," conservatively dressed in a long-sleeved sweater and ankle-length knit skirt. When the police questioned her about the car, she claimed she didn't know to whom it belonged. The officers asked if she lived alone, and she replied that she shared the home with her mother, who happened to be at work at the time. She gave her name as Vanessa Smart, smiled a lot, and invited them in for coffee. They declined, but not before glimpsing several hand-sewn samplers on the walls behind her.

That night when his mother got home from the salon, Vincent Thresher cut her throat, fried and ate her tongue in a sandwich with A.1. steak sauce, and piled the body into the back of the VW bus. The bus was later discovered abandoned at a rest stop along I-10 outside Phoenix, but they never found Margaret Thresher's body.

For the next two years, Vincent Thresher vanished from

sight. During this time, he lived under a variety of guises and killed any number of people—the wilder estimates put the figure at more than a hundred—taking what money he needed to survive from his victims. He might have evaded capture forever, but the FBI created composite photos that depicted what Thresher looked like dressed as both a man and a woman and distributed them to all the major media outlets. One of these photos, shown on *America's Most Wanted*, ultimately led to Thresher's arrest as he shopped in drag at a Wal-Mart in Albuquerque, New Mexico.

Even then, Vincent Thresher might have won a not guilty verdict in court, for the prosecution had no physical evidence against him and none of his victims could identify him with any certainty . . . except one. Nora Lindstrom summoned Margaret Thresher in court, and the mother's shrill denunciation reduced her accused son, normally smug and sardonic, into a blubbering child. Natalie knew that it was for this humiliation, even more than for his ultimate conviction and execution, that Vincent Thresher had resolved to torment Nora till death and beyond.

Natalie picked up the small drawing tablet that lay next to the true-crime books and opened it to the sketch she'd made of the impostor nurse who'd killed her mother, trying to match the features with those of the Violets she knew. She doubted that the killer was actually a woman. The voice she'd heard in her mother's memory sounded masculine, and Thresher was notorious for his female disguises.

Sliding *Needle, Thread, and Blood* out from the piled books, Natalie opened it to the slick center pages where the composite picture of Thresher as a woman had been reproduced beside an unaltered version of a photo of the killer as a young man—perversely handsome with his strong chin and delicate, boyish features. She mulled over the mug shots for a while, then tore the sketch of the nurse out of the drawing tablet and set it to one side.

With a fresh, blank page in front of her, she selected a well-worn charcoal crayon from a box she'd brought with her and started to redraw her sketch of Nora's killer, removing the makeup and hair and adding tattooed node points on the scalp. Though her skill as an artist hadn't been good enough to get her a gig painting with Da Vinci in the Corps' Art Division, it served her well in police work.

Long before she finished the portrait, she felt the stubble of hair beneath her wig stand straight up in apprehension. Steadying her hand, she added a bushy mustache to the drawing.

The face of Lyman Pearsall frowned up at her.

"Good Lord." Natalie put a hand to her mouth as a few of the college students at the surrounding computer carrels gave her curious glances.

Setting the sketchbook aside, she returned to the keyboard and typed "Vincent Thresher Lyman Pearsall" in the Yahoo! search window. She hit ENTER, and the horizontal thermometer onscreen slowly filled with blue to indicate the search in progress. This time a single hyperlink appeared, Web Site 1 of 1, with the names she selected in boldface:

Possible Needlepoint Victim Discovered.
Police in Saugus have
recovered . . . Needlepoint Killer VINCENT
THRESHER. Discovered by hikers . . . Corps
conduit LYMAN PEARSALL to assist . . .

Natalie clicked on the link as if unlatching a forbidden attic door. A small single-column article from the *L.A. Times* appeared onscreen:

Possible Needlepoint Victim Discovered

Police in Saugus have recovered the bones of a young woman they believe may be a victim of executed Needlepoint Killer Vincent Thresher.

Discovered by hikers in the Angeles National Forest, the skeletal remains bore no trace of clothing, jewelry, or other items, indicating that the woman's death was not accidental, a police spokesperson said. During the summer of 1979, the nude bodies of at least eight Thresher victims were discovered on or near the park's grounds.

Condemned to the gas chamber at San Quentin in 1982, Thresher died without ever making a full confession of his crimes. Convicted of 12 murders, he is implicated in the deaths or disappearances of more than 50 people.

The skull is missing from the newly discovered corpse, making dental identification of the victim impossible. Police have called in North American Afterlife Communications Corps conduit Lyman Pearsall to assist with the investigation.

Natalie noted the date of the piece—January of last year. About six months before the trial of Avram Ries.

"My God, Lyman," she breathed, "what did you do?"

23

Outgoing Message

WADE LINDSTROM HAD THE MONEY TO STAY AT hotels rather than motels, and it was nearly midnight before Natalie reached his room on the fifth floor of the Hilton near Disneyland. He answered the door in his silk pajamas, squinting at the sudden glare of light from the corridor and smoothing the cowlicks of his bed hair.

"Natalie! I wasn't expecting you till tomorrow."

"I know." Glancing left and right to make sure no one in the hallway was watching, she pushed him back into the room and locked the door behind them. "It's an emergency."

A single shaded lamp between the two queen-size beds lit the room. The bedcovers had been pushed into a heap on one bed, while Callie sat in the other, brushing sleep from her eyes. "Mommy?"

"Hey, honey." Natalie drew close to her father, lowered her voice. "Dad, would it be all right if Callie and I stayed with you and Sheila for a while?"

Wade wrinkled his face, his comprehension slowed by shards of shattered slumber. "In New Hampshire? Jesus, Natalie, what's going on?"

"It's Thresher, Dad. He really has come back."

"That's impossible—"

"No, it isn't. He *did* come to Mom for years, entering her

mind so often that she believed he was always with her. Now he's inhabiting another Violet, Lyman Pearsall, using him to kill again."

Wade glanced with concern at Callie, who was now wide awake and watching them. "But I thought you guys learned how to kick out souls you didn't want."

"That's the problem. I think this Violet *wants* Thresher to use his body."

"Why, for heaven's sake? What could he possibly have to gain?"

Natalie thought of Scott Hyland and the fortune he stood to inherit, imagined how much Scott would pay to be a rich, free man.

"Thresher might have done him a favor." She sighed. "That's why I think we should go away until I can have someone investigate Lyman. Thresher knows about me. If he knows about me, he might know about Callie, might know where we live. Think Sheila can put up with us for a couple weeks?"

"She'll survive. Question is, can you put up with her?"

"Uhhh . . ."

They both laughed at her hesitation.

"Are we going to Grandma and Grandpa's?" Callie asked, as if invited to tour Santa's Workshop at the North Pole.

Natalie queried Wade with a smile.

He chuckled. "When did you want to leave?"

"Now, if possible. The first flight out. And I think we'd better stay in a place with lots of people around till then."

Her father smiled, but the shadows deepened around his eyes. "Well, let me call the missus and tell her we're coming."

"At this hour? It must be past two on the East Coast."

"That's all right. Builds character." Sitting on the edge of the bed, he took his cell phone from the nightstand, pressed a couple of buttons, held it to his ear. "Besides, I haven't been able to reach her all day. She's sure to be home now, probably wondering where the heck I am."

He absently rubbed his nose and sniffed, waiting for an answer. It came. His face slackened, whitened to ash, and the phone slipped from his fingers.

"Dad?" Natalie crouched beside him, grabbed his wrist to check the pulse. "Dad, what's wrong?"

"No, no, *no.*" Wade put his shaking hands to his forehead. "Not my Sunny. *No!*"

As his words disintegrated into slurred sobs, Natalie snatched up the cell phone, listened, heard nothing. She hung up and hit the REDIAL and SEND buttons. The phone at the other end rang twice before the answering machine picked up.

"Hello," a familiar male voice greeted with snide joviality. "You've reached the Lindstrom residence. Mrs. Lindstrom can't get to the phone right now because I'm cutting a hole in her throat. Leave your name and number after the tone and I'll come for you when she's dead."

The beep droned like a flatlining EKG, then left a blank silence for Natalie to fill.

24

Aunt Inez and Uncle Paul

WHEN THEY PULLED UP OUTSIDE THE MENDOZA residence in Gardena, Inez and her husband, Paul, came out onto the front porch in slippers and heavy robes, hugging themselves to ward off the chill of early morning. Natalie carried a half-asleep Callie up to the doorstep, while Wade waited in the Volvo, eyes staring inward.

In response to his emergency call, the local police in Nashua, New Hampshire, dispatched a patrol car to the Lindstroms' address to check on Sheila. The cops called back a half hour later. Wade hadn't spoken since then.

"Sorry to get you up at this hour," Natalie said as she stepped onto the porch. "Our flight leaves at a quarter to two this morning, and I didn't know where else I could leave her. Who else I could trust."

"I don't blame you. Particularly if what you said about Pearsall is true." Inez grimaced as she said the Violet's name.

"Besides, we love having kids in the house," Paul Mendoza said, cheeks dimpling with a grin. A round-faced man with a thin black mustache who was as effusive as his wife was stoic, he scooped Callie out of Natalie's arms and bounced her against his ample tummy. "You don't mind staying with your uncle Paul, do you, *mija?*"

She responded with a sleepy groan, and he laughed.

"How long are you going to be gone?" Inez asked.

"Only a day, I hope." Natalie glanced back toward Wade's shadowed figure in the Volvo. "Longer if Dad needs me. I'll let you know."

"I'll take a couple sick days. I'm sure Hodgkins won't miss me," she said dryly. Up for reelection this year, L.A. District Attorney Philip Hodgkins was reportedly furious about Inez's handling of the Hyland case.

Natalie bit her lip in hesitation. "I hate to ask another favor . . . but I was wondering if you could contact Quantico for me and see if they have any artifacts from the Thresher case left in their archives. Especially anything having to do with his mother."

Inez gave her a hard look. "Don't play with Thresher. You don't want to end up like your mom."

You don't want to end up like your mom. How many times had Natalie received that particular warning in her lifetime? Only now did she take it seriously.

"I'll be careful," she said.

Inez huffed. "I'll see what I can do."

"Thanks. To you, too, Paul."

He smiled and waved, careful not to disturb Callie, who'd fallen asleep on his chest.

"Well, I'd better get going." Natalie hugged Inez and started down the cement walk to the curb.

"Watch your back," Inez called after her.

Natalie walked backward a few steps. "You, too."

She went around to the Volvo's driver's side, quickly scanning the street before she got in. At least two people observed her as she and Wade drove off that night, but the only one she noticed was Horace Rendell, glaring at her through the windshield of his Hyundai like a beggar at a banquet-hall window.

Like Natalie, Rendell did not take note of the dilapidated white Bronco, which lingered at the curb behind him while he waited for the Lindstroms' car to vanish from sight and for the Mendozas' porch light to wink off. Nor did the Corps Security agent see the man behind the Bronco's wheel, who watched with growing interest as Rendell slunk out of the shell of his Hyundai and crossed the street to case the house where Callie Lindstrom now slept.

still sanded and mushy from the winter's snows. She refused to go over 25 miles per hour in slush, and reckless drivers spattered their car with highway grime as they zoomed past her.

The trip took more than twice the usual hour to make, giving Natalie plenty of opportunity to dwell on the change that had occurred since last night's phone call. Yesterday she'd felt a camaraderie with her dad that she'd never known before; now he seemed more distant than ever.

Of course, that was partly due to the fact that the only two women he'd loved in his life had been viciously murdered within days of each other. Natalie knew that and chastised herself for the petty neediness she felt, resenting that he was thinking of Sheila rather than her.

Natalie had never considered her stepmother as more than an appendage of her father, a cancerous growth that had sprung from his side and that she hoped would go away someday. Seeing her dad weep for this woman forced Natalie to view Sheila not as an enemy but as a person. That smile, both condescending and ingratiating—had it also been sincere? If Natalie had looked beyond that irritating, prissy veneer, would she have found someone who truly wanted to befriend her . . . someone she might even have come to love?

Such questions were academic now. All that remained was the guilt for shortsighted grudges and squandered opportunities.

They didn't reach Wade and Sheila Lindstrom's two-story, Colonial-style house until four in the afternoon. They resided in a quiet, affluent Nashua suburb where one rolling green lawn melted into another without fences to mark the property boundaries. The winter storms had pulled a cotton comforter of snow across the grass, and the huge maple trees

25

Grandma's House

THE TRIP TO MANCHESTER WAS THE FIRST TIME NATALIE had been on a plane in almost six years—since those harrowing cross-country flights with Dan—yet the old phobia of flying barely troubled her. With so many crises pressing in upon her, the fear of a jet crash seemed ridiculously remote, like worrying about a meteor impact while standing chest deep in floodwater. Yet she still wished she had Dan sitting beside her. Now more than ever, she wanted to feel the warm grip of his hand on hers.

Instead, her father sat next to her, gazing out the oval window at the inappropriately blue sky above the clouds. In these economy-class seats, they touched elbows on the armrest, yet he might as well have been in New Hampshire already. In some ways, he was.

"Dad . . ." Natalie took hold of his hand, but he yanked it away.

"Let her sleep," he snapped, as if Sheila were dozing in the aisle seat across from them.

She didn't try to touch him again, and they hardly spoke to one another, even during the long drive from the airport to Nashua. Natalie volunteered to take the wheel of her dad's Mercedes, but regretted it when she saw that the roads were that lined the street bared bristles of stark branches. In a tell-tale sign of warming weather, though, several daggers of ice had dropped from the rain gutter along the Lindstroms' roof to splinter on the asphalt driveway.

A Nashua police car waited for them at the curb, its tailpipe puffing like a Franklin stove as the officer kept the motor running to stay warm. When they parked behind him, he switched off the engine and got out, zipping up his parka and donning the sort of broad, flat-brimmed Scoutmaster hat favored by New England police.

"Mr. Lindstrom?" he asked as they crunched out into the snow.

"That's right." Wade swung a limp arm toward Natalie. "My daughter."

The officer gave a tight-lipped nod. "Sam Runyon. I reported to the scene last night."

"We appreciate your waiting for us." Natalie shivered in her down jacket and jeans, wishing she had a stocking cap and a pair of thermal underwear; a decade of living in southern California had thinned her blood. "We would've been here at three, but the roads are still pretty bad."

"No problem. Are you ready, Mr. Lindstrom?"

Wade billowed steam from his mouth as if purging himself of hope and bobbed his head.

Runyon led them across the flagstones to the porch. "Watch your step. These things are still pretty slick."

He tore the yellow POLICE LINE DO NOT CROSS ribbon off the front door and unfastened the makeshift latch and padlock the police had bolted to the door frame. The door's regular latch had been forced, leaving a useless, wood chip–lined gouge in the jamb. "They removed the body early this morning. We already have a positive ID on it, but I'll take you to the morgue if you want to see her for yourself."

Natalie watched her father's face, but he seemed to be viewing some scene other than the one that surrounded them. If he were a Violet, Natalie would have assumed from his expression that he felt someone knocking.

The air in the house was as chilly as it ever got in L.A. Evidently, the cops had left the thermostat set just high enough to keep the plumbing's pipes from freezing. His breath still coming in clouds, Runyon guided them through the living room and up the polished hardwood stairs. "I have to tell you, we're not really used to this kind of thing here. Anything you can tell us to help catch this guy, we'd be much obliged."

Natalie almost spoke, thought better of it. How could she get the police to take her theory about Vincent Thresher and Lyman Pearsall seriously? Even more troublesome, how could she get the Corps to admit that one of their own had betrayed them?

Although she'd spent her early childhood here, Natalie hadn't even visited the place since Callie was born. She now experienced an amnesiac's sense of *jamais vu*—an utter lack of recognition or emotional attachment—as she walked through what had once been her family home. Her stepmother's redecorating had erased all traces of Natalie and Nora: pastel paint had replaced the floral wallpaper, and stark contemporary furnishings had deposed their plush antique predecessors. An open doorway on the second-floor landing revealed that Sheila had even turned Natalie's former bedroom into an upstairs den.

She never wanted me here, Natalie thought. But was that true, a voice inside her argued, or had Sheila simply given up hoping that her stepdaughter would ever want to rejoin the family?

Guilt doused the flare of old resentment the moment they entered the master bedroom where Sheila had died.

Officer Runyon removed his hat in a belated show of respect for the victim. "No signs of a struggle, and the neighbors didn't hear a thing. Near as we can figure, he drugged her while she was sleeping."

The king-size bed had been stripped of its coverlet and sheets, which were most likely taken as evidence along with the corpse. Deep maroon splotches had soaked all the way through to the mattress, however, making the rough outline of a spread-eagled human figure on the gold-stitched cushioning. Sheila's visage superimposed itself on that negative space like the gumdrop face on a gingerbread man.

Wade braced himself against the wall, fist to his mouth as his stomach heaved. Already unwinding the Twenty-third Psalm in her head, Natalie rushed to support him. "Dad?"

He shook his head, and swatted her away with his hand.

She turned back to Runyon. "Did the killer leave any clues?"

"Plenty. We have strands of at least four different colors of hair and trace evidence of a dozen different cloth and carpet fibers."

"Oh." *Should've known,* Natalie thought. Thresher was notorious for taking evidence from past victims and planting them on his current prey to confuse the forensics experts. She lowered her voice to a whisper. "What was the condition of the body?"

Runyon glanced at Wade. "You sure you want to talk about that now, miss?"

"Yes. I've worked murder investigations before."

"I see." The officer's expression of discomfort made his face look squashed. "Well, the victim was discovered nude with her throat cut—cut out, I should say—"

"What was the design sewn on her body?"

Runyon lowered his gaze as if leveling a gun at a suspect. "It was a giant wolf's head," he said slowly, "its jaws opening to eat a little girl in a red cape. Why do you ask?"

Lips quivering, Natalie looked back at the blood-blotted mattress where Sheila had died. Of course: this was Grandma's House, and Thresher was the Big Bad Wolf. Which meant that Little Red Riding Hood was . . .

"I should've been here," Wade said suddenly. He stood upright now, but he kept his back to the bed.

Natalie returned to him, put her arm around his back. "I'm sorry. If I'd found out sooner . . ."

Her father shook his head. "No. I should've come back yesterday, like I planned."

"That wouldn't have saved her, Mr. Lindstrom," Officer Runyon said. "The M.E. says she'd been dead more than twenty-four hours when we found her last night."

"But the message . . ." Natalie faltered, not wanting to put the thought into words. "Dad, you said you tried calling Sheila several times yesterday and didn't get an answer."

Wade nodded.

"But the message on the answering machine didn't change till last night?"

"Yeah." He frowned. "Did the sick bastard stay with her a whole day after she was dead?"

"I'm afraid not." Natalie didn't know whether the numbness in her face and fingers was from the cold or from Sheila knocking. "Does your machine have its remote access number printed on it?"

Wade's look answered for him. "You mean . . ."

". . . he could have changed that message from anywhere. Even California." She snatched her father's cell phone from his pocket and punched in Inez's number, unable to feel the buttons under her deadened fingers.

Callie . . . .

26

A Deeper Sleep

CALLIE LINDSTROM AWOKE IN WHAT USED TO BE Lance Mendoza's bed and saw that the lights were off. But she wasn't scared. She was a big girl—almost six—and darkness didn't frighten her the way it used to. Not since talking to Grandma Nora.

Aunt Inez had left the bedside lamp on when she tucked in Callie that evening. She then seated herself in a chair across the room, an open book in her lap, and promised to wait with Callie until Mommy got back. Aunt Inez didn't appear to be in the room now, but Callie didn't worry. Mommy would be back soon. She said so.

Only when Callie reached over to the lamp with its baseball-shaped night-light and flicked the switch did she begin to feel afraid. The bulb didn't light. Maybe it was burnt out.

She pushed back the covers, all of which were emblazoned with the Dodgers' logo, and lowered herself off the high bed. The night outside the room's window was cloudy and moonless, and Callie shuffled forward with her small fingers stretched out in front of her. No cracks of light outlined the bedroom door, but she found it by memory and touch. It stood ajar.

Callie poked her head out into the dark and unfamiliar

hallway. *It's okay*, she thought. *Aunt Inez said it's safe. And Mommy's going to be back soon.*

Mommy had called that afternoon to say she was coming back. Callie had been watching TV in the living room when she heard Aunt Inez talking on the telephone in the kitchen, saying, "Don't worry, she'll be *fine*. I'll stay with her every second till you get here, and we'll keep the doors and windows locked."

Callie had crept into the room, the waxed linoleum sticky on her bare feet, and hunkered by the refrigerator to listen.

"What time does your plane get in?" Aunt Inez caught sight of her then. "Oh, wait, she's here. You want to say hi? Okay." She offered the receiver. "It's your mom."

Callie scampered to take the phone. "Mommy!"

"Hey, baby girl!" Her mother's voice sounded funny, and not just from the conch-shell hollowness of long distance. "I'm so glad to hear you."

"Me, too. I miss you, Mommy."

"I miss you, too, sweetheart. Are you having a good time with Aunt Inez?"

"Yeah. I guess."

"Well, be nice to her. Do everything she tells you, okay?"

"Okay." Callie twined the old-fashioned, curlicue phone cord around her fingers. "Mommy, are you sad?"

Her mother didn't answer for a long time, and when she did, her voice sounded even funnier than before. "No, sweetie, I'm happy. I'm glad you're all right."

"Okay. When are you coming back?"

"As soon as I can. If I had a magic carpet, I'd be there right now."

Callie giggled. "Yay! I love you, Mommy."

"I love you, too, honey. I'll see you soon. Can you let me talk to Aunt Inez again?"

"Uh-huh." She gave back the phone, and Aunt Inez went on talking about some man and how she was sure he couldn't get in the house without her knowing about it, but Callie didn't listen after that. All she needed to know was that Mommy was coming home.

Now, as she ventured out of the bedroom into the tar-black hallway, Callie remembered what Aunt Inez had said, about the man who wanted to get into the house. She also remembered Mommy talking about someone who might be mean to them because they could hear Whos.

Someone who might want to hurt them.

Across the hall, a rectangle of slightly paler darkness indicated that the door to the Mendozas' bedroom was open. Maybe Aunt Inez had gone to bed with Uncle Paul after all. If she asked really nicely, Callie thought, they might let her sleep in their room . . . at least until Mommy got back.

She pattered over to the door and tiptoed into the master bedroom. The windows here were bigger, allowing more ambient light from outside, and Callie could see a hill of sheets on the bed that looked like Uncle Paul's size. But he seemed to be alone in bed.

"Aunt Inez?" Callie whispered, as she moved around to the other side of the bed.

Her foot hit something firm yet pliable. Looking down, she saw that she'd nearly stumbled over a pair of outstretched legs: Aunt Inez sprawled on the floor, still wearing the baggy sweat suit she had on when she put Callie to bed. The receiver of the bedroom phone lay beside her slack hand.

Neither Aunt Inez nor the phone made a sound.

But there was a noise in the room—a liquid sniffing. Callie spun around in time to see the ebony outline of a man surge from the corner. He peered at her with what looked like bug eyes, a cross between a pair of binoculars and a skin diver's goggles. Callie shrieked, and the man extended his arm toward her, a black tube sprouting from his fist. A loud puff sounded, like someone blowing through a straw, and she felt the mosquitolike sting of a needle on her neck. Then the room spun into blackness, sucking her down into a sleep deeper than sleep.

27

Lights Off, Lights On

NATALIE'S FLIGHT DIDN'T GET HER BACK TO L.A. UNTIL 11 P.M., but that didn't stop her from ringing the doorbell of Inez's dark house at sometime past one in the morning. She had to take Callie away *now*.

The doorbell did not play its signature snatch of Mozart's Symphony No. 40. Natalie's skin prickled with gooseflesh. She tried the bell again, then rapped on the door, then pounded on it. No answer.

Maybe they couldn't hear her. She tested the doorknob but found it locked. Skirting the perimeter of the house, Natalie let herself through the gate into the Mendozas' back-yard and walked around to tap on the window of the master bedroom.

On the other side of the glass, someone moaned.

"Inez? It's me, Natalie."

"*Help,*" the voice cried weakly.

If she'd had a brick in her hand at that moment, Natalie would have hurled it through the window in order to get into that room. As it was, she ran around to the house's back door and wrenched its locked knob in vain.

"*CALLIE!*" she yelled, throwing her weight against the door. Its glass pane shivered, but it didn't budge. She staggered back for another run at it when she noticed that the adjacent window was open. The mesh of its screen had been slashed from its frame and a neat circle cut from its glass right below where the latch would have been.

Heedless of the evidence she might be contaminating, Natalie crawled over the sill into the living room and groped down the hall toward the master bedroom where she'd heard the voice. Inside, she saw Inez struggling to lift herself from the floor. In the bed, a lump that must have been Paul rolled over with a groan.

Rushing to her side, Natalie helped Inez sit upright, bracing her back against the side of the bed. She turned the switch of the nightstand lamp, but it failed to light.

"Flashlight," Inez mumbled, rubbing her brow. "Top drawer."

Natalie took out the flashlight, which Inez must have put in the nightstand during California's last round of rolling blackouts. Its batteries weak, it drizzled sickly yellow light on the bed and floor as Natalie swept it around the room. "What happened?"

"Don't know." Inez clamped her eyes shut, pained by the dim light. "When the lights went out, I heard Paul yell, so I ran in here. Tried to call 911, but the phone was dead."

The flashlight beam fell on the derelict receiver lying on the floor. "Yes. And?"

"I felt something hit me here." Inez touched the skin beneath the open collar of her sweat suit. A nickel-size bruise with a pinhole tear in the center dripped a tiny trickle of crusting blood down her chest, like the bite of a one-fanged vampire.

Natalie trailed the flashlight beam down from Inez's clavicle to the floor. There lay what looked like a miniature missile, its needle tip stained burgundy.

With quivering fingers, Natalie picked up the empty tranquilizer dart, studied its glint under the flashlight. "Where's Callie?"

"Callie? She was in Lance's bedroom—" Inez gaped at the dart. "Oh, God, Natalie, I'm sorry."

Leaving her friend in the dark, Natalie rushed to check the rest of the house, calling Callie's name. She knew it was useless, though. *He* had her.

By the time she got back to the master bedroom, Paul Mendoza had rolled up onto his rump, Inez embracing him as he grumbled at the headache the tranquilizer had given him. A red spot on the stomach of his white extra-large T-shirt circled the hole where the dart had penetrated.

"Where's your cell phone?" Natalie asked.

Inez indicated a door behind her. "My handbag. In the bathroom."

"You guys all right?" she said as she fetched the phone and dialed 911.

Inez pulled up the tail of Paul's shirt to examine his puncture wound. "I think so."

The emergency operator answered, and Natalie gave him the Mendozas' address and told him that her friends had been drugged and her daughter kidnapped. She requested both police and paramedics and started to say that the man they should look for was Lyman Pearsall, registered member of the North American Afterlife Communications Corps, but the operator interrupted her.

"Keep calm now, ma'am," he said in the gently patronizing tone of emergency personnel. "We'll get some officers over there right away to investigate. We're going to do everything we can to get your daughter back safe and sound, okay?"

She exhaled. "Okay."

But it wasn't okay. She knew Thresher had taken Callie, and she knew that she'd find both of them if she tracked down Lyman Pearsall. Let Inez try to tell the whole story to the cops.

With help on the way, Natalie handed the phone to Inez and took the flashlight outside to the back of the house, where the electric meter and breaker box were located. As she suspected, someone had cut the padlock from the box and switched off all the circuit breakers. She flicked them back on, and several lights inside the house resumed glowing.

"I have to go," she said as she returned to the bedroom. "Will you two be okay?"

Inez nodded. "Find her."

"I will."

Leaving the house, Natalie compressed the fear in her mind to concentrate on action. She had other friends in law enforcement and in the Corps, as well. If she called in some favors, one of them could surely tell her where Lyman lived, what car he drove, what the license plate number was, and so on.

She was so busy strategizing that she walked right past Arabella Madison, who waited for her on the Mendozas' front porch.

"Having a pleasant evening, Ms. Lindstrom?" the Corps Security agent greeted her.

Natalie stalked around to the Volvo's driver's side without looking at her. "Not tonight, Bella. I'm not in the mood and I don't have the time."

"Oh, really? I thought you might be curious about your daughter."

Natalie slammed the door she'd just opened and glowered at Madison over the car's roof. "What about her?"

"She's perfectly safe." The agent smiled. "With us."

"What do you mean?"

"She's in protective custody until we find out who's murdering your family."

Protective custody. Natalie felt the ambivalent relief of a Pole who's been freed from Hitler only to find Stalin in charge. "When can I see her?"

Madison gave a pitying shake of her head. "I'm afraid that won't be possible right away. Callie's location is being shared on a need-to-know basis at present, for her own safety."

"I'm her *mother.*"

"Yes, but you're also a potential victim. This killer has methods of extracting such sensitive information, and you wouldn't want to put your own child at risk, would you?"

Natalie chuckled without a trace of humor. "Thanks for your concern."

"I knew you'd see it our way. Of course, if you'd like our protection, as well, we'd be happy to—"

"I'll take my chances with the killer."

The agent shrugged with feline insouciance. "Your choice." She headed off toward her Acura, which was parked across the street.

"You don't have to look far to find the murderer," Natalie called after her.

Madison turned. "What?"

Natalie nearly said Pearsall's name then, but stopped short. If the public learned that Lyman Pearsall had conspired with a serial killer to give false testimony in court, it would cause a scandal that might threaten the existence of the Corps itself. Would the Corps choose to expose his crimes . . . or bury them? Not to mention the fact that, as long as the person who'd murdered Nora and Sheila Lindstrom remained at large, Corps Security would have the excuse to keep Callie in "protective custody" forever.

"Never mind," Natalie told the agent. "I'll take care of it."

She got in her Volvo and drove off, leaving Madison to stare after her and wonder.

28

Bad Babysitters

CALLIE AWOKE IN A COT WITH STIFF WHITE SHEETS and a scratchy gray blanket, surrounded by cold white walls. Her head hurt. She rubbed the itchy patch on her neck that felt like a bug bite and pushed herself upright to look around, her fear muted by a residual fuzziness of thought.

Across the small room, she saw a man with pale, blotchy skin seated on a metal folding chair next to a card table. He held a mug of steaming liquid under his large nose, making bubbling noises as he inhaled the vapors.

When he noticed her watching, he self-consciously set aside the mug and got up. "It's a honey-lemon thing. Supposed to clear the sinuses."

She stared at him. "Where are we?"

"Don't worry. We're in a safe place—a safe house." He opened a McDonald's Happy Meal box that sat on the card table and pulled out a paper-wrapped cheeseburger. "You hungry? There's a microwave out there." He gestured to the door. "I could heat it up for you."

Callie shook her head. "I feel sick."

The man nodded. "That's the trank. It'll wear off soon. Drink lots of this." He handed her a small bottle of water.

She cupped her hands around the bottle, thirsty but too

suspicious to drink. "Where's Aunt Inez? Mommy told me to stay with her."

"You weren't safe at her house. That's why we brought you here."

"But where's Mommy? When do I get to see her?"

"When you're out of danger." After unlocking the dead bolt on the door, he opened it and leaned out. "She's come out of it."

He stepped back to allow a bald man in a white robe to enter. "I don't approve of your techniques, Rendell," the bald man said. "If any harm's come to her, you can forget about your early retirement plan."

"She's fine. I adjusted the dose for her age and weight." Rendell shut the door. "You wanted the job done; don't quibble about the means."

The bald man bent to touch Callie's cheek. "Are you all right, child?"

She shied away. "You were at Grandma Nora's funeral. Your name's Simon."

He smiled, sat on the bed. "Yes, that's right. *Master* McCord. I taught your mother. Did you know that?"

Callie shook her head. "What did you teach her? Math or something?"

He chuckled. "Nothing so tedious. Would you like me to show you what it was?"

She sucked the tip of her index finger a moment, nodded.

"Splendid! But first, I have a present for you."

Master McCord pointed to a bag on the card table, then looked at Rendell as if directing a golden retriever. The agent curled his lip but fetched the bag as ordered. McCord reached inside and brought out a bread-loaf–size bundle wrapped in a baby's blanket.

"This is very old, so you must take great care with it." He peeled away the cloth to reveal a doll in a deep burgundy Victorian dress with lace trim. The painted blush had dulled on the fat baby cheeks of its stiff celluloid head, and one of its blinking translucent blue eyes had stuck half open, its iris tarnished as if blind. It smelled like dusty drapes.

Callie made no move to take the toy, but Master McCord took the water bottle from her and pressed the doll into her hands. "Go on, child. It's yours, if you want it."

A stinging tingle buzzed through Callie, like the time she licked the top of a nine-volt battery. She gasped, then found she couldn't let her breath out. The vision of a park she'd never seen before wavered inside her, ornamental flower beds surrounding a lake where swans glided over the sun-dappled water. The caramel stickiness of a hard nougat—the kind she hated, the kind that stuck your teeth together—buttered her tongue, and she was running to take a bouquet of dandelions to her mother, her legs sweating under hot petticoats, fast breaths hissing around the stone of the candy that filled her mouth. It lodged in the back of her throat, she yawned her mouth open for air, saw the skin of her hands turning blue . . .

Mummy, Mummy, help me! the piccolo voice of an English girl piped in Callie's head. *Where are you?*

"That's it, my child," Master McCord murmured as she shivered and twitched. "Good."

But it wasn't good. Callie didn't want to feel the other girl's death. For an instant, she thought about calling for Daddy, asking him to make the girl go away, but Mommy had told her not to do that anymore. What did she say to do when the bad Whos came?

The next time the bad ones come, I want you to say your

ABCs. Say 'em over and over without stopping until the bad ones go away . . .

"Aaayyyyyyy . . . buh-buh-BEEEEEEE . . . suh-suh-SEEEEEE . . ."

Her mouth felt all mushy at first, like when the dentist filled two cavities in her baby teeth, but it got easier as she went along, saying each of the letters and then the entire alphabet faster and faster.

"ABCDEFGHIJKLMNOPQRSTUVWXYZ! *ABCDEFGHIJ-KLMNOPQRSTUVWXYZ!*"

The English girl's soul dissolved, the way a bad dream faded once the lights came on. *And I did it all by myself,* Callie thought, breathing normally again. She gave the old doll back to Master McCord. "I can't have this. It's someone else's."

He put the toy away, violet eyes shining with shrewd delight. "Excellent. Most impressive. It seems your mother *has* passed on a bit of what I taught her. How would you like to learn more?"

Callie gave a noncommittal shrug.

McCord sweetened his voice. "Do you like horses?"

She bobbed her head.

"Well, I own a big ranch out in New Mexico, and I know we have a pony there who'd love for you to ride him. Would you like that?"

Another nod.

"We also have a bunch of little boys and girls there just like you. I know you'd make good friends there. Would you like that, too?"

Nod.

"Do you have many friends here?"

Callie shook her head.

"I know. It's hard to make friends when you're different. When you're *special.* But I know everyone at my ranch would like you. You could have a lot of fun there and learn to do all kinds of amazing things. Would you like that?"

She sucked her finger again. "Would I have to cut all my hair off?"

Master McCord laughed. "That won't be necessary any-time soon."

"Could Mommy come with me?"

The smile lines at the sides of his mouth turned cross. "She can *visit* you. And you can visit her, when you're not studying."

"But I want to see her! I want to see her *now.*"

He patted her shoulder. "All in good time, child."

"My name's Callie. And I won't go to your stupid ranch until I see Mommy." She folded her arms with a determined scowl.

Master McCord chuckled again. "You really *are* like your mother."

He rose and headed for the door, glancing back at Rendell. "I'll be back in two days. Make sure you take good care of her until then. And get her something better to eat than *that,*" he commanded, indicating the Happy Meal.

When McCord was gone, Rendell shut and locked the door, made a face to mock the Violet's supercilious sneer.

He plopped back in his folding chair and picked up his mug of honey-lemon liquid, now gone cold. "Well, kid, it's just you and me now. Make yourself at home."

Callie looked at the pale, bored man in front of her, at the locked door, at the cold cheeseburger on the card table, at the itchy gray blanket over her knees. And she started to cry.

29

Ringing Phones and Wringing Hands

THAT NIGHT, FOR THE FIRST TIME IN NEARLY A WEEK, Natalie went home. Or, more accurately, she returned to the ugly condominium where she lived, since everything that had made it a home was gone. Only now did she realize that she'd never enjoyed a true home before since she'd never really had a true family before.

Until Callie.

She spent the larger part of the following morning in the kitchen, calling the N-double-A-C-C in a vain attempt to get information on where they were keeping her daughter. "I'm afraid that information's classified," they told her. "But if you want to write to her, we'll happily forward any mail addressed to her care of Corps Headquarters in Washington."

Finally, she demanded to speak to Delbert Sinclair, the authoritarian Director of Corps Security himself.

Age had mellowed neither his mood nor his manners. "The last time we conversed, Ms. Lindstrom, you led me to understand that we had nothing left to say to one another. Why are you bothering me now?"

"My daughter."

"Yes? What about her?"

Natalie pressed her lips together, as if to seal the words in ner mouth. She let them out anyway. "If you let her go, I'll come back."

Sinclair chuckled. "I think we both know that the time for that offer has long since expired. Although, if you want to reinstate your membership, we might arrange for visitation rights—"

She hung up.

Later, when she'd boomeranged from anger back into despair, Natalie called her father in New Hampshire to explain why she might not make it to Sheila's memorial service.

"Do whatever it takes," Wade told her. "Catch the man who killed my Sunny. And get Callie away from those vultures."

"I will. Somehow."

"And Natalie?"

"Yes?"

"Watch out for yourself. You and Callie are all I've got left."

That was Natalie's cue to tell her father that she loved him, and she wanted to. But after years of bitter division, she suspected her own sincerity, didn't trust herself to say something that she might not really mean when the emotions of the past week cooled into memories.

"I'll be careful," she said, hoping it was enough for now. "You take care, too, Dad."

"I will. Thanks, honey."

With a groan, Natalie hung up the phone and looked at the answering machine beside it. The digital display told her she had thirty-two messages waiting, the most the device could hold. Thirty-one of them turned out to be from reporters. One was from Inez.

"It's me," the prosecutor said, as Natalie's finger shied back from the SKIP button. "I know I'm probably the last person you want to talk to this morning, but I got some stuff on Pearsall and Thresher and thought you should know. Call or come to my office anytime today if you can." A blank hiss followed. "About Callie . . . I can't tell you—"

But Inez had paused too long and the machine cut her off.

Natalie went to the condo's front window, nudged aside the drawn drape. Outside, a gauntlet of photographers and minicam crews milled about on the street, smoking cigarettes and slurping coffee from paper cups. Every now and then, one of them glanced toward the house the way a housecat might eye a canary's cage.

"Well, guys," she murmured, "this is your money shot. On your marks, get set . . ."

The connecting door into the garage allowed her to reach her car without being mobbed. Locked safely inside the Volvo, she was able to inch her way through the jabbering mass of reporters outside without too much trouble. A few of the news vans attempted to follow her car, but George had given Natalie plenty of practice in how to shake a tail, and with a few well-timed turns and red lights she lost them all. Only the tan LeBaron pulled in beside her when she parked in a pay-by-the-half-hour lot outside the L.A. Criminal Justice Center.

The automatic window on the LeBaron's passenger side rolled down. *"Tu es une conductrice diabolique, mon amie,"* George said when Natalie lowered her own window to hear him. "You almost lost *me."*

"Merci." She couldn't manage a smile.

"I heard about Callie. Want you to know I don't think it's

right." He didn't look at her, either from shame or from the fear that someone might be watching them.

Natalie had no such fear, and fixed her gaze on him. "Where is she?"

"I don't know. They're keeping it hush-hush."

"Can you find out?"

George's expression roiled like crawling lava. "Aw, hell. Wanted a career change anyway." His shaded eyes swung toward her. "I'll see what I can do."

She did muster a smile then, if only a small, sad one. "Thanks. Pizza's on me next time."

"Better be." He grinned.

Her smile widened a bit, and she got out of the car.

The offices of the Los Angeles deputy district attorneys were located on the Justice Center's seventeenth floor, and Natalie had to ask the white-shirted guard at the desk in the foyer to call Inez for permission to come up. Though not given to public displays of affection, the prosecutor greeted Natalie with a hug.

"Welcome to Purgatory," she said, holding open the office door.

Despite the ostensible importance of Inez's position, her office was cramped and functional. Piles of papers and file folders covered every available square inch of space on her fake-walnut desk and surrounding shelves, and an enormous corkboard covered one wall, a mosaic of crime-scene photos, three-by-five cards, and yellow Post-it notes.

Indicating a vacant chair as she passed, Inez returned to her seat behind the desk. "Any news?"

Natalie remained standing. "Callie's alive, and in the Corps' tender, loving care. Could've been worse. How're you doing?"

"Better than you, I'll wager. Paul and I felt a bit silly going to the hospital, actually, because we were both fine by the time the paramedics came." She shook her head. "I'm sorry. We should have taken her somewhere else."

Natalie didn't answer, and she paced to the opposite corner of the office so Inez wouldn't see the flash of anger on her face. Though she wanted to absolve her friend of guilt, she couldn't help but think how her whole life started to unravel the afternoon that the prosecutor showed up at Callie's school. "What do you have for me?"

"You know, the Corps hates bad publicity. If you got a good lawyer and told the press about Callie—"

"What did you find out?"

"Sorry. Just trying to help." Inez shifted a pile of manila folders off her desk blotter and pulled a thick FedEx envelope in front of her. "I couldn't get much on Pearsall, since we don't have enough on him to go to a judge for subpoenas. What's more, the D.A.'s livid about the Hyland case and wants to try Avery Park for the murders before this year's election, so he's confined me to paper-shuffling for the foreseeable future. My job here's hanging by a thread, but I did my best for you.

"I tried calling Pearsall's apartment here in L.A., but there was no answer. Surprise, surprise. When I contacted the N-double-A-C-C, they said he'd requested a week's leave of absence to recover from his ordeal at the Hyland trial, and they generously granted him four days."

Inez indicated the stack of folders. "I couldn't find any leads on where he might be, but if he and Thresher are after you, then he's probably still in the area. I asked some friends in the LAPD to red-flag his ATM and credit cards and put out an APB on the license-plate number of his Ford Escort, the only car I could find registered in his name.

"I did find one interesting thing in Pearsall's Corps file, though. Early last year, he took out a seventy-thousand-dollar loan against his retirement benefits. No indication where that money went; the purpose stated on the application was 'personal expenses.'"

"Would've been just in time for the Ries trial," Natalie mused. "What about Thresher?"

"That wasn't easy, either. Quantico didn't want to loan out any of their artifacts from the Needlepoint Killer case because the last time they did, they didn't get back one of the main items in their collection—a jackknife Thresher was carrying when they arrested him. Care to guess who had it last?"

The name clung to Natalie's tongue. *"Lyman."*

"Yep. After he summoned the victim found in the Angeles National Forest, Pearsall visited the Quantico archives to do some 'research' that he said might lead to the discovery and identification of other Thresher victims. The archivist later discovered that the knife was missing from the articles Pearsall examined. Pearsall, of course, denied even seeing the knife. The archivist has been reluctant to let anyone touch the remaining artifacts since. He did, however, send us this."

Inez opened the FedEx envelope and upended it. A folded floral-print blouse slid out into the prosecutor's hand, wrapped in gossamer plastic as if fresh from the cleaners. "It's the one your mom used to summon Margaret Thresher."

Natalie made no move to take the blouse when Inez held it out to her. "Thanks. Put it back in the envelope and I'll take it with me."

"Okay. But take care of it, or the guy from Quantico will personally fly out from Virginia to wring my neck."

"Will do," Natalie said, unsure whether she'd be able to keep that promise.

She put the envelope under her arm and said good-bye to Inez, heading home with only a vague idea of how she might use the blouse to find Vincent Thresher—and a growing certainty that, if she didn't find him soon, he would find *her*.

30

Special Delivery

STILL NURSING A COUGH THAT THREATENED TO become bronchitis, Horace Rendell was dozing on the couch in the living room of the Corps Security safe house when the doorbell rang.

Probably the blasted Mormons, he thought as the bell sounded for the third time. He sat up and sniffed at the underarm of his short-sleeve dress shirt. You could tell by the smell that he'd worn it three days in a row, but he went to the door without caring that he stank.

Peering through the peephole, he saw a squat UPS driver with mirrored sunglasses standing on the doorstep, a flat, paper-wrapped box under one arm, an electronic clipboard under the other. The brown shirt of his uniform looked about two sizes too small for him, its threads ready to snap as the man's paunch bulged beneath them.

Idiot must have the wrong address, Rendell groused, still half asleep. Leaving the chain and security latch in place, he pulled the door open just enough to shout through. "You got the wrong place. Try next door."

"Address is right, sir." The driver held up the box. "Package for Miss Lindstrom?"

"You've got to be kidding." Griping under his breath, Rendell threw aside the chain and latch. The Corps was supposed to route all mail for safe-house occupants through the local office, to be delivered later by Security agents. This would not be the first time, though, that the bureaucracy had screwed up.

"Let me see it." Rendell took the box from the delivery man and read the mailing label. It was addressed from Natalie Lindstrom to Callie Lindstrom, care of the North American Afterlife Communications Corps, Washington, D.C., with a desperate PLEASE FORWARD! request written in red block letters. Another label gave the Corps' Washington headquarters as a return address and redirected the package here to the safe house in Silverlake. The mother evidently paid for overnight delivery, so the package had bounced from one coast to the other and back again in two days.

Rendell regarded the box as if it were a brick of solid C4 explosive. If it were up to him, he would've stamped it RETURN TO SENDER and thrown it back in the UPS guy's face, but the Corps bureaucrats, in their infinite wisdom, insisted that their freaks be able to receive approved mail from immediate family "in order to maintain conduit morale." Part of the whole PR thing, keeping up the appearance that they weren't oppressing anyone. Like, who were they kidding?

"All right. I'll take it."

The UPS guy handed him the clipboard and a pen-shaped plastic stylus. "Sign in the black rectangle."

Rendell scrawled his name invisibly on the touchpad, became annoyed when he saw his signature converted to a first-grade scribble on the liquid-crystal display above it. "There."

The UPS guy shoved the clipboard back under his arm. "Thanks, pal."

He trundled back toward the brown truck he'd parked at the curb, and Rendell slammed and locked the front door.

Taking the box to the Formica-topped dining-room table, the agent squeezed, prodded, and shook the package like a kid trying to guess his birthday present. He doubted that the Lindstrom woman would booby-trap the thing when there was a chance that her kid might open it first, but it paid to be cautious.

Rather than unwrapping it in the conventional fashion, Rendell got a steak knife from the kitchen and stabbed right through the cardboard in the center of the lid to saw a silver dollar–size disc from the box top. When no poison gas poured out, he peeked through the hole and saw multicolored strands of yarn interwoven with a grid of coarse thread.

Deciding that the contents looked innocuous, he cut around the lid and took out the only item inside the box—an old-fashioned sampler in a thick wooden frame. The kind old ladies hung in their parlors, filled with cutesy animals and cherubs and boasting such timeless pearls of insight as "Today Is the First Day of the Rest of Your Life" and "It Takes a Whole Heap o' Lovin' to Make a House a Home." What a load of hooey.

A typewritten note had been taped to the front of this one, signed with a pair of barely legible initials:

> To Whom It May Concern:
> Please give this to my
> little girl. Thank you.
> Sincerely,
> Natalie Lindstrom

A coughing fit hit Rendell, causing him to hack up phlegm, which he spat into an empty coffee cup that he kept close at hand for that purpose. Knocking back a swig of cough syrup straight from the bottle that sat on the table, he tore the note off the sampler, balled it up, and tossed it at the wastebasket by the wall, where it bounced off the rim and landed among the soggy, wadded tissues littering the floor.

The sampler featured two teddy bears, one large and one small, surrounded by flowers and flitting butterflies. The larger bear, obviously the mother, touched a loving paw to the head of its cub, and the bright red letters above them read I'LL ALWAYS BE WITH YOU. Rendell brushed his fingers over the tight mat of bumps, the stitched pixels of yarn that made up the picture. Nice work, he had to admit; the Lindstrom woman must have stayed up all night to finish it so quickly.

He felt around the wide frame and flipped the picture over to examine the back, making sure there were no weapons, lock picks, or other tools of escape attached to the gift. Not that he had much to fear from a five-year-old, but he wasn't taking any chances with that four-hundred-grand bonus at stake.

Satisfied that the picture was harmless, he let himself into the kid's bedroom without knocking and tossed the sampler in front of her on the foot of her bed. "Here. A present from your mom."

Wearing an ill-fitting dress and shoes Rendell had obtained for her, Callie looked up from the cheap coloring books he'd bought to keep her occupied, a glow of hope lighting her face. "Mommy? What did she say? Is she coming?"

But Rendell shut the door on her questions, coughing spasmodically as he locked the dead bolt.

When the mean man left without telling her what Mommy had said, Callie slumped back into dejection. Since her mother was not there to hug her, she crawled forward on the bed to look at the picture. She'd never seen needlework like this before; it was pretty. She liked the bears and butterflies especially. Had Mommy made it for her?

Callie made several abortive attempts to read what the words said, sounding out each letter as best she could. Mommy wanted to tell her something, and she had to find out what it was since the mean man wouldn't tell her. As she often did with her reading workbooks, Callie put her little index finger on the big *I* at the beginning of the message to keep track of which letter she was saying.

The instant her skin touched the fuzzy mat of yarn, a bolt of pure will shot up into her brain. She collapsed on top of the sampler, convulsing and frothing at the mouth as if in a grand mal seizure.

Callie frantically stuttered the alphabet in her mind, but now couldn't remember all the letters. *A-B-C . . . A-B-C-D . . . D-E-F . . .*

A barrage of images assaulted her, colored black and red and blanched blue-white, visions so heinous that her innocent mind mercifully did not possess the knowledge to comprehend them. Cold hatred, like liquid nitrogen, flash-froze her consciousness into icy brittleness.

This was a *bad* Who. The worst Callie had ever known. She wanted to vomit it out like poison, but the soul clamped on her thoughts and squeezed, a hand crushing a flower blossom for its fragrance.

She lay still for a moment, the expectant lull of a jukebox changing discs. Then clarity returned to her eyes—even a glint of childish mischief. She wiped the spittle from her mouth and stood up on the bed, stretching her little body and bouncing on the mattress with Christmas-morning eagerness.

When she glanced down at the sampler, however, her expression took on an unusual maturity of determination. Glancing at the locked door apprehensively, she put the picture between her knees and tugged at the top of the frame with both hands, growling in frustration at the weakness of her young muscles. Finally, by leveraging what little weight she had, she pried apart the upper left corner of the frame, which was held together with a single thin nail.

There, drilled down into the diagonal cut at the top of the frame's side bar, was a deep hole about the diameter of a fountain pen. Callie turned the frame upside down, and a small syringe slid out of the tube onto the cot's scratchy blanket. The hypodermic's finger pads had been shaved off so it would fit into the hole and its needle capped to keep the clear fluid inside—a particularly potent barbiturate solution—from leaking.

Smiling, Callie hurled the sampler with its loosened frame onto the floor with as loud a clatter as possible.

"Mister! Mister!" she yelled, picking up the syringe and pulling off its cap. "I need help!"

As a key rattled in the bedroom door's dead bolt, Callie knelt on the edge of the bed, her small hand cupped around the top of the hypodermic, which she held close against her left thigh.

Rendell opened the door and leaned inside, the bags beneath his bloodshot eyes quivering with irritation. "What now?"

"It fell." Callie cast a glum look down at the sampler and twisted frame on the floor beside the bed. "Can you fix it?"

"Oh, for Chrissake—"

Grumbling, Rendell stepped over and stooped to collect the pieces of the picture. With his head bent down before her,

Callie drove the needle into the side of his neck, pushing the plunger down with the palm of her other hand. Her mouth stretched into the gargoyle grin of a fiend.

Rendell cried out and staggered back, the syringe still lodged in the fleshy folds of his skin. His eyes and mouth gaping into rings of astonishment, he yanked out the hypodermic and peered at it. "What the hell . . . *you little minx!*"

He lunged forward to swipe his fist at her, but his movements were already becoming slow and clumsy. Callie easily dodged him and jumped off the bed, giggling girlish triumph.

Rendell waggled his head and weaved to intercept her but tripped over his own feet and dropped to the floor. He pushed himself up, yet only made it to his knees.

Straining to lift the weight of his eyelids, he clawed at Callie, who danced just beyond his reach. As his gelatinous body slumped into immobility, she laughed and sang a playground taunt. A single sucking noise, like the last rasp of a clogged vacuum cleaner, escaped Rendell's mouth before he started to turn a cyanotic blue.

Keeping a prudent distance away from his body, Callie watched him for any signs of life. She inched forward, gave his head a practice kick, scampered back. He didn't move. Tittering, she stamped on the dead crab of his outstretched hand. Horace Rendell didn't seem to mind.

Callie took the CO_2-powered dart pistol from the leather holster under the agent's arm, then wormed her little hand into his pants pocket to grab his keys before strolling out the door, which Rendell had left open. Although no one had responded to the commotion in the bedroom, she moved through the Corps safe house with caution in case there happened to be another agent lurking around. When she made it through the front door and onto the suburban street, she started to hum, skipping daintily all the way to the battered white Bronco that Pearsall had parked along the curb.

"Took you long enough," he muttered as she climbed into the passenger seat beside him.

She dropped the pistol into the glove compartment and grinned at him. "Awwwww! Were you worried about me, Lyman, buddy?"

Pearsall was sweating even more than usual. "I'm worried about *me*. I can't keep taking chances like this."

"You dispose of the UPS truck like I told you?"

"Yeah. Left it downtown, hazard lights flashing. How long you think it'll take the cops to figure out it doesn't have a driver?"

"At least half an hour."

The mirrored shades hid Lyman's eyes, but not his discomfort. "What *did* you do with the driver, anyway?"

Callie snickered. "Trade secret."

"I bet." Pearsall quailed under the five-year-old's gaze. At least he was out of that cursed uniform, so tight it felt like wearing the dead man's skin. "After this, I'm out of it, right? You're done with me. That's what you said, right?"

"Sure, Lyman. Once I've got a replacement." The girl buckled her safety belt and relaxed in the seat with a lazy smile. "Now, drive."

Lyman did as he was told. Better to have him in the girl's brain than his own, he thought, even for a little while.

31

Good Things

EVEN IF SHE HADN'T TALKED TO GEORGE THAT DAY, Natalie would have feared the tiny parcel that awaited her on the doorstep when she got back to the condo. The small cube fit in the palm of her hand and was barely wide enough to accommodate her full address and a meter stamp for postage. For a return address, the paper-wrapped box merely offered the initials *VT* printed in block letters in one corner.

From what George had told her, Natalie knew the parcel was a trap. She also knew she had no choice but to open it.

"Good things come in small packages," she muttered, and took it into the kitchen.

She had sensed that something was wrong when she walked out to get the morning paper and noticed that the tan LeBaron was not parked at the curb.

Two equally disturbing possibilities occurred to her. The first was that George had been caught trying to learn where the Corps was keeping Callie and had been summarily fired—or worse. The second was that the Corps simply decided that they didn't need to keep her under surveillance anymore. They had what they wanted now, and Natalie had become unimportant to them. If the Corps was that confident of keeping Callie under their control, it meant that Natalie might never see her daughter again.

A third possibility, worse than the first two, did not occur to her until she left the Fullerton Public Library that afternoon. The moment she shut the Volvo's door, a dark voice emanated from behind her car seat.

"Don't freak out and don't look at me," it warned her. "Pretend you're putting on makeup or something."

Natalie found her breath. "Jesus, George! You scared the crap out of me." She tilted the rearview mirror toward her, feigned vanity. "What are you doing back there?"

His grumble rose from below her; he must have curled up on the Volvo's backseat. "Waiting for you, and, believe me, it wasn't easy. I thought you'd be in that stupid library all day."

"I was doing some research." She'd read everything she could find on Thresher and Pearsall, sifting for any hint as to where they'd holed up. "How did you get in here?"

"Popped the lock with a slim-jim. I can't be seen talking to you."

Natalie tried to steady her hand as she applied superfluous lipstick. "Why? Did you find where they're keeping Callie?"

"Yes and no. The Corps lost her."

She overshot one corner of her mouth, smearing red on her cheek. *"What?"*

"Someone got into the Corps safe house yesterday, killed Rendell, and took your girl. They'll deny it if you ask them, of course; they'll tell you she's snug as a bug in a rug, but secretly they're in an uproar over it. Simon McCord himself is gonna summon Rendell to find out what happened."

Natalie stopped listening at "took your girl." *"Thresher..."*

"Hate to bring bad news, but I thought you should know."
George waited for her to speak. "Nat?"

"I've got to go . . . I've got to do . . . something." She wiped
the lipstick off with a dirty tissue from her purse and fumbled
for her car key.

"Do me a favor," George said before she could put it in the
ignition. "Go in the library for ten more minutes. I'll be gone
by the time you get back."

Natalie lapsed into an angry silence but got out of the car
as he asked. Later, she would feel guilty for not even thanking
George for the risk he'd taken in talking to her.

Forced to loiter in the library for the longest ten minutes
of her life, Natalie could only think of her failure to save Callie. She didn't even know where to begin looking for her.

The box waiting for her on the doorstep at home solved
that problem.

Pulling on a pair of Playtex gloves to protect any evidence the
small package might offer, Natalie briefly considered taking
the box to the police but decided she didn't have time for
that. Whatever was in the box wouldn't hurt her directly, she
knew—Thresher wanted to *see* her suffer—and if there was
even an infinitesimal chance of saving Callie's life, Natalie
needed to discover it *now*.

Restraining the impulse to rip the thing open, she peeled
the tape off as if the scrap of brown paper were a sheet of fancy
wrapping she wanted to fold and save for a future birthday.
With only a moment's hesitation, she took a knife and slit the
single strip of tape that held the cardboard box shut. She lifted
the hinged lid to find the interior filled with cotton wadding.

Swaddled in its white center lay an irregular bluish-black oval with crumpled ridges, resembling a soft-bodied mollusk that had been torn from its shell and left to shrivel in the sun. The object looked so strange, so utterly alien, that only when Natalie picked it out of its cotton nest and saw the crusts of paper-dry skin on its underside did she realize what it was.

An ear.

She yelped and dropped it on the kitchen table in abrupt disgust. Though the ear lay perfectly still, she stared at it, gasping, afraid to blink lest it scuttle away to nest under her stove. *Oh my God . . . Callie!*

But, as the initial horror retreated, she saw with ironic relief that it couldn't be her daughter's ear. It was too big. This ear belonged to an adult.

Like her mother.

It might not be hers, she thought, but knew she was in denial. Of course it was her mom's ear. Thresher had saved it, preserved it, just for her. Why?

Because it's a touchstone. He wants to get in my head.

The thought petrified Natalie, the way it had that day at the Institute when Thresher clawed toward her with Nora's fingers. Both her mother and Lyman Pearsall had become vessels for his monomaniacal will, their flesh magnetized like lodestone by the lightning bolt of his soul's energy. Would Natalie be strong enough to push him out of her mind when they could not?

She had to try. Even with all the research she'd done, Natalie had no idea where Thresher and Pearsall might be hiding Callie. The only hope of finding her daughter lay in the mind of the man who'd abducted her.

Whispering her spectator mantra, Natalie stripped off her gloves.

The mummified ear seemed to squirm between her fingers as she picked it up, but she kept it cupped in her palm. *"Row, row, row your boat, gently down the stream . . ."*

A sensation like a menthol muscle rub tingled through her body and her mind, both hot and cold at the same time. Hot from an unquenchable rage that longed to scorch to cinders everything alive. Cold from a stunted psyche incapable of feeling anything more than a joyless delight in sadism. A sickening endorphin rush of orgasm accompanied memories of needles and blood and faces contorted by agony, and Natalie bent double over the table, dry-heaving with revulsion. She squeezed the ear in her fist and kept whispering.

Greetings, Natalie. She had never heard the voice now in her head, but recognized the hatpin invasiveness of its inflection from her visits to Nora. *I hoped this ear might help you hear me better.*

"Where's Callie?" she demanded, monitoring Thresher's thoughts for any telltale images that might reveal her child's location.

She's fine, if that's what you're wondering. In fact, I went to all this trouble to invite you to come visit us.

"You mean walk right into your torture chamber. How do I know she's even alive?"

Because I've only started to enjoy her. Why, just look at how much fun we've had already! And he treated her to a mental movie of how he'd killed Horace Rendell with Callie's tiny, innocent hands, how he'd danced and skipped and kicked the corpse with her little feet.

Natalie balled her hands into impotent hammerheads. *"BASTARD!"*

I realize you're probably feeling left out right now. That's why I thought you might be interested in negotiating a little trade.

She clenched her teeth against further screams and considered. Should the mongoose follow the cobra into its hole?

"All right," she said, her voice the whisper of wrath that exceeded screaming. "What do I need to do?"

He gave her explicit instructions to follow, his soul snickering like the cuckoo about to hatch in another bird's nest. *And remember that this is a private party, so please don't invite any guests,* he admonished her. *Otherwise, Callie and I will have to play without you—and there's so much more fun we could have together.*

Bile rose in Natalie's throat, but she swallowed it. "I understand."

I knew you would. You seem much more reasonable than your late mother, bless her. I'm sure we're going to be the best of friends.

And with that, he left her.

Shuddering, Natalie dropped into one of the kitchen chairs and rubbed at her face and bare arms with the fervor of an obsessive-compulsive, wishing she could shower the soul-deep stink off her but knowing it was impossible. The taint of his memory festered like a fresh brand, red and sizzling, marking her as chattel.

32

Los Niños

WITH THE EYE-SHADOW APPLICATOR STILL POISED IN her fingers, Natalie stood back from the mirror, comparing her reflection to the photographs of Margaret Thresher in the copies of *Tapestries of Flesh* and *Needle, Thread, and Blood* propped open on her makeup table. She'd used the eye shadow to deepen the hollows of her eyes, rouge to harden her cheekbones, dashes and smears of eyebrow pencil to darken the furrows of her brow and turn her smile lines into frown lines. Several times she had to stop in the middle of brushing on her mascara and tilt her head back to keep tears of futility pooled in her eyes, to stifle the fear that everything she was doing was in vain.

She'd matched the hair as best she could: her brown wig, with a lock on each side held back with black barrettes. Margaret's hair had been dead straight, but Natalie didn't have time to brush the curls out of the wig. Her flight departed in less than three hours, and she'd need about half that time to get through security.

Resigned to the fact that her physical appearance was as close to Margaret's as she could make it under the circumstances, Natalie put aside the makeup and picked up the plastic-wrapped blouse Quantico had sent Inez. She opened one end of the bag, but hesitated to reach in.

Dressed only in a bra and the sort of knee-length skirt Margaret wore in the pictures, Natalie had told herself that she'd waited to put the blouse on last because she didn't want to get makeup on it. Now she had to admit that she dreaded wearing the dead woman's garment, wrapping herself in Margaret Thresher's soul. But without it, the rest of her preparations really would be worthless.

"*The Lord is my shepherd,*" she whispered before touching the cloth. "*I shall not want.*"

Continuing to murmur the protective mantra in her mind, Natalie put on the blouse and buttoned it up. The reflection in the mirror made her midriff clench as her resemblance to Margaret leapt from passing to uncanny. She felt Margaret knocking—*hard*—or maybe it was only her own paranoid imagination.

Whichever it was, Natalie took several deep, even breaths and kept the Twenty-third Psalm spiraling in her brain as she put on her raincoat and zipped up her near-empty suitcase. She wasn't about to let Margaret inhabit her.

Not yet.

She'd booked the flight to Sacramento out of John Wayne Airport in Orange County, saving her a trip to LAX. As Thresher instructed, she told no one where she was going. Despite that precaution, she still had one small problem.

George.

"Not today," she groaned when she saw the LeBaron in her rearview mirror.

There wasn't time to go through the whole I'm-going-shopping-at-the-mall sham, so she tried to lose him on the surface streets before hitting the freeway. He tailgated her all the way, though, running at least three red lights in the process.

Remember that this is a private party, Thresher's voice replayed in her head, *so please don't invite any guests. Otherwise, Callie and I will have to play without you—and there's so much more fun we could have together.*

Natalie shook her head at the reflection of the LeBaron's driver as it followed her into the parking garage at John Wayne. "George, George, what am I going to do with you?"

She hoped in vain that he would wait for her in his car, the way he did when she went shopping, but instead he trailed her into the terminal, stayed a discreet distance behind her in line as she waited to pick up her electronic ticket and boarding passes. Should she try to talk to him, tell him to go away? Was Thresher watching her right now? What would he do to Callie if he saw Natalie speaking to a Corps Security agent?

Her heart sank further when George showed up at the gate where her flight waited to board. She tried to catch his eye as he sat across from her with folded arms, to signal him to nix the surveillance, but he ignored the slashing motion she made across her throat. His eyes walled off by the wraparound shades, he seemed no more interested in her than any of the other listless passengers around them.

Natalie tried to slow her heartbeat with measured breaths but ended up hyperventilating by the time she entered the gangway to the airplane. George remained a distracting shadow in her peripheral vision, like a fly that buzzed where she couldn't swat it. As she put her suitcase in the bin above her seat, she saw him sidling past other travelers in the aisle. He didn't carry any luggage. Maybe she could slip him a word as he went past. . . .

Natalie shut the overhead bin and turned to block the aisle as he approached. "George—"

His chest slammed into her shoulder, nearly knocking her back against her seat's headrest. She staggered, and he grabbed her right arm with both hands to steady her.

"*Pardonnez-moi, madame.*" He squeezed his right hand, big as a catcher's mitt, against her forearm, and she felt smooth plastic against her skin. "*Gardez-vous.*"

He slid the concealed item down her arm and pressed it into her hand, staring at her with the twin reflections of her own dumbfounded expression.

She closed her fingers on the object. "*Merci.*"

He bobbed his head once and pushed past her to a row at the rear of the plane.

Natalie lowered herself into her seat and surveyed the passengers around her. When she felt sure no one was watching, she peered down at the black plastic box cupped in her fist. Smaller and thinner than a pager, the electronic device was nearly featureless but for one tiny, rectangular green light that flashed with the deliberate oscillation of a lighthouse beam. No technological expert, Natalie guessed the gadget was some kind of GPS tracking device like the Lojack auto locator she'd installed in the Volvo, although the Corps obviously had access to better miniaturization technology.

As soon as the plane was in the air and the captain had turned off the FASTEN SEAT BELT sign, Natalie went to the lavatory and hid the device in her panties. Maybe Thresher wouldn't think to look there—at least, not right away. She padded the box with toilet paper to keep its outline from showing against the loose folds of her skirt, but it still rubbed against her pubic area and dug into her thighs when she took her seat again. She found the discomfort oddly reassuring, however, like the snugness of a safety belt or the tug of an umbilical cord.

Though a starry night sky was visible outside the window, the cloud cover beneath the plane thickened into an opaque black mat, obliterating the view of the glowing grids of cities on the ground. As they descended into Sacramento, blackness swamped the stars and raindrops strafed the aircraft.

"Hope you brought your umbrellas, folks," the pilot drawled over the P.A. system as they taxied to their arrival gate. "El Niño's throwing another little tantrum here."

Having checked the weather forecast, Natalie *had* brought an umbrella, but it hardly helped her once she got outside the Sacramento International Airport terminal. No matter how she angled the umbrella, gusting winds spattered her face with water as she shivered at the curb, waiting for the courtesy van that would take her to pick up her rental car. The world beyond the airport remained invisible except when lightning cracked the sky, its stroboscopic flash silhouetting the distant mountains and trees and freezing the rain into a meteor shower of silver streaks.

So much for my makeup, Natalie thought, wiping the dripping water from her eyes and scanning the area to see who might be watching her. Sacramento was a small airport—almost quaint by LAX standards—and few people lingered along the oval drive that curved past the terminal. One of them was George, who didn't have an umbrella. Stoic and sopping wet, he stood a few yards to one side and faced the opposite direction, the way someone waiting in line at an ATM will hang back far enough to avoid seeing the PIN number of the person in front of him.

He dogged her in that same circumspect manner to the

Avis lot, waited patiently while she filled out her paperwork before renting his own car. She, in turn, lingered in her rented Toyota Corolla until he came out to claim his Buick LeSabre. Despite the tracking device wedged between her thighs, she made sure to keep the watery blur of George's headlights framed in her rearview mirror as she left the airport and headed north on I-5.

Following Thresher's instructions, she drove through miles of dark, flat farmland to the town of Williams, an agricultural community that offered travelers a truck stop, an Italian deli, a couple of gas stations, and a KFC, all of which were closed by the time Natalie sped past them. From there, she turned off onto Route 20, the desolate two-lane highway that wound over the mountains surrounding Clear Lake. Between the rain that pelted the windshield and the tar blackness of the night, the landscape that flanked the road remained virtually opaque, except when a lightning flash illuminated a flooded rice paddy or cotton field.

Water sheeted the road and crested in the Toyota's wheel wells as if under the prow of a ship. Natalie felt a fishtailing swerve when the car started to hydroplane, and she eased down on the brake pedal, panting anxiety until she regained control. Nearly invisible under the sheen of wetness, the yellow line in the center of the highway alternated between a broken dash and a double bar as the road sloped upward into a series of switchback curves walled in by trees and boulders.

Natalie slowed to an exasperating crawl, squinting to read each road sign in the fleeting clarity provided by the swipe of the windshield wipers. At the same time, she glanced at the rearview mirror to make sure George's headlights were still behind her, fretted every time they disappeared around a bend. The radio station she'd switched on to take her mind

off where she was going—and who was waiting for her—
dissolved into asthmatic white noise, the signal blocked by
the surrounding mountains.

Finally, a small blue rectangle bearing the white words
VISTA POINT appeared at the side of the road, directing vehicles
to a scenic turnout. As instructed, Natalie steered the car into
the semicircular detour, switched off her engine and headlights, and turned on her blinking orange hazard lights.

On the road to her right, George's car—or the car she assumed was his—whizzed past her in a spray of water. Had he
seen her turn off? Was he planning to wait farther up the
highway to tail her?

She touched the hard lump of the transmitter between
her legs and prayed that it actually worked. It occurred to her
that George might be trying to retrieve Callie for the Corps,
but that hardly mattered now. Not if he could save her child's
life.

Natalie gazed out the windshield at the black vacancy of
the view. Time stretched to intolerable length, drawn out by
the nerve-racking click of the emergency blinkers. Did she
have the meeting time wrong? Was this the right scenic
turnout? It was the first one she'd noticed. Had she missed
one somewhere? With the rain and the dark . . .

The rearview mirror ricocheted the blinding glare of a
pair of high-set headlights toward her, and Natalie shaded
her eyes. A moment later, a man's fist rapped loudly on the
driver's side window. She rolled it down, narrowing her eyelids against the rain that blew inside.

Lyman Pearsall bent forward to peer at her from beneath
the brim of his water-soaked fisherman's cap. Seeing him
without his mustache for the first time, Natalie knew he was
the "nurse" who killed her mother.

"Let's go," he said.

It wasn't until she got out of the Toyota and into his white Bronco that she saw the long-barreled gun in his hand.

She brushed the sodden strands of her wig off her forehead. "You don't need that."

"Maybe. And maybe I don't need these, either." Still pointing the gun at her, he plucked two ratcheted plastic bands out of the pocket in the driver's side door. "You know how this works, don't you?"

Natalie sighed and held her hands out to him, wrists together.

With comical clumsiness, Pearsall tried to bind her wrists with one hand so he could keep the gun trained on her with the other. He even tried to pull the band tight with his teeth.

"Don't make me use this," he muttered as if doing a bad '30s gangster impression, shaking the gun at her before laying it on the dashboard.

Obviously, Vincent Thresher was elsewhere. As Lyman fumbled to bind her ankles together and buckle her seat belt, Natalie scanned the rear of the Bronco, which was vacant. "Where's Callie?"

"She's all right. She's . . . being cared for."

With Natalie's limbs immobilized, Pearsall gave her a cursory pat-down search for weapons. As she'd hoped, his quivering hands skimmed over her breasts and crotch, and he seemed relieved to withdraw to the driver's seat. Natalie gathered that women made him uncomfortable. Given what she'd read about his past, she almost pitied him.

She glanced at the gun that still lay on the dashboard, considered making a grab for it and forcing Pearsall to take her to Callie. But Thresher was already with her daughter— *inside* her daughter—and if anything went wrong . . .

"You don't have to obey him," Natalie said softly as Lyman started the engine.

Without appearing to hear her, he threw the SUV into gear and squealed out of the turnout. The gun nearly slid off the dash, but Pearsall caught it and shoved it in the basket attached to the driver's seat.

Natalie waited about a mile's distance and tried again. "Look . . . those things you did—I know that wasn't *you*. I know you aren't capable of anything like that."

"Shut up." The wetness on his face gave it a waxy sheen.

"I can help you get rid of him."

"SHUT UP!" He snatched the gun out of the basket and aimed at her, his head swiveling between her and the road ahead. "There's only one way to get rid of him. You'll find out. Now, are you gonna keep your mouth shut, or do I have to gag you?"

Natalie shook her head and lay back against the headrest. Her gaze flicked to the convex mirror attached to the passenger door, the one that cautioned that reflected objects might be closer than they appeared. A pair of headlights had swung in behind the Bronco. Was it George?

Pearsall noticed them, too. His eyes squinting with suspicion, he pulled over into the slow lane as soon as a brief passing lane became available. The car behind them refused to pass.

Cursing, Lyman waited until the road's shoulder widened enough for him to pull over and stop. The tailgating car zoomed ahead of them, too fast for Natalie to be sure it really was George.

Exhaling pent-up breath, Pearsall resumed driving, but before long another set of headlights—or was it the same set?—trailed their rear bumper. Lyman pulled over again, and again the vehicle sped past them. Only this time it was a red pickup, not George's car. Pearsall shook his head and drove, but then another pair of lights appeared . . .

They continued to play leapfrog with every car that came along as they wound their way up one side of the mountain and down into the valley on the other side. The rain grew so heavy that the windshield resembled the rippled refraction of a shower door. After more than an hour, they turned off Route 20 onto Route 29 toward Lower Lake, the road leveled, and patches of civilization appeared along the highway: a Wal-Mart, a convenience store, a half-dozen vineyards, and a couple of small wineries.

A green sign with reflective white letters gave the number of miles to the nearest towns, Lakeport among them. The name jarred Natalie's memory. Dan's family lived around here somewhere, his parents and his . . . brother, was it? He'd never told her how to contact them, and she hadn't taken the trouble to find out. She didn't know how to tell the Atwaters that she'd conceived a child out of wedlock with Dan and that she was at least partly responsible for his death, since he'd been shot while trying to save her from the Violet Killer. Now, since Pearsall had forbidden idle conversation in the car, Natalie had no choice but to dwell on how she'd denied Callie another set of grandparents.

I swear I'll make it up to you, baby girl, she silently promised, but couldn't help adding the qualifier: *if we get out of this alive.*

They left the highway and wound down the road that wormed between the edge of Clear Lake and the base of Mount Konocti, a brush-covered extinct volcano. A single pair of headlights followed them into the stand of towering evergreens that a road sign labeled BLACK FOREST. The car mimicked every wrong turn and detour Pearsall made to lose it, and he mumbled a continuous string of expletives, frustrated as a snake trying to shake the rattle from its tail. Every now and then, he glared at Natalie, but she gazed blankly out the side window, acting as if she hadn't noticed either the car pursuing them or the distress it caused him.

Then, of its own accord, the car steered down a side street, leaving them alone among the trees. Lyman watched the rearview mirror more than the road as he made several more false turns, waiting for the pursuer to reappear. It didn't.

Natalie tightened her thighs around the hidden tracking device.

When the road remained dark behind them, the tension on Pearsall's face eased a bit, and he navigated the Bronco out of the woods and back into a more open, cultivated area of vineyards and pear orchards. Once confined safely to the horizon, lightning now split the air directly ahead of them. The crack of the thunderclap came so close behind the bolt that they seemed simultaneous.

Lyman hung a right onto a country lane in which runoff from the surrounding cow pastures and walnut orchards sluiced down to meet rising floodwaters from the lake. The Bronco nearly sank to its bumpers as it rolled past empty houses where water lapped at the doors. The SUV came to rest at the end of the street in front of a two-story house that resembled a painting askew on its hanger.

Natalie assumed the cockeyed cant of the house was a trick of perspective caused by the water churning around it. That was before Lyman cut her ankles loose and commanded her at gunpoint to wade through the front door. The moment she splashed into the entryway, Natalie instinctively leaned to counter the house's tilt, resulting in a sense of seasick disequilibrium.

She gaped in outraged horror at the interior lagoon that overspread the hardwood floor. "You left my daughter here? Alone?"

"Not alone." Pearsall ignited the cold moon-fire of a fluorescent lantern and waved her forward with the barrel of his gun.

Skirting the central stairway, they splashed into the mildew-spotted living room, where empty rectangles of white on the dirty walls framed the ghosts of absent pictures. Here the floor sloped downward like the bottom of a swimming pool, the water growing deeper toward the rear of the house. The shag pile of the saturated carpet oozed like tide-pool algae under Natalie's boots.

The only furnishing in the room was a tarnished brass bed, which faced the sliding glass door that overlooked the man-made channel behind the house. The channel had overflowed the wooden pylons that held back the soil of the bank, submerging the backyard and bringing the lake into the living room. The bed now resembled a raft, the tails of its sheets floating on the surface of the rising water. Sitting cross-legged on the mattress, lit by another fluorescent lantern and surrounded by half-eaten packets of Oscar Mayer Lunchables and empty water bottles, Callie gazed out the glass door at the flashing tempest over the lake with calm, even avid, fascination.

Please don't let her turn around, Natalie prayed, staring at the slim crescent of her daughter's cheek that was visible from that angle. *Don't let me see her with his smile.*

As if in response to her thoughts, Callie suddenly straightened her posture and cocked her head to one side, like a cat sensing the proximity of a mouse. Despite the oversized down jacket she wore, she suddenly began shivering, as if a heavy blanket had been yanked from her shoulders. Then she looked over her shoulder, and Natalie saw her little girl's face, lonely, longing, and afraid. "Mommy?"

Heedless of Pearsall and his gun, Natalie ran to the bed and looped her bound arms around Callie, crushing her to her chest and pecking kisses on the top of her head. "Yes, baby girl, it's me."

"Can I go home now?" Callie sniffled.

"That depends on your mama." Pearsall's voice interrupted before Natalie could answer.

She glanced back at where she'd left him, the lantern in one hand, the gun in the other, both directed at Natalie. He stood straighter now, and the nervous palsy in his expression had vanished, replaced by an arrogant amusement.

Natalie grimaced. "Mr. Thresher, I presume."

He smiled and gave a slight bow.

"I came to accept your offer, whatever it is, as long as you let Callie live." Natalie rocked her daughter to soothe her. "Kill me if you want, just let her go."

Callie's arms tightened on her. "No, Mommy!"

"Hush, sweetheart." Natalie cast a defiant glare at Thresher. "Well?"

He chuckled. "You've got me all wrong. I don't want to kill you." Lightning flickered in the window behind him. "I want to *be* you."

33

Family Reunions

NATALIE'S FACE BECAME AS CLAMMY AS HER WATER-soaked feet. "What do you mean?"

Thresher clucked Pearsall's tongue. "Oh, come on, Natalie. You can see my buddy Lyman isn't good for much longer." He gave a wry glance down at his host body's paunch. "Now, *you*—you look like you take care of yourself."

Vomit hiccuped in her throat as she imagined sharing his orgiastic glee for torture, carrying out his depravities. "You want me to be your puppet."

"I find the term 'personal assistant' more flattering, don't you? But you've got the general idea."

"And if I won't?"

"Well . . . I've got other options." His gaze lowered to Callie, who whimpered and tried to burrow deeper into Natalie's bosom.

"And if I cooperate? You'll leave her alone forever, for the rest of her life?"

"Absolutely." He raised his right hand, which still held the gun. "On my honor as a gentleman."

"All right, then." *Come on, George,* she thought, clenching her thighs around the tracking device again. *I don't know how much longer I can vamp here.*

"I knew you'd see it my way. Your mom, she resisted me for twenty years, but I could tell you were a more reasonable sort. In place of a handshake, shall we seal the deal with . . . a little display of trust?" His expression stiffened from condescending to commanding. "Tell me your protective mantra."

A shudder fluttered inside her like a panicked canary, but she threw a sheet over the cage. Her protective mantra enabled her to reconnect with her body when another soul inhabited her. If Thresher knew it, she'd have no defense against him. It was like giving him the key to her house; he could come and go as he pleased.

"It's Hamlet," she said. "You know—the 'To be or not to be' speech."

Thresher laughed. "That's cute. You've got a sense of humor—I like that. Let's brush up our Shakespeare, shall we? Come on. Summon me." He aimed the gun at Callie. "Now."

"Okay." Natalie gently disengaged herself from her daughter. "Don't worry, honey," she whispered, and backed away from the bed.

When she saw Pearsall's face soften to its usual sullen befuddlement, Natalie shut her eyes and started murmuring *Row, row, row your boat* in her mind.

For an instant, she could feel Margaret Thresher's soul pushing at the boundaries of her consciousness, drawn by the touchstone of the blouse Natalie wore. Mother and son threatened to reunite inside Natalie's head. Knowing from experience that such a multiple summoning could induce a seizure, Natalie focused on the thoughts that would attract only Vincent Thresher—the visions of pinprick torture and dewdrop blood she'd seen when he last inhabited her.

He snapped into her skull as if jerked there by stretched elastic.

Natalie opened her eyes to find her hands already outstretched toward Callie, a vision in her mind of what it would be like to twist that small head around on its neck until it came off in her hands . . .

"Mommy?" The pitch of Callie's voice rose in fear as her mother advanced toward the bed. "Are you okay?"

Immediately Natalie switched to the Twenty-third Psalm. Eavesdropping on Thresher's thoughts, she heard him make it as far as "perchance to dream" before he slipped back into the ether.

Pearsall let out a cry, dropping the lantern in the water and stumbling back against the windowsill behind him as if he'd been struck. He held on to the gun, though, and by the time he pushed himself upright, he was already laughing. Ripples of light from the submerged lantern drifted across his shadowed face, as if he were standing over an aquarium. "O ye of little faith!"

"You lied," Natalie shot back. "You said you wouldn't hurt her."

"And I wouldn't have. That was a test, and you failed." He shook his head with a *tsk-tsk* sound. "Now, are you going to give me the *real* protective mantra, or will Callie end up like poor Nora? I can do that, you know. Even if she kicks me out every time, I'll keep knocking, every second of every day, for the rest of her miserable little existence."

Time to play the hole card, Natalie thought. "Speaking of which, I feel someone knocking right now . . ."

She was about to summon Margaret Thresher when silver lightning shimmered in the window behind Pearsall. The flash outlined a looming figure that might have been his shadow, for it, too, held a gun.

Vincent Thresher saw Natalie's gaze shift and wheeled around.

Thunder magnified the gunshot and crash of glass as shards exploded into the room. The bullet grazed Pearsall's right shoulder, but Thresher kept the Violet on his feet. George aimed his Glock through the jagged hole in the window for another shot, but Thresher fired first. Rather than the expected report, the gun made a spitting sound and launched a needled dart into George's left eye. It was the first time Natalie had ever seen him without his trademark shades, and he'd paid the price for it.

Yowling, George dropped the Glock into the water and clapped his hands over his eye as a tear of blood streaked down his cheek. The tranquilizer dose must not have been strong enough for his hulking size, however, for he vaulted over the windowsill, streaming water like an enraged merman, and caught Thresher in a flying tackle.

Natalie lunged to scoop Callie off the bed. She also grabbed the remaining fluorescent lantern, brandishing it like a weapon.

The dart still lodged in his eye, George grabbed Pearsall's hair, but the toupee slid off the Violet's bald scalp. When Thresher flailed to throw George off him, the Corps agent pushed him in the water.

"Get out of here!" He struggled to hold Pearsall down as bubbles streamed from the Violet's submerged face. "The key's in my car. Take it."

Natalie didn't have time to thank him. With a wrestler's roll, Thresher flopped George onto his back. He now held an open jackknife in Pearsall's hand, and he plunged its blade into George's chest. There was a sickening rip and George screamed.

Thresher raised the knife for another stab but saw Natalie running toward the front door, Callie in her arms. Tearing himself from George's weakened grasp, he charged to intercept them, driving Natalie back from the door with swipes of his blood-sheened blade.

Natalie deflected the knife feints with the lantern, Callie clutched in the crook of her left arm, crying into her ear. Thresher pressed forward, nicked the back of Natalie's hand with one slash, made her back up until she felt her heel hit the base of the staircase. He was herding her, forcing her to retreat upstairs, where she and Callie would be trapped.

Sweeping the heavy lantern around in an arc at arm's length, Natalie hurled it at his head. It smacked his brow, knocking him off balance, and he let out a furious growl as he dropped to the floor. The lantern clattered beside him, bathing the hardwood in pale fairy light.

Hands grasped at Natalie's ankles as she leapt for the front door again. She shook her legs free but stumbled. Top heavy with the child she carried, she couldn't stop the momentum from taking her down.

Like a football fumbled on the five-yard line, Callie slipped from her hands.

She yelped in pain, and Natalie scrambled toward the sound. A boot-kick to her ribs left her gasping. Unable to move as the impact sent shock waves through her body, Natalie heard Callie's shriek rise to crystal-shattering pitch, then recede into hollowness. Bootsteps thudded up the stairs, thumped on the ceiling over Natalie's head. Somewhere in the house, a door slammed.

"NO!" Natalie crawled over to the stairs and pulled herself upright with the baluster. Holding her throbbing side, she stooped to pick up the fallen lantern but wavered, torn by conscience.

She shone the light into the living room but couldn't see around the corner. "George?"

"I'm okay." He coughed, rasping phlegm. "Get her."

Natalie pictured him lying there on his back, unable to rise, the tail of the dart still sticking out of his eye, red fluid welling from his chest only to dissipate in the surrounding water.

"I'll come back," she promised. Bracing herself against the banister, she limped up the crooked staircase.

Three closed doors awaited her on the uneven second-floor landing. Natalie listened, but heard only the rat-patter of rain on the roof. She advanced to the first door, hesitated only a second when she saw the red *X* plastered on it like the crossed bones on a poison bottle.

Afraid Thresher might be waiting just over the threshold, she pushed the door in and skittered back, thrusting the lantern in front of her like a crucifix. Only the dull glint of aluminum foil emerged from the room. Yet as Natalie swept the light around the chamber, saw its interior sealed with insulation and metal and recognized it for what it was, its apparent emptiness made the bristles of hair beneath her wig stand up.

A soul cage.

She barely had time to register the thought before the knocking started. The lantern fell, forgotten, as her arms went slack, her fingernails gouging the heels of her clenched hands. She slumped to the floor and jittered there, every muscle in her body contracting at once, while the wheels of two souls ground her consciousness between them. Natalie's mind fragmented as she witnessed the same scene from three points of view simultaneously—hers and theirs.

The door to the master bedroom burst open while they were unwinding in bed before sleep. He glanced up from his business records, she from her book. The figure they saw before them would have been laughable but for the double-barreled shotgun in its hands—an overgrown trick-or-treater in a thrown-together Halloween costume. The black turtleneck and jeans, the New Balance basketball shoes, and that navy ski mask with the diamond pattern—why, she'd given that mask to Scotty that last time he went to Park City.

The whole outfit revealed more than concealed the identity of the slim boy who wore it, who aimed the gun at the father who'd taught him to shoot. The father was about to ask if this was some kind of a sick joke when the first barrel fired, slamming a meteor crater into his chest.

As the father's corpse fell back, the mother pitched forward. "WHAT ARE YOU DOING?" she screeched at the face behind the ski mask. In answer, the figure lifted the shotgun until her right eye nearly looked down the second barrel. In the instant between the click of the cocked hammer and the eruption of smoke and lead, she saw the figure in the ski mask pinch his eyes shut . . .

Twin revenants, Press and Betsy Hyland vied to breathe their fury into Natalie's brain, the outrage at their son's betrayal and their imprisonment after death. She pushed against them with her protective mantra, crowded them out of her mind by filling it with her psalm.

He restoreth my soul . . .

Her limbs relaxed, fully hers again. She didn't take time to recover but instead seized the lantern and hobbled to the next bedroom.

Yea, though I walk through the valley of the shadow of death, I will fear no evil . . .

She threw open the second door seared with a red X, and again a soul insane from anguish and solitude sank desperate, clinging claws into her thoughts. Natalie could feel how her naked skin had stuck to the vinyl upholstery of a car's backseat, could smell the musk of aftershave and sweat of the half-nude man who sat on top of her, could see Avram Ries grit his bleached-white teeth in ecstatic frenzy as he tightened the bra around her neck . . .

Natalie nudged Samantha Winslow's spirit from her mind, but gently, as if encouraging a captive bird to fly free.

A quick scan of the bedroom's foil-lined interior confirmed that it was vacant. That left only one door to open. The one without an X.

Once again Natalie twisted the knob, shoved the door, and shied back. She needn't have bothered; Thresher placidly waited for her at the back of the room, at the limit of the lantern light's reach. The burgundy blot on his right shoulder had smudged Callie's cheek as he coiled a hand over her mouth to keep her quiet.

"Ah! I wondered how long it would take you to join us." He idly tapped the blade of his jackknife on his lips. "Now, as I recall, we had discussed a business arrangement before we were so rudely interrupted. Have you reconsidered my offer?" Thresher jerked Callie's head back and brushed the edge of the knife's blade over the delicate baby fat of her neck. "Think carefully before you answer."

Measuring her breaths, Natalie slowly lowered herself to the floor and set the lantern beside her. "I've made my decision."

"And?"

Row, row, row your boat . . .

"I'll open myself." She ran her hands over the sleeves of Margaret Thresher's blouse as numbness tingled in her fingertips. "But not to you."

Vincent Thresher shouted something then, a warning not to play any tricks, but Natalie barely heard it, for Margaret poured into her like spillage from a dam's floodgate. She heaved forward, mop-string hair falling over her face as she convulsed to the tempo of the lightning that strobed in the windows.

"What's going on? What are you doing?" For the first time, Thresher's voice lacked its customary cockiness.

. . . life is but a dream.

With the detachment of a passenger staring out a train window, Natalie felt her body stop thrashing, watched it get to its feet. Parting the hanging draperies of Natalie's wig, Margaret Thresher shot glances around the abandoned bedroom—at the storm flashing outside, at the pond of flourescent light on the barren floor, at the stranger in the shadows who held a knife to the throat of a little girl.

"What is this place?" There was no panic in her voice, merely the pessimism of a cynic for whom hell holds no surprises. "Who are you?"

Maybe the rain had straightened the curls of Natalie's brown wig, or perhaps the makeup she'd applied held up better than she expected. More likely, Margaret replicated her characteristic scowl on Natalie's face, her gaze sweeping over Lyman Pearsall's form like a prison searchlight. Whatever the reason, Vincent Thresher trembled inside Pearsall's skin.

"Mama." He let the hand that held the jackknife fall to his lap.

"Who are you?" Margaret snapped again. "What are you doing with that girl?"

That's your son, Vincent—or Vanessa, if you prefer, Natalie told her in the mind they now shared. *The man you see there brought his soul back the same way I brought yours back.*

"Vanessa? Ha!" One corner of Natalie's mouth curled up in a bitter half grin. "I only *wish* I had a daughter."

Thresher raised the knife to Callie's throat again, but couldn't keep the blade steady. "Make her go away. I'm telling you, *get rid of her.*"

He wants to kill that girl, Natalie said, *just like he killed you.*

Margaret approached Pearsall until she loomed over him, studying his face with dark amusement. "So you found some sucker to hide in, eh, little boy? Couldn't take your punishment like a man."

Thresher looked up at her with the terror of a small child about to be beaten. "Go away! Go back where I sent you."

She snorted her disdain. "I should've known it was hopeless to try to change you. You always were like your father, Vincent—he killed me *years* before you did."

"You don't understand, Mama . . ."

"I understand that I should have smothered you in your cradle the moment I saw that thing between your legs!"

Thresher groaned, a buckling board about to break. "You don't get it! I wanted to make you happy. *I'm going to be a girl,* like you always wanted. If you'd leave me alone—"

"A girl?" Margaret laughed, a sound like corn being husked. "You aren't fit to be a man, much less a woman."

"*STOP IT!*" With one arm still clamped around Callie, he thrust the knife toward his mother. Toward Natalie's midriff.

Watching from the back of her own mind, Natalie gave a mental gasp, but Margaret didn't even blink. She leaned over the exposed blade to peer directly into Pearsall's eyes. "You think that scares me? You may have got the better of me with your needles and knives when we were alive, but you were no match for me dead, were you? By God, if I ever get you to myself again, I'll make you homesick for the gas chamber."

Thresher dropped the knife and cowered against the wall, wetness seeping from his shut eyelids. "D-don't l-l-look at me like that."

"Like what, Vincent? Like the pathetic worm you are? Not such a big man without a knife in your hand, are you? Disgusting little wretch! Why, that girl you're holding is stronger and smarter than you'll ever be—"

A wail, half banshee howl, half baby's bawl, shrilled from Pearsall's throat. When it ended, the fat cheeks sagged into a look of dumb astonishment. Vincent Thresher was gone.

Natalie immediately switched to her protective mantra, exiling Margaret Thresher from her body. *The Lord is my shepherd, I shall not want . . .*

Lyman Pearsall blinked Thresher's tears out of his eyes. Callie renewed her wriggling in his grasp, and he let go of her, shrank from her as if she had the plague. She scuttled back from him to hug Natalie's thigh.

Like Rip Van Winkle, Pearsall trembled as he gaped at them, at the dark bedroom, at the wound in his shoulder, for he sensed that his world had changed irrevocably.

"Where are you?" He searched the dust-laden air, a slave terrified of sudden liberation. "You can't leave *now. Come back here!* Come . . . oh, God, no."

Lyman's fat hands fluttered to his head, his cheeks quivering as he moaned. Natalie drew back, tugging Callie with her, in case Thresher had answered Pearsall's plea.

The tremor that began in his head rippled through the rest of his bulk, until he looked like a rag doll thrashed by an angry child. Drool frothed over his lower lip. "No! Stop! *I didn't kill you! One penny, two penny, three*—NO!"

Pearsall's protective mantra couldn't save him. Without Thresher to inhabit him, to act as his armor, Lyman lay open to the souls of three murder victims he'd imprisoned, who dove and tore at his mind like eagles ripping a bleeding rabbit.

As his cries devolved into a blubbering yammer, Natalie hoisted Callie into her arms and hurried toward the stairs. Huffing yogic breaths to soothe the pincerlike pain in her side, she lurched down to the ground floor, guiding herself with the banister and descending one step at a time in the darkness.

When she got to the bottom, she set Callie down and pulled her into the living room to check on George. Much as Natalie had imagined, he lay in the rising floodwaters, the submerged lantern behind him limning his body with a corona of silver-blue luminescence. By some superhuman effort, he'd pulled the tranquilizer dart out of his eye, which brimmed in the socket like a smashed egg.

She ran and knelt beside him, saw that his chest still rose shallowly. "George? Can you hear me?"

"Yeah. But you—you better get a doctor . . . or I'm gonna be the next one knocking on your head." His chuckle became a cough, and red spittle ran from his mouth.

Natalie peeled back the hand he held against the right side of his chest, revealing a gash that ran between his ribs. Dark bubbles surfaced when the wound whistled.

She tried to keep a nurse's calm in her voice. "Do you have a cell phone?"

"Car," he said in a drowsy mumble.

"Okay, George. Hang on while I move you to higher ground." Taking hold of his feet, Natalie leveraged her weight to drag his golem body a few feet toward the shallow end of the living room. "Hope—your—Corps insurance is paid up," she grunted, grinning, as she pulled.

"No Corps. Quit." He raised his head as if lifting the earth, turned his remaining eye toward Callie, who stood behind her mother, watching intently. "Is she . . . ?"

"She's fine." Natalie pressed her hand on top of the one he held over his chest, but couldn't find words to express her gratitude.

George gave one nod, let his head rest.

Water filled her vision. *"George!"*

His right eye reopened.

"I'm going to get help. Don't go to sleep. Understand?"

He nodded.

Natalie gave him a shaky smile. "You'll see. This'll make a great scene in your book."

The corners of his mouth bent upward. *"Oui."*

His eye closed again, and Natalie palpated his neck. The pulse was faint but there. She swept Callie into her arms again and dashed out the front door into the sparking storm.

George's rented Buick sat a few yards behind Pearsall's Bronco, its wheels nearly engulfed by the churning current in the road. Water sloshed over the door frame to soak the interior carpet when Natalie opened the car to set Callie in the passenger seat. Two electronic devices had been tossed on the dash: a PDA-style unit that appeared to be a portable global positioning system map display and a small Nokia phone. Natalie punched 911 on the handset's keypad and held it to her ear, praying that the storm wouldn't interfere with the connection.

Mute from apparent shock until then, Callie kicked and fussed with hysterical impatience. "What are we waiting for?" she whined. "Let's *go*, Mama! I want to go *NOW!*"

A click and a crackle in Natalie's ear. "Emergency services," the operator said, his voice fuzzed with static. "How may we help?"

Natalie didn't answer. Her damp skin goose-pimpling, she laid the phone on the dashboard and looked at her daughter.

Callie had never called her Mama.

"What's your favorite bedtime story?" Natalie asked her.

"What? What are you talking about? Let's *go*." She pouted, her hand fidgeting in the right pocket of her man-size jacket.

Natalie ignored the squeaking of the 911 operator. "What have you got there?"

Callie's petulant frown abruptly inverted, became a vulpine smirk. "Let me show you."

She lashed out with Vincent Thresher's jackknife, the blade biting Natalie's cheek.

Natalie tried to grab her arm, but Callie parried and jabbed, slashing her mother's hands. With a gasp of pain, Natalie caught hold of the blade itself to twist it from Callie's grip. Snarling, the girl yanked it back, leaving a deep, leaking slit in Natalie's palm.

Callie put the pointed tip of the knife to her own jugular, her teeth gritted in Thresher's grin. "Last chance, Natalie. Let me in *now*."

She held back the despairing wail in her throat. "Callie, I

know you're in there. If you can hear me, call Daddy. You hear me, Callie? *Call Daddy.*"

Dismissive at first, Thresher's smile faltered. The knife quivered as two expressions seemed to fight for Callie's face.

"*No.*" Thresher fought to steady Callie's hand, but her brows knit in pleading. "Don't. You can't send me back to *her* again. I—must—stay . . ."

Natalie's breath quickened. "That's it, Callie. Bring Daddy inside you. He'll make the bad Who go away."

Her daughter shuddered and dropped the knife, pressing her hands over her ears to shut out a harangue only Thresher could hear. "Shut up, Mama! Just shut up! *I'd kill you again if I could, you old hag!*" His terror shrilled Callie's voice to a shriek, and he pulled her body into a fetal ball as if to shield himself from the vise of Margaret's embrace. "SHUT UP SHUT UP SHUT UP—"

A strangled sob of exorcism choked off the words. Natalie snatched up the knife, watching warily as Callie's face smoothed into a blank mask with no identity to mold it. Gradually familiarity returned to the features—the wry crinkle at the corners of the eyes, the impish jut of the chin—but with a more mature attitude than Callie possessed.

She looked more like her father than ever.

"Hello, Natalie," she said.

"Dan." She extended a hand, realized she'd be caressing her daughter, not her lover, and withdrew her touch. "Thank God you came."

"You know I can never resist you two." Callie's face flared with the brightness of his wistful smile, grew somber again. "I'm glad I could help . . . but I can't come back anymore."

Sharp sorrow pierced Natalie's relief. "What do you mean?"

"I feel it calling to me—the place beyond—and I know I have to go there. I know it's the right thing."

Natalie let her head droop. "For Callie's sake."

"No. For yours."

Her face crumpled, and salt strands trailed down her cheeks. It was like losing him all over again.

She realized then that this was what death was for most people—the rending certainty of separation, the absolute end of hope for resurrection and reunion in this world. As a Violet, she had kept Dan's immaterial presence as a crutch in her life, leaning on it and limping long after an ordinary person would have walked unaided and alone. Now Natalie snatched at the shared memories of their love as if they would fly into the void with Dan, leaving her with nothing. They were all she would have of him until the next time they met, when she went to him.

"I miss you," she said. "Even when you're inside me, I miss you."

"I know. I'll miss you your whole life." Callie's eyes twinkled with sudden humor, and she smiled Dan's smile. "By the way . . . has anyone ever told you you look good as a brunette?"

Natalie mopped the scraggly strands of her drenched wig off her forehead, sniffed, and chuckled. "Not for a long, long time."

"Someone will." The smile broadened. Neither Dan nor Natalie said good-bye, for that would have been unnecessary and unbearable.

Then Callie's lips shrank back to a small oval, and her eyes grew shiny with sadness. She had never looked so much like her mother before.

"We can't call Daddy anymore, can we?" she asked.

"No, honey." Natalie swallowed the tightness in her throat. "We won't have to. He'll never really leave us."

And though she still needed to phone the paramedics and the police and attend to George's wounds, Natalie took a few precious moments to hug her daughter as they both wept.

34

Hysterical Inhabitations

THE NEW RESIDENT OF ROOM 9 AT THE LOS ANGELES Mental Health Institute was screaming again. The latest sedative had worn off half an hour earlier, and now he pressed himself into one corner of the room, his hand swatting at his head as if trying to stave off a swarm of bats.

"*One penny, two penny, three penny*—GET AWAY FROM ME! GET AWAY!"

His violet eyes rolled in their sockets, and a V-shaped sweat stain darkened the neck of his cotton hospital robe. Black stubble had grown on his legs, arms, face, and scalp, but one could still see the constellation of node points on his crown.

Natalie peered at him through the door's open peephole. "Well?" she asked Inez, who stood beside her.

The prosecutor shook her head. "They doubt he'll ever recover enough to stand trial. Not that it matters, since the Corps won't let us charge him anyway."

"Should've seen that coming. Anything to keep it out of the papers." She glanced at the uniformed LAPD officer posted at the door. "Is security tight enough here?"

"For the time being. Now that we've done the psych evaluation, we hope to send him to Atascadero."

Natalie nodded, watching Lyman Pearsall cower in his madness. "Are the souls still knocking?"

"Not according to the SoulScan readings. Whatever they did to his mind, he's now doing to himself."

Just like Mom, Natalie thought, sliding the peephole's door shut.

"How's Callie?" Inez asked as they walked back toward the entrance of the locked ward.

"Getting better." This was an overstatement rather than an outright lie. Her daughter only woke screaming once last night rather than four or five times, and she remained silent and withdrawn for mere hours at a time rather than entire days. She demanded to sleep in Natalie's bed and insisted that the bedside lamp stay on all night.

"What about the Corps?"

"They still want her, of course. They say the fact that Thresher inhabited her only proves that she needs the School's protection and training." Natalie recalled Callie's sweet visage slashed by Thresher's scimitar grin. "Maybe they're right."

"You can protect and train her better than any School." The steely Patton determination had returned to Inez's voice. "Where is she now?"

"With my dad. We're staying at a different hotel every night and going to Disneyland every day, just in case the Corps tries to take her into 'protective custody' again. I've got a lawyer now, but . . . you know what they say."

" 'You can't fight the N-double-A-C-C'? Don't believe it. Keep your daughter, Natalie."

She remembered George saying almost the same thing in French. George now lay in critical condition in an ICU at Sutter Lakeside Hospital in Lakeport. The doctors managed to replace the blood he'd lost but said he might lose his left lung as well as his right eye. The small tranquilizer dose the dart gave him might actually have saved George's life by preventing him from going into shock due to exsanguination.

Natalie pushed away the image of George in his hospital bed with a respirator hose, IV tubes, and EKG wires all sprouting from him, and changed the subject. "What are you doing with Avery Park?"

"Letting him go," Inez said. " 'Upon further investigation, we found that the Hylands were killed by an unknown assailant whom the victims mistook for Park' . . . or at least that's the cock-and-bull story the D.A. and the Corps are feeding the press."

Natalie made a face. "So Scott Hyland gets to spend his parents' money happily ever after."

An orderly—a white guy about seven feet tall—let them out of the ward. Andy had either taken an extended sabbatical or retired from the mental health care profession entirely.

As they emerged into the lobby, Inez gave a fatalistic half smile. She'd taken to wearing her crucifix prominently even when outside the courtroom. "I guess we'll have to leave Scott to the Last Judgment."

"I suppose."

But the injustice of the situation niggled at Natalie like a sliver embedded in her side. It pricked her again when she went out to her car and saw George's replacement—a bored, buttoned-down yuppie in a black VW Beetle—waiting beside the Volvo. She wished she could teach both Scott *and* the Corps a lesson.

Digging through her purse for her keys, Natalie came across the creased and grimy business card Sid Preston had given her during the Hyland trial. She'd meant to throw it away, but now grinned with wicked glee that she'd forgotten about it.

As soon as she got in the car, she took out the cell phone she'd bought to keep in touch with Wade and Callie and entered the number on the card.

"Mr. Preston?" she asked when his flat, nasal voice answered. "This is Natalie Lindstrom. Look, I've thought it over and . . . would you still be interested in that exclusive interview with the Hylands?"

35

Scott Free

THE DAY THE ARTICLE CAME OUT, SCOTT HYLAND
awoke around noon, having partied at a rave in Westwood
until almost three the night before. He'd been going out a lot
lately, with or without Danielle. He needed to keep active—it
kept his mind off . . . things.

Lounging in the rumpled hipness of red-white-and-blue
Tommy Hilfiger sheets, hands folded behind his head, he
surveyed with sleepy satisfaction the amenities of his new
custom-designed bedroom, which the contractors had finished redecorating only yesterday: tiled mirrors on the ceiling,
full wet bar in the corner, flat-screen plasma television and
entertainment center, Jacuzzi in the bathroom—everything
just the way he wanted it.

Until recently, this room had been an upstairs lounge and
library for his parents, and it cost Scott a bundle to convert it.
But it was worth it. Although he was now the legal master of
the Hyland mansion, Scott did not use the master bedroom.
Indeed, he never set foot in that chamber, despite the fact
that every inch of blood-matted carpet had been ripped out
and replaced with fresh, polyester-scented shag, white as a
nun's conscience.

Still lazing in bed, Scott grabbed the cordless phone from
its cradle on the nightstand and punched in Danielle's num-

ber, holding the receiver over his face so he didn't have to lift his head from the pillow. He'd wanted to spend his first night on this new king-size mattress with her, but her dad had grounded her. Truth be told, Mr. Larchmont loathed Scott and used any excuse to keep Danielle away from him, but she'd promised to meet him later that day, maybe have a late lunch at Jerry's Deli.

The phone rang once before a recorded voice informed him that he had been blocked from calling that number.

Annoyed, he tried the number again to make sure he'd dialed correctly. Same result.

Probably her old man, he thought, and entered her cell phone number instead.

He got the same canned female voice, telling him that that number had also been blocked.

Cursing, Scott sat up and dialed again but still couldn't get through. Whatever. He'd drop by her house later if she didn't call first.

He left the phone on the unmade bed and ambled downstairs in his boxer briefs, rubbing his left eyebrow where a small silver hoop now jutted. Scott had been without the ring so long that he'd had to have the stupid brow repierced, and it pinched his skin. After pouring himself a bowl of Lucky Charms in the kitchen, he carried his breakfast into the living room and switched on the big-screen.

As he levered up his feet in the Barcalounger and shoveled cereal in his mouth, ESPN returned from commercial to cover the final round of a poker championship: two guys staring at each other across a green felt tabletop. Why didn't they just film paint drying? Scott thumbed the remote control balanced on his armrest to flip to ESPN2. Some lumberjack contest. Make that a *lame*berjack contest.

Laughing at his own joke until milk nearly came out his nose, he started to surf through the thirty-odd satellite channels between the sports networks and MTV. Like a roulette ball landing on a losing number, the television happened to pause at CNN, where Scott saw his own grinning face in a boxed graphic over the anchor's left shoulder.

"—revelation of witness tampering has caused a scandal for the criminal justice system and the North American Afterlife Communications Corps," intoned the attractive brunette woman, who wore glasses that gave her a cute-librarian look. "Earlier this month, a jury found Hyland not guilty of murdering his parents based largely on the victims' dramatic courtroom testimony—testimony that now appears to have been fabricated to secure Hyland's release."

Scott lowered his spoon, his mouth full of half-masticated cereal.

"The deception came to light in a front-page article in this morning's *New York Post*," the anchor continued over footage of a newsstand vendor selling tabloid papers with the headline SCOTT DID IT! SAY SLAIN PARENTS in giant type. "When summoned by former N-double-A-C-C conduit Natalie Lindstrom, murder victims Prescott Hyland Sr. and Elizabeth Hyland both accused their son of shooting them, contradicting the testimony attributed to them during the trial."

An old family photo showed Scott's parents smiling proudly, arms around their three-year-old son.

"The Corps issued a swift denial of any wrongdoing and called Ms. Lindstrom's credibility into question, but several members of Congress have already demanded a full investigation. Immune from further prosecution due to double-jeopardy laws, Prescott Hyland Jr. could not be reached for comment but is presumed to be staying at the Bel Air home he inherited . . ."

An aerial shot of the house, like the glaring gaze of God, appeared onscreen, and Scott's skin crawled. There at the top of the driveway was the security gate that he'd had installed last week to keep the gawkers and paparazzi at bay. Behind it seethed a mass of camera crews, pulsing like a thirsty leech.

Spitting obscentities, Scott jumped from the easy chair, capsizing his cereal bowl onto the carpet. He ran to one of the front windows and looked out. A dozen telephoto lenses zoomed in on him. They hadn't been able to reach him by phone because he'd channeled all incoming calls through an answering service ever since the trial. But they knew he had to come out sometime, and they waited at the gate with the patience of buzzards, bloated with questions to ask.

A cold certainty settled on Scott, like the dripping, steaming quiet that follows the screeching crash of a head-on collision. He scrambled to the Rolodex beside the phone in the study and called everyone he knew, beginning with his closest friends and ending with those whose names he could barely remember. The same recording answered each time, another back turned to him.

He put down the phone and looked up from his dad's desk toward the gun cabinet. It, too, had been restored, its smashed front replaced by a pristine pane of glass. One notch of the rack inside remained glaringly empty, for the police kept the shotgun as evidence. But Scott's dad still possessed plenty of other guns, all of them loaded and ready for action.

Scott crossed to the cabinet and pushed the spring-loaded catch hidden in the carved wooden trim that opened the "locked" door. The keyhole was only for show: As Dad once told him, "You don't want to mess with keys if there's a God-damned killer in the house."

He fingered several of the handguns mounted on the

cabinet wall as if choosing what to wear from a closet full of suits. Scott knew which one he wanted, though. The shiny .44 Magnum revolver had always been his favorite when he and Dad went out for target practice at the range. Now that he thought about it, shooting was the only activity they ever really enjoyed doing together.

You want to blow the bastard's brains out, that's the gun to use, his old man's voice said again as Scott unhooked the .44 from its mounting brackets and squeezed the grip in his fist. The remembered words now sounded like a suggestion.

I don't need to do this. He spun the cylinder, made sure every chamber was full, snapped it shut. *I'm rich. The cops can't touch me. I can go to Mexico or Tahiti or wherever. I have my whole life ahead of me. My whole life . . .*

From the living room's entertainment center, Danielle Larchmont whined in stereo. "I didn't have a choice. He hit me, told me if I didn't help him, he'd do me like he did his parents."

The .44 dangling at the end of his slack right arm, Scott shuffled back to stare at the big-screen, where Danielle sniffled for the cameras. Reporters shouted questions, but they were silenced by the raised hand of Malcolm Lathrop.

"That's all Ms. Larchmont is able to tell you at the moment," the lawyer said, curling a protective arm around the girl and speaking into the microphones thrust at her. "Clearly, Scott Hyland is a disturbed individual who deceived us all, and any suggestion that Ms. Larchmont should pay for his crimes is an outrage. She's as much a victim of this sociopath as Prescott and Betsy Hyland, and we're prepared to prove that in court. Thank you—that's all for now." Ignoring the fusillade of follow-up queries, Lathrop shepherded Danielle into the seclusion of his limousine, the camera panting for them like an abandoned puppy.

With a throat-grating yell, Scott fired five shots at the big-screen, perforating it with bullet holes. Since the television used a projection system, however, he couldn't stop the image of Danielle riding away from him in the lawyer's stretched Lincoln.

His roar degenerated into a snivel, and he stumbled back to land butt-first on the floor. It didn't matter what he did or where he went, he realized. He would spend the rest of his life as he was now.

Alone.

No, not alone. Mom and Dad would never leave him. They were here now, all around him, *inside* him. You didn't need to be one of those violet-eyed freaks to hear the dead, he thought. They practically shouted at you if you listened.

Scott Hyland, who'd never listened to his parents when they were alive, could now hear nothing else. The strangled rage of his father's death rattle, his mother's shriek when he leveled the shotgun at her, the pumpkin crunch of her head as it blew apart . . .

With the same blank determination that propelled him on the night of last August twenty-first, Scott got to his feet and climbed the stairs. As he ascended, he checked the .44 again, confirming that one bullet remained.

An hour ago, it had been so easy to forget it all. To pretend that someone else really had done it. A burglar. Avery Park. Someone.

Entering the remodeled master bedroom for the first time, Scott crossed the Dacron snow of carpet to the handsome leather-upholstered couch that rested where his parents' bed had once been. The contractors had done a nice job.

The room was bright and white and pleasant, and still smelled of fresh paint. Scott sat on the sofa and cocked the pistol.

His parents called to him: *Scotty! Scotty!* Their tone wasn't angry. It was encouraging, the way they once urged him to take his first plunge off the swimming pool's diving board.

Eager to please them, he put the .44's barrel in his mouth and pulled the trigger.

36

One to Grow On

NATALIE CAPPED THE TUBE OF RED CAKE-DECORATING gel and stepped back to evaluate her artwork. She'd done her best to draw and color a wide-eyed Horton the elephant, copying the picture from one of her daughter's Dr. Seuss books. "WHO's six?" the pink-frosted cake asked. "CALLIE!!!"

She was about to put the candles on when she heard her dad unlock the cabin's front door. Natalie shoved the cake in the fridge and hid the decorating paraphernalia an instant before Callie bounded into the kitchen ahead of her grandfather.

"Look, Mommy! Look what Grandpa and I picked!" Beaming, she held out a small McDonald's drink cup that had been rinsed out and filled top-full of fresh wild blackberries, the first of the season.

"Wow! Those look scrumdillyumptious." Natalie ruffled the six-year-old's hair, grateful to see her child smile again for the first time in months. "Did you like your hike through the woods, baby girl?"

"Yeah. And look what else I got!" Callie stretched out two accordion-folded birthday cards for her admiration. "One from Aunt Inez and Uncle Paul, and one from Grandma Jean and Grandpa Ted. And they both had *five-dollar bills*."

Natalie smiled. Dan's parents had been wary and a bit

nonplussed when she first contacted them by phone back in April to set up a visit. As soon as they saw how much Callie resembled their late son, though, they embraced her as an Atwater, born and bred.

"We stopped by the post office on the way back," Wade explained, and handed her a postcard of the Arc de Triomphe in Paris. "You got this."

She flipped the card over to read the cramped handwritten text squeezed into the small white square not taken up by the French postage stamps, the Par Avion sticker, and the U.S. Post Office forwarding label:

> *Bonjour, ma chère Natalie!*
> *Paris est magnifique! Monica and I spent 4 days just going through the Louvre. Got my glass eye now, but she still has me wear the patch now and then—calls me her Pirate King!* ☺ *Gotta run: Versailles today, Chartres tomorrow. À bientôt, mon amie! G.*
> *P.S. 72 pages of novel . . . and counting!*

She barely had time to chuckle before Callie tugged at her blouse. "When can we have our hot dogs? I'm starving."

Wade held up his hands. "Say no more. I'll go fire up the grill."

"Thanks, Dad." Natalie moved to catch his eye as he headed out to the patio. "Uh . . . do you mind if Callie and I have a little talk while you're busy?"

His look told her that he knew this would be no idle chat. "Sure. Take your time." He winked at Callie. "See ya soon, kiddo."

He exited out the back door, and Natalie offered Callie her hand. "Come on. Let's take a walk."

They stepped out of the cabin into a crisp June afternoon. Though it was nearly five o'clock, the sun remained high above the horizon; on the first day of summer, it would stay light past eight in the evening. However, a late-spring cold front and the shade cast by the surrounding maple and oak trees, now covered with fresh green leaves, conspired to prickle the short hair on Natalie's scalp. Wade had rented this two-bedroom summer cottage as a place to stay until he decided whether he could stand to live in the house where Sheila had been murdered. He invited Natalie and Callie to stay with him while the fallout from the Hyland trial scandal expended its media half-life.

"Where are we going?" Callie asked as Natalie led her down the shoulder of the rural lane, which was still full of the sand road workers had spread in winter to coat the icy asphalt. "Can't we talk with Grandpa?"

"Not now, honey. I want to tell you some secrets."

Callie's face brightened. "Birthday secrets?"

"Yeah. You could say that."

Natalie gave a small, sarcastic salute to Arabella Madison, who sat across the road on the hood of her Acura. Looking less smug and more spiteful than ever, she was the last of the three original Corps Security agents still assigned to Natalie, Horace Rendell and George having been replaced by rookies. The Corps had backed off from its demand that Callie attend the School; Natalie had attracted too much press attention for exposing Lyman Pearsall's fraudulent conduit testimony, and the NAACC was being scrutinized from all quarters. But they made clear that they weren't about to leave the Lindstrom family alone. As long as Natalie refused to cooperate, Bella's job was secure.

A fallen tree lay almost parallel to the lane, and Natalie

used it as a bench, lifting Callie into place beside her. She took her daughter's hands in hers. "I want to talk about the Bad Who."

Callie let her gaze wander, the birthday dimples gone from her cheeks. *It's him, Mommy!* she had shrieked after each nightmare. *He's inside me!* Yet whenever Natalie asked her about that night in the crooked house, Callie pretended not to hear her.

"You worry he'll come back, don't you, sweetheart?"

She tried to pull away, but Natalie tightened her grip.

"No!" Callie whimpered, struggling. "I want to go back. It's my *birthday*."

"Shh. It's all right, honey." She clasped Callie to her chest, rocking her when she started to cry.

"He comes in my dreams," Callie sniffled. "I'm afraid he'll make me do more bad things."

"I know. He comes in my dreams, too." Natalie knew from experience that those dreams would only grow worse as Callie got older, as she began to comprehend the visions of blood and pain that Thresher had sewn into the fabric of her psyche. "That's why I brought you here. To give you your birthday present. Your birthday secret."

The girl quieted, sought guidance from her mother.

As far as Natalie knew, Thresher hadn't actually knocked since Dan cast him back into limbo. Maybe Margaret Thresher had vacuumed her son's soul into hers, to scold and scourge and emasculate him for eternity. Natalie couldn't take any chances, however. Callie needed to learn how to defend herself from Thresher and every other Bad Who, and her mother wasn't about to let the School teach her.

"You need to find your special, secret magic words," she told her new pupil. "We call those words your mantra. When you say them, you can call the good Whos like Daddy and make the bad ones go away. Would you like to do that?"

Callie nodded, wide-eyed, her tears drying to brown streaks on her face.

"Let's try it. Let's see if you can bring Grandma Nora here for a visit and then send her away again."

Callie puckered her lips dubiously. "Won't she get mad if I tell her to go away?"

Natalie smiled, her violet irises radiant without their contact lenses. "I'm sure she'll understand."

About the Author

Stephen Woodworth, author of the previous Dell novel *Through Violet Eyes*, is a graduate of the prestigious Clarion West Writers Workshop and a first-place winner in the Writers of the Future Contest. His short fiction has appeared in such publications as *The Magazine of Fantasy & Science Fiction*, *Weird Tales*, *Aboriginal Science Fiction*, *Gothic.Net*, and *Strange Horizons*. He is currently at work on the next two volumes of the Violet series.

Acknowledgments

The author would like to thank the following individuals for their invaluable support and assistance: Anne Lesley Groell, my patron editor, and the whole crew at Bantam Dell; my stalwart agent, Jimmy Vines; my foreign rights agent, Danny Baror; my family and friends; and, ever and always, Kelly.

Be sure not to miss

The next exciting
Violet novel from

Stephen Woodworth

Here's a special excerpt.

As he did every morning, Nathan Azure rose at dawn, dressed, and shaved in the musty canvas confines of his private tent, scrutinizing the aristocratic severity of his Mayfair face in a travel mirror to make certain that not a whisker remained and that every strand of blond hair was in its proper place. He then opened the carved wooden box next to his cot and selected a pair of leather driving gloves from the dozens of pairs inside. Although he wore gloves as a matter of habit, he donned these with special care, like a surgeon wary of infection.

He had not touched another human being nor allowed himself to be touched in more than a decade.

Seated on the edge of his cot, Azure idled away half an hour skimming Prescott's *History of the Conquest of Peru,* lingering over passages that he had long ago committed to memory—those that described the abundance of gold sixteenth-century Spanish explorer Francisco Pizarro and his conquistadors had extorted from the Inca people, who tried in vain to purchase the release of their leader Atahualpa. A king's ransom, indeed.

Azure's gloves made it awkward for him to turn the pages, however, and he soon tossed the book aside. Snatching the .45 automatic out from beneath his pillow, he chambered a round and shoved the gun, barrel down, into the hollow of his back between the waist of his slacks and his oxford shirt. He put on a cream-colored linen jacket to cover the butt of the pistol and stalked out of the tent.

Outside, the Andean air, thin and crisp, pricked the inside of Azure's windpipe, as if he'd inhaled a handful of asbestos. The sun had yet to ascend above an adjacent peak to the east, leaving the camp in a pall of predawn gray. Nevertheless, the camp already bristled with activity, Peruvian laborers bustling to and fro with spades and sifters, men delicately brushing dust off bits of broken metal and stone at makeshift tables. Azure had created this dig with painstaking detail, accurate enough to fool an expert. One expert, in particular.

It was all a sham. Azure had purchased the artifacts here at auction and then planted them on this Andean slope. The Peruvians he'd assembled to pose as his assistants were actually mercenaries—some of them former

Shining Path terrorists, others drug runners from the Huallaga Valley cocaine trade. Men whose loyalty Azure could purchase and whose silence he could ensure. Men to whom all work, whether menial labor or murder, was the same, as long as it paid well. Not unlike the conquistadors themselves.

The performance was proceeding as scheduled, but the audience—the expert for whom Azure had staged this mock expedition—was missing. It seemed that Dr. Wilcox, the only true archaeologist on the site, had chosen to sleep in.

The closer Azure drew to his prize, the more impatient he became with delay. Intent on hastening today's drama to its climax, he made his way down the path his crew had cleared in the spiky brush that carpeted the mountain slope. Erected wherever the ground leveled off for a few feet, the haphazard tent encampment formed a terraced village of canvas and plastic, with Azure's large shelter at the hill's summit. At its base, a medium-sized tent rested near the edge of a precipice, where the mountainside abruptly plunged into the valley below. Clouds blanketed the dell, a comfortable illusion of cushioning that hid the screaming descent.

A young man in a creased white dress shirt and chinos sat in a director's chair outside this last tent, head bent over a book, legs crossed as if he were lounging at a Parisian café. He must have sensed Azure's approach, though, for he slapped the book shut and hopped to his feet before the Englishman arrived at the tent's entrance. A *gringo* like his boss, he differed from Azure in nearly every other respect: his hair and complexion dark instead of fair, his face broad rather than narrow, his manner expansive, not calculated.

"Looks like I got up before you did today." He displayed the book's cover, smiling. He smiled a lot—a monkey appeasing an alpha male. "I've even been studying, see?"

Conqueror and Conquered: Pizarro and Peru read the title copy above an artist's rendering of a composite face— half Pizarro, the other half Atahualpa, the Incan leader he overthrew and executed. Below the dual portrait was the author's name: Dr. Abel Wilcox.

Nathan Azure did not smile. He never smiled. "There'll be plenty of time for that on the plane, Trent," he commented in a clipped Cambridge accent. "Do you have the cuirass?"

With exaggerated flair, Trent snapped his fingers at one of the nearby laborers, who hurried up with a mud-encrusted, rust-stained breastplate in his hands. The men had done an admirable job of simulating centuries of exposure to the elements. The armor had been polished to a museum-ready sheen when Azure had purchased it from an underground "antiquities dealer" in Lima—a glorified fence for grave robbers and artifact thieves.

Azure noted that the center of the breastplate had

been rubbed clear of dirt, revealing the ornate engraving of a family crest. He registered his satisfaction by withholding criticism. "What about Wilcox?"

Trent glanced at the tent behind him, shrugged. "Still asleep."

"Wake him."

Trent smiled again and pulled his own pair of leather gloves out of the back pocket of his pants. He put them on and ducked under the black plastic flap that served as the tent's door. A drowsy grumble came from inside, followed by the shuffle and clatter of hasty activity.

A few minutes later, Trent emerged with a man who could easily have been his brother. The latter stood an inch or two taller and lacked Trent's muscular development, but they shared the same almond-shaped eyes, high forehead, and black widow's-peak. The resemblance was not a coincidence; Azure had chosen Trent for his appearance as much as his skills.

"Good morning, Dr. Wilcox," Azure greeted the second man. "I trust you slept well."

"Until now." A day's growth of beard darkened the archaeologist's face, the fly of his jeans was only half buttoned, and his untied bootlaces trailed in the dust. He put on a pair of oval spectacles and scowled at Azure. "I hope you have something worth getting up for this time."

"Perhaps." Azure thought of the string of worthless daggers, swords, coins, and other flotsam he'd tossed in front of Wilcox like a trail of bread crumbs over the past month, gradually luring him to this remote Andean peak. "We just found this piece, and it seems promising—*very* promising. Naturally, I couldn't wait to get your professional opinion."

He held a gloved hand toward the cuirass that the impassive laborer still held. Wilcox sniffed dubiously and glanced at the breastplate as if scanning the headlines of the morning paper. As he moved close enough to see the crest inscribed on it, his expression flared with stifled excitement—a prospector afraid that the mother lode he's discovered is actually fool's gold. He shot a look at Azure. "Where did you find this?"

Azure's face remained as immobile as a bas-relief. He *asked* questions, he didn't answer them. "Is it genuine?"

Wilcox pushed his glasses higher up on his nose and reached out to touch the breastplate's insignia.

Azure snatched the archaeologist's wrist with one leather-clad hand. "Look, don't touch. Rust damage—the engraving might crumble."

Wilcox made a face but nodded. He relaxed his arm until Azure let go of it, then bent forward and squinted at the armor.

"Well? Is it *his*?" The archaeologist's silence rankled Azure. He knew at least as much about Peruvian history as this ivory-tower effete, and yet . . . had he been wrong about the cuirass? Had he blown a million quid on a clever forgery? If he hadn't wanted to be absolutely sure of the breastplate's authenticity, he wouldn't have put up with Wilcox this long. Although Nathan Azure would never admit it, he needed to commandeer the man's knowledge as much as his identity.

The archaeologist did not respond directly to Azure's questions. Instead, he pointed to the design on the breastplate, mumbling as if to himself. "The family escutcheon . . . but with the black eagle and twin pillars of the royal arms. And here: an Indian city and a llama. Charles the Fifth's seal of approval for the Peruvian conquest."

"But is it *his*?" Azure pressed. "Could one of his men have worn it?"

Wilcox shook his head, voice quavering. "Pizarro wouldn't have *allowed* anyone else to wear it."

"Then we can use it to summon him?"

"Yes." The archaeologist straightened. "You have a Violet?"

Azure's face returned to its dour placidity, the closest he ever came to expressing pleasure. "We have one in mind."

"But I thought all conduits were controlled by the N-double-A-C-C," Wilcox said, using the popular acronym for the North American Afterlife Communications Corps.

"Not all." Azure pictured the photos he'd collected of Natalie Lindstrom, the classical lines of her face turned skeletal by her shaved scalp, her violet eyes weary yet intense. Although he had yet to secure her services, he knew that she would agree to assist him. Especially after the good Dr. Wilcox helped lure her here to these isolated Peruvian peaks. A pity the archaeologist would never get to meet the Violet . . . at least, not until Azure had finished with her.

"If you're right about Pizarro's gold, this could be the biggest find since King Tut." Wilcox's words grew heavy with a kind of lust. He did not appear to notice the two Peruvian workers who flanked him from behind, gloved hands clenched into fists. "Everyone's going to want a piece of it. Customs, the Peruvian government—everyone."

"I agree. That's why they mustn't find out about it." With a shift of his eyes, Azure signaled the men, who seized the archaeologist's arms.

Wilcox wriggled in their grasp, more from astonishment than fear. Then he laughed, as if he were the butt of a fraternity prank.

"You can't be serious." When Azure failed to smile, the archaeologist's own grin fell. "I'll be missed. If I die, *they'll bring me back.* I'll tell them all about you."

Azure sniffed to indicate his amusement. "You're under the mistaken impression that I care."

He pulled the .45 from its niche at the small of his back and emptied it into Wilcox's chest.

The impact of the shots threw the archaeologist backward, but the men holding his arms kept his body from falling. His eyes white-rimmed and staring, Wilcox lifted his head, gurgling and hacking as if struggling to utter a final curse.

"*Madre Maria,*" one of the Peruvians gasped.

In the instant before they dropped him, Wilcox spat in Nathan Azure's face.

"*Bastard!*" Azure recoiled, dropping his gun and slapping at the viscous spittle on his cheek. A film of crimson mucus smeared the palm of his driving glove, and he tore it off his hand and flung it in the dust at his feet, nearly doubling over with nausea. He'd gone to great lengths to avoid establishing any quantum connection with Wilcox, but now the man's soul would adhere to him with the tenacity of a lichen. He'd have to keep that dead-talker Lindstrom from touching him, or Wilcox's spirit might ruin everything.

The Peruvians laid out the bleeding corpse while Trent rushed up to put his gloved hand on Azure's shoulder. "You okay, boss?"

Azure swatted his hand away. "*Don't touch me!*" He pointed at the dead archaeologist. "Find his passport. Then get rid of him and everything else he came in contact with. We're moving camp by nightfall."

Trent smiled, but Azure staggered away from him, compulsively wiping his contaminated cheek.

As commanded, Trent and the other men gathered everything Abel Wilcox had touched—his tent, his bedroll, his books and notes, his campfire cookware—and tossed them all over the cliff's edge into the valley below. Last of all, they pitched the body itself off the mountain. Before it dropped beneath the cloud cover, the drifting limbs of the corpse spread-eagled in the air, as if the archaeologist were about to take flight.

They never heard the body hit ground.

4/05

OLD CHARLES TOWN LIBRARY
CHARLES TOWN, WV 25414
(304) 725-2208